Cade Clenched His Jaw As Kylie Approached Him. She Was Twenty-Seven Years Old And She Was His Boss!

The situation was ridiculous, but true. And his *boss* was a knockout. Kylie Brennan was blessed with natural beauty. She appeared both sultry and sweet; wholesome yet enticingly sexy. All in all, a fascinating contrast that evoked an immediate and tangible response from Cade.

He was appalled at his reaction! The last thing he needed was to be turned on by this woman, who could single-handedly wreck his future. Yet here he stood, conjuring up what was definitely a sexual fantasy.

And during office hours, yet!

Dear Reader,

There's something for everyone this month! Brides, babies and cowboys...but also humor, sensuality...and delicious love stories (some without a baby in sight!).

There's nothing as wonderful as a new book from Barbara Boswell, and this month we have a MAN OF THE MONTH written by this talented author. *Who's the Boss?* is a very sexy, delightfully funny love story. As always, Barbara not only creates a masterful hero and smart-as-a-whip heroine, she also makes her secondary characters come alive!

When a pregnant woman gets stuck in a traffic jam she does the only thing she can do—talks a handsome hunk into giving her a ride to the hospital on his motorcycle in Leanne Banks's latest, *The Troublemaker Bride.*

Have you ever wanted to marry a millionaire? Well, heroine Irish Ellison plans on finding a man with money in *One Ticket to Texas* by Jan Hudson. A single mom-to-be gets a new life in Paula Detmer Riggs's emotional and heartwarming *Daddy by Accident.* And a woman with a "bad reputation" finds unexpected romance in Barbara McMahon's *Boss Lady and the Hired Hand.*

Going to your high-school reunion is bad enough. But what if you were voted "Most likely to succeed"...but your success at love has been fleeting? Well, that's just what happens in Susan Connell's *How To Succeed at Love.*

So read...and enjoy!

Lucia Macro

Lucia Macro
Senior Editor

Please address questions and book requests to:
Silhouette Reader Service
U.S.: 3010 Walden Ave., P.O. Box 1325, Buffalo, NY 14269
Canadian: P.O. Box 609, Fort Erie, Ont. L2A 5X3

BARBARA BOSWELL

WHO'S THE BOSS?

SILHOUETTE *Desire*®

Published by Silhouette Books

America's Publisher of Contemporary Romance

SILHOUETTE BOOKS

ISBN 0-373-76069-8

WHO'S THE BOSS?

Copyright © 1997 by Barbara Boswell

This edition published by arrangement with Harlequin Books S.A.

Printed in U.S.A.

Books by Barbara Boswell

Silhouette Desire

Rule Breaker #558
Another Whirlwind Courtship #583
The Bridal Price #609
The Baby Track #651
License To Love #685
Double Trouble #749
Triple Treat #787
The Best Revenge #821
Family Feud #877
*The Engagement Party #932
The Wilde Bunch #943
Who's the Boss? #1069

*Always a Bridesmaid!

BARBARA BOSWELL

loves writing about families. "I guess family has been a big influence on my writing," she says. "I particularly enjoy writing about how my characters' family relationships affect them."

When Barbara isn't writing and reading, she's spending time with her *own* family—her husband, three daughters and three cats, whom she concedes are the true bosses of their home! She has lived in Europe, but now makes her home in Pennsylvania. She collects miniatures and holiday ornaments, tries to avoid exercise and has somehow found the time to write over twenty category romances.

One

Though he knew they were first cousins and shared the Brennan gene pool, Cade Austin had never seen such a dissimilar pair. From his vantage point at the end of the corridor, he watched Kylie Brennan and her younger cousin Bridget walking toward him. Conversation between the cousins appeared minimal and a bit strained.

He saw Kylie slant a covert glance at Bridget, and a slight smile tilted the corners of Cade's mouth. He was willing to bet his fifteen percent stock ownership in BrenCo that Kylie had never worn a tight, tiny, belly-button-exposing, black ribbed T-shirt, like the one Bridget was wearing now. Bridget had matched it with a brilliant lime-colored faux leather skirt that scarcely covered her behind, black stockings and little-girl style shoes with thick black straps and jarring lug soles. Bridget was one of BrenCo's receptionists, but rarely dressed like one. Cade had seen movie hookers whose outfits were more conservative than some of Bridget's.

Kylie's light gray suit, white silk blouse and traditional pumps looked professional and classy. *She* dressed like the attorney Cade knew she was.

However, as president, Cade enforced no company dress code, though he was somewhat relieved that the rest of the staff chose more traditional attire for the workplace. Employees could wear whatever they liked at BrenCo as long as they showed up on time and got the job done. Which Bridget did. She was both reliable and competent. The old "never judge a book by its cover" adage definitely applied to Bridget Brennan.

Cade reminded himself not to make that mistake with her cousin Kylie, either. She may or may not be what she seemed; he needed time for a thorough assessment.

His eyes focused more intently on her. The last time he'd seen Kylie Brennan had also been the first time, exactly fourteen months ago at her uncle Gene's funeral, right here in Port McClain, Ohio. She had flown in shortly before the service and been unable to stay for the post-funeral festivities. Her parents explained she was in the middle of a trial and had only that day off before court resumed.

The other Brennans hadn't been pleased by Kylie's abrupt arrival and departure. "She inherits controlling interest in the company from Gene and she can't even stick around long enough to eat some corned beef and cabbage at his wake?" complained Lauretta Brennan.

"Kylie must have been Uncle Gene's favorite, and I don't understand why." Ian Brennan sulked. "She didn't grow up in Port McClain, and she saw the old man only once a year at most."

"Ever hear the one about familiarity and contempt? Mystery solved, Ian," replied his cousin Bridget.

Ian had shot her a killing glance, the one he reserved for most of his relatives.

Cade smiled at the memory. Twenty-two-year-old Bridget often said what he was thinking himself but was too polite to share. At least *some* of the time he was too polite. Other times he, too, just said what he thought, a trait that hadn't endeared him to most Brennans.

He didn't care because he'd had the approval, confidence and full backing of the one Brennan who counted, Gene Brennan. Gene, the man who had hired him eight years ago and eventually made him president of BrenCo, who had given him the job opportunity of a lifetime and all the challenges and privileges that went with it.

Until fourteen months ago, he'd had only to answer to Gene Brennan, but the older man's sudden death had changed everything. Gene had left fifty-one percent of BrenCo stock—controlling interest—to his niece Kylie, the daughter of his favorite brother Wayne. Since Cade already owned fifteen percent due to the generous stock options afforded him as CEO of BrenCo, the remaining thirty-four percent of the company's stock had been equally divided between Gene's two younger brothers, Artie and Guy, lifelong residents of Port McClain. Gene's house and personal effects had been willed to brother Wayne, a retired navy captain.

The local Brennans—Artie and his ex-wife Bobbie and their kids Brenda, Brent and Bridget; Guy and his wife Lauretta and their kids Ian, Todd and Polly—hadn't been shy about vocalizing their displeasure with the terms of the will. It was one of the very few things they all agreed upon.

The out-of-town Brennans—Wayne, wife Connie, son Devlin and daughter Kylie—remained apart from the grousing and the grumbling, separated from the rest of the clan by more than mere geographical distance. Of course, one could argue that branch of the family had done very well by Gene Brennan's last will and testament. The other Brennans often argued that point.

For the past fourteen months, Cade had continued to run BrenCo as before, the only difference being the absence of Gene Brennan himself. Cade sometimes wondered if he were the only one to miss the man. Certainly, Gene's relatives here in Port McClain didn't even pretend to. As for his niece-heiress, financial statements were regularly sent to Kylie Brennan at her address in Philadelphia along with Cade's written offers to discuss company business with her at any time, but she'd displayed no interest in either his offer or the business.

Until two weeks ago. Two weeks ago, Cade had received a note from Kylie Brennan stating her intent to come to Port McClain. She would be staying in her uncle Gene's house for the duration of her visit, but she hadn't specified why she was coming or how long she intended to stay. That bothered Cade. An open-ended visit? He didn't like the sound of it.

Even more ominous was Artie Brennan's phone call, announcing that he and Guy had already talked with Kylie about the possibility of selling the company. "Kylie is the majority stockholder and that makes her the boss, *your* boss, Cade." Artie had reminded him with gleeful malice. "If she votes to sell BrenCo, it gets sold."

His boss. Cade clenched his jaw as *his boss* approached him. She was twenty-seven years old and she was his boss! The situation was ridiculous, it was unthinkable, untenable. But true.

Gene, how could you do this to me? Cade's eyes flicked heavenward as he silently invoked his departed mentor. Of course, Gene's death at sixty-two had been completely unexpected. Given his parents' longevity—Ma and Pa Brennan had lived well into their eighties—Gene had probably intended to alter his will at some later date, after Cade had bought enough stock to own controlling interest in BrenCo as planned.

But time had run out and they were stuck with the one and only will he'd written, naming Kylie Marie Brennan his major heir. Making her Cade Austin's boss.

"Hey, Cade!" Bridget greeted the company president the same way she greeted her peers at Club Reek, her favorite night spot along the banks of McClain Creek.

"Hey, Bridget," he replied gamely. He saw the glimmer of humor in Kylie's eyes, saw the sudden smile cross her face. Cade inhaled sharply.

Kylie Brennan was blessed with natural beauty: high cheekbones, wide-set china blue eyes, and a heart-shaped face framed by her thick, dark slightly-below-the-chin-length bob. But that smile of hers transformed her classic good looks into something more compelling, more intriguing. She had a wide, generous mouth and a dimple on her left cheek, and when she smiled she appeared both sultry and sweet, wholesome yet enticingly sexy. All in all, a fascinating contrast that evoked an immediate and tangible response from Cade.

He felt the stirrings deep in his groin and was appalled. The woman was his boss! The last thing he—or BrenCo—needed was for him to be turned on by this alluring young woman who had the power to sell the company out from under him.

Who could single-handedly wreck his future plans and take BrenCo from him with one crucial decision. Sell.

Damn, why did she have to be so attractive? He studied her soft full lips and imagined...

"So I guess you two know each other, huh?" Bridget's voice jerked him from the erotic fantasy he'd been drifting into.

Cade was grateful for the reality check. What was happening to him? He never daydreamed while he was working, not unless the subject had to do with environmental engineering, and then it was called brainstorming. Nor was he prone to sexual fantasizing in his spare time; he'd outgrown that puerile pastime long ago. Yet here he stood, conjuring up what was definitely a sexual fantasy. During office hours. Starring his could-be-trouble beautiful young boss! *Was he losing his mind?*

"Cade Austin," he said, briskly extending his hand to Kylie. Hopefully, his inner turmoil wasn't evident. "We haven't been formally introduced but I saw you at Gene's funeral."

"Kylie Brennan." She put her hand in Cade's and was immediately struck by the size of it. His fingers were long and strong and closed around hers. "I'm sorry I haven't kept in touch. I received all your company updates but I've been very busy..." Her voice trailed off.

It was a lame excuse and she knew it. Cade Austin was a busy man, but he had taken the time and effort to send those business communiqués to her. Reflexively, she lifted her eyes to his. Their gazes met and he raised his dark brows in a gesture she couldn't quite interpret. Was he merely acknowledging her explanation? Or silently berating or mocking her for it? She couldn't tell.

And then it occurred to her that he was still holding her hand, that their handshake had lasted longer than the conventional introductory shake, which elevated it to an altogether different realm. When she felt his thumb glide lazily over her knuckles, she felt a sharp thrust in her abdomen, stunning and swift, as if she'd been kicked. Except the sensations jolting through her were pleasurable not painful. Alarmingly pleasurable.

Kylie felt a hot flush of color spread upward, heating a path from her belly to her suddenly very pink cheeks. She quickly removed her hand from his.

What on earth was the matter with her? she wondered, a little frantically. She was twenty-seven years old, not a schoolgirl who hadn't yet tamed the swirling rush of hormones in her system. Yet she was reacting to Cade with a wild surge of awareness, appallingly similar to her teenage crushes on certain cute boys all those years ago.

There was nothing cute or boyish about Cade Austin, far from it. He was thirty-five years old and six feet four inches of solid masculinity, with a muscular frame and well-defined features. Kylie's gaze took in his strong jaw and square chin, the sharp blade of a nose and firm, hard mouth.

She was standing close enough to see that his eyes were hazel, flecked with green, and watched her with an alert, assessing intelligence. What if he knew the turmoil he was so effortlessly evoking within her? The possibility made her cringe.

Her mouth felt dry, and Kylie quickly flicked the tip of her tongue over her lips. She felt Cade's eyes follow the small movement. Kylie took a step backward, then another. Hopefully, putting some physical distance between them would enable her to put an end to her distraction and his domination.

And he was dominating her, with his greater height and strength and sheer virility. Kylie understood body language; she'd made good use of it in court but never before had she been so personally affected by it.

"What brings you to Port McClain at this particular time, Miss Brennan?" Cade asked, his tone impeccably polite.

And yet...Kylie swore she heard a mocking note in his tone, subtle enough to be indiscernible if one wasn't paying close attention. She met Cade's eyes again and set her mouth in a determined line. She always paid attention.

"I wanted to visit my relatives and to be brought up-to-date on BrenCo. This month seemed like the perfect time to come here to—"

"The perfect time to come here," Cade echoed. There was no mistaking the taunt in his tone this time. "Yeah, sure. March in Ohio is a veritable paradise, especially when a place is as close to Lake Erie as Port McClain. We've got the notorious lake-effect winds, temperature *and* record snowfalls. Port McClain, the perfect place, the perfect time. Wonder if the Chamber of Commerce could pitch the town as the newest winter vacation destination?''

''We get enough snow in Port McClain to be a ski resort,'' Bridget stated. ''Except it's totally flat here. We don't even have a hill. But it would be cool to have a ski lodge anyway, wouldn't it, Cade?'' She completely ignored Kylie.

''What's the point of a ski lodge without any skiing?'' Cade was clearly not taken with Bridget's idea.

''It could be like a Club Reek with a fireplace,'' Bridget explained. ''Sort of an antiski lodge.''

''An antiski lodge, hmm?'' Cade echoed, smiling.

Or was he grimacing? Kylie found it difficult to differentiate. ''Let me rephrase from a perfect time to visit to a convenient time to visit,'' she suggested quickly, before Bridget went off on another tangent.

''And has your visit been convenient so far?'' Cade asked.

He sounded so unctuously solicitous that Kylie guessed he was aware that so far her visit had been anything but convenient. ''No,'' she admitted grimly. ''No, it hasn't.''

''You arrived in Port McClain last night, I believe? And planned to stay in Gene's house,'' Cade prompted.

''Uncle Gene's house is currently uninhabitable.'' Kylie was sure she wasn't telling him anything he didn't already know. ''I'd written to both Uncle Guy and Uncle Artie two weeks ago and asked them to have the electricity, water, gas and phone service turned on in the house and to hire a cleaning service to prepare the place for occupancy.''

''Let me guess, nothing had been done,'' Cade surmised. ''Your first mistake was asking both Artie *and* Guy, and then letting them know you'd asked them both. You unwittingly set up a Brennan double play. Artie and Guy could each claim that he thought the other was taking care of the house, while each did nothing. Meanwhile, both your uncles could enjoy a hearty laugh imagining you showing up at Gene's place, which has been vacant since his funeral.''

Kylie thought of her phone calls last night to her two uncles who had each claimed he thought the other was handling her requests. It had seemed a logical, albeit annoying, slipup. But

to think it was premeditated, that they'd relished the idea of
her standing in the creepily dark, cold, damp and musty old
house...

"That's an awful thing to say," Kylie scolded, rejecting his
premise.

She glanced at Bridget, expecting her to second the objection. After all, Cade had insulted her father and their mutual
uncle Guy.

Bridget merely shrugged. "So where'd you stay last night?
Not at Uncle Gene's Haunted Mansion, I'm sure."

"I stayed at the Port McClain Hotel."

Cade and Bridget looked at each other and laughed.

"That place has all the ambience of the House of Usher.
And you must've been one of the few guests who rented a
room for the night, instead of by the hour." Cade's eyes
gleamed. "You'd have done better to stay at one of the motels
off the interstate exit."

Kylie thought of the sounds she'd heard last night in the
room above her, the steady traffic through the halls. Cade's
remarks explained a lot. She shuddered. "When I talked to
Aunt Lauretta last night and asked her where to stay, she said
the Port McClain Hotel."

"Wow! She deliberately sent you there?" Bridget laughed
harder. "Chalk one up for Aunt Lauretta."

"You should have contacted me about the house," said
Cade. "I would've taken care of all the arrangements and the
place would have been ready for you. I suggest that you rely
upon me, not the Brennans, while you're here in Port McClain.
Now, would you like me to have my secretary Donna make
those calls to the utilities and a cleaning service for you?"

"I've already done all that from my hotel room this morning." Kylie was irked by his condescending, paternalistic attitude. Did he think she was incapable of making a few phone
calls? "And I intend to rely on myself while I'm here in Port
McClain," she added coolly.

"Is it true you lost your job, Kylie?" Bridget suddenly interjected. "That's what my brother, Brent, heard from my dad
who heard it from Uncle Guy. They all think you'll be glad
to sell the company 'cause if you're out of work, you'll need
money, right? That's what they're hoping for. *They* want to

sell real bad and get big bucks for their shares. Aunt Lauretta and Ian are really pushing for it, too, and—''

''Bridget, this is company time and you're wasting it.'' Cade interrupted her, his tone stern, all signs of friendliness gone. ''Get back to work right now.''

Bridget smoothed her hands over her short, spiky black hair. ''I didn't say anything that everybody doesn't already know,'' she said defensively. ''Why would Kylie be here if she didn't want to—''

''Bridget, if you're not gone by the time I count to three, your pay will be docked, one hour for each number I reach.'' Cade's voice was calm but steely enough to send Bridget heading down the corridor before he even uttered ''one.''

Kylie shifted uncomfortably. ''I've never found bullying to be an effective tactic to use in dealing with—''

''You've obviously never had to deal with your relatives. I've found it effective in dealing with some Brennans, at times the *only* effective method of dealing with them.'' He folded his arms in front of his chest and stared down at her.

It was as if he were looming over her, a most unfamiliar sensation. Kylie felt her stomach tighten. At five foot eight, she wasn't used to feeling small and powerless in a man's presence, but Cade Austin's big muscular frame seemed to dwarf her. It was a disconcerting sensation. No wonder Bridget had taken off. At a petite five-two, she was like a mouse facing a lion.

Cade's face was hard and still, and his hazel eyes watched Kylie with the same concentration said lion might focus on his intended prey. She swallowed and willed herself to maintain her composure. She was no scurrying little mouse.

''I know what you're doing and it's not going to work,'' she said, summoning up the necessary bravado. A useful trick of the legal trade. How many times had she faked a bold confidence she was far from feeling in the courtroom?

''What am I trying to do, Kylie?''

It didn't escape her notice that he'd used her first name for the first time. Big deal. Everybody called everybody by their first names these days; formality had gone the way of the TV antenna. So why did Cade's use of her given name seem to create an aura of intimacy between them?

"You're trying to physically intimidate me, Cade." She used *his* first name in an attempt to counter his effect on her. To turn the disturbing intimacy into everyday, meaningless informality.

"If that's what you think, I apologize. Physical intimidation isn't my style." Even as he spoke the words, his fingers closed around her upper arm. "Come into my office. We have a lot to discuss."

"May I suggest making your invitations sound less like orders?"

A grin slashed his face. "Now why would I want to do that? There are times when one must be persuasive, Kylie." He led her into his office, his fingers still encircling her arm.

"I believe you mean coercive. And I don't appreciate it. Cade."

She was excruciatingly aware of his hand on her arm, of his nearness as he walked closely alongside her. If he wasn't physically intimidating, he was certainly physical, and she was reacting to him with a primal feminine awareness.

Inside his office, Cade dropped his hand and closed the door. "Is it true you lost your job?" he asked, as frankly as Bridget had blurted it out.

Kylie winced. "Unfortunately, yes. There were budget cuts—" She paused to see his dark brows arch, his glance unmistakably skeptical.

"It's true!" she exclaimed, stung. "What did you think, that I'd been fired for—"

"Incompetence? Such a possibility never crossed my mind."

Right words, wrong tone. He was deliberately baiting her. Kylie resolved not to rise to it. "I don't know what, if anything, you knew about my job. But I was with the Public Defender's office in Philadelphia. The new governor made big cuts in the state budget and left the counties to decide where and how to downsize services."

"I'm going to take a wild guess that your department was downsized and your job along with it?"

Kylie nodded glumly. "The Philadelphia Public Defender's office staff was one of the agencies to feel the budget ax. They cut nine full-time investigators and twelve attorneys, on the basis of seniority. I was one of the newest hires, I'd been working there since I graduated from law school two years ago."

She gazed out the window. Cade's big corner office had a spectacular view of Lake Erie, which lay in the distance. The rippling waters almost seemed to blend into the cloudy gray skyline. "I don't know how the people left in the PD's office will ever get the job done now. Even at full staff, we were shorthanded and had too many cases. Our clients will have to bear the brunt of—"

"I'd better warn you that I'm not a bleeding heart who cries over the rights of all those unfortunate, misunderstood criminals. My sympathies lie with the victims of crimes who are usually forgotten while the legal eagles enjoy their competitive courtroom jousts."

Kylie stifled a groan. She'd heard that rhetoric before, too many times to count. She'd given up trying to defend herself against those who had no use for defense attorneys, especially ones paid for by state tax dollars. She stood silently, staring at the lake.

"Don't I even rate a rebuttal?" Cade was unaccustomed to the silent treatment. He stared at her profile, his eyes lingering on the porcelain texture of her skin, the graceful curve of her neck. He couldn't keep his eyes off her, he acknowledged resentfully, while she couldn't seem to tear her eyes away from Lake Erie.

She appeared so aloof and unreachable, very much in control. He felt an inexplicable urge to shatter her poise. To get under her skin, the way she'd so effortlessly gotten under his.

"I'm waiting for your righteous 'even-the-most-heinous-criminal-has the-right-to-a-lawyer-who'll-try-to-get-him-off' spiel." His tone and stance were as challenging as an opposing counsel's. "So what if a homicidal psychopath walks on a technicality? It's all in a day's work, and then you lawyers go off and have a drink together afterward."

But he didn't succeed in putting even a minor dent in Kylie's composure.

"It's not like your views toward defense lawyers are unique, you know," she said dryly. "Even my parents and my brother hated that I wasn't on the prosecution team. You haven't said anything I haven't already heard a few thousand times."

"I think you just called me a repetitive, predictable bore. Ouch."

Now what? For the first time in his memory, Cade wasn't certain what to say or do next. He was floundering and unfocused, just like this meeting. An unheard of lapse in the professional history of Cade Austin. If only she weren't so attractive, if only she were less verbally adept. If only...

Stalling for time, Cade pressed a button on the intercom. "Donna, bring Miss Brennan and me some coffee," he ordered. Donna's coffee was strong enough to power a space shuttle. Hopefully, a dose of it would jolt him out of this uncharacteristic mental morass.

A few moments later Donna entered, carrying a tray with a coffeepot, two cups and containers of cream and sugar. She placed the tray on the wide square table that stood between a charcoal gray leather sofa and two matching armchairs.

"Can I get you anything else?" Donna hovered, solicitous.

"This is fine." Cade motioned her away, and Donna obediently headed for the door.

"Thank you very much, Donna," Kylie said, smiling warmly. She did not approve of Cade's cavalier manner toward his secretary and hoped that she sounded gracious enough to make up for it. He'd ordered Donna around and hadn't even asked or thanked her properly for the favor she'd done for them!

Cade sat down on the sofa with his coffee. Across the office, Kylie stood stiffly beside his desk, making no move to join him.

He sighed. It was obvious she was displeased. Well, that was par for the course. Brennans were invariably ticked off about something. There was nothing too trivial to escape their wrath. Gene excepted, of course.

"I know you're upset about something." He'd decided long ago that the best way to deal with the ever-edgy clan was to be up-front with them. Kylie was one of them; he better follow his usual procedure. "Are you offended by my opinion of the criminal justice system?"

"Hardly. You're certainly entitled to your own opinion."

"I agree. But if that isn't it, what is? I'm not a mind reader so unless you tell me what's wrong, we're at a standstill."

"I'll be happy to tell you." Kylie's eyes flashed. "It bothers me the way you autocratically make assumptions and then imperiously act on them. For instance, you didn't ask me if I wanted coffee, you simply demanded that Donna bring it. And when she did, you never even thanked her, you simply flicked her off like she was a—a gnat."

"I did no such thing!" Cade jumped to his feet, indignant. The hot coffee spilled over the sides of the cup onto his fingers. He muttered a curse under his breath.

"Are you all right? Did you burn yourself?"

"I'm fine!" His fingers felt as if they were on fire as he set the cup on the table, though he would've rather faced amputation than to admit pain to *her!* "As for your accusation, it's ridiculous and unfair. I treat Donna and everyone else at the company with respect."

"Of course, you're denying your dictatorial behavior because it is so ingrained that you aren't even aware of how you're perceived."

"Donna has worked for me for the past six years and I can assure you that she does *not* perceive me as brushing her off like a gnat!"

"Maybe not." Kylie shrugged. "Because she's grown accustomed to such treatment. Just as my cousin Bridget accepted your threat to dock her pay if she didn't instantly obey your command. It's obvious to me that your management style is of the 'when you say jump, the employees must reply how high' school."

"My management style is what made this company the success it is today, *Miss Brennan*. BrenCo is thriving. We're not only prosperous, we're the biggest employer in this town. Your uncle certainly had no complaints when I refocused and expanded BrenCo from a small household waste disposal firm to a regional environmental cleanup leader in its field. This past year has been BrenCo's most lucrative yet, and within the next five to ten years we'll—"

He abruptly broke off. "Damn, I see where you're headed. Typical attorney trick, create a smoke screen to obscure the facts. You're complaining about Donna when what you're really trying to do is to set up a—''

"Let me set the record straight. I was not using a smoke screen to obscure any facts, *Mr. Austin*. I was criticizing your management style and being quite forthright about it.''

"Don't bother to equivocate. I read your agenda loud and clear, lady. You're in cahoots with your uncles to sell BrenCo,'' Cade said harshly. "You know that Gene's will set up provisions for BrenCo's management to remain the same until one year after his death. Now the time is up. And here you are.''

Kylie guessed that health workers learning the Ebola virus was in their midst looked a lot like Cade Austin did at this moment, faced with her presence. And he seemed to be waiting for her to say something.

"Here I am,'' she agreed, noncommittally.

Her simple statement seemed to further infuriate him. "That this year happened to be the most productive one in the company's history has only whetted your family's urge to sell.'' Cade glared at her accusingly. "They have delusions of striking it rich when in reality selling the company is akin to killing the goose who laid the golden eggs. Not that I expect the Brennans to grasp the implications of something as intricate as an allegory.''

"I'm a Brennan and I have no trouble understanding allegories,'' Kylie countered.

Cade might know her relatives better than she, but they were *her* relatives and she was getting a little tired of listening to him take verbal swipes at them. "And I'm not in cahoots with anybody. I don't have a hidden agenda. Are you one of those paranoid types who sees a conspiracy lurking behind every remark and every action? Your motto is Trust No One?''

"If I have a motto, it would be Trust No Brennan.'' Cade glowered at her. "Gene excepted, of course.''

"Of course.'' Kylie was exasperated. "Sounds like you and Uncle Gene had yourselves a merry old time, sitting around trashing the rest of the Brennans. You delighted in taking offense at perceived slights and misinterpreting everything that was said and done. Yes, I'm beginning to get a very clear picture of things now.''

"Oh, are you?"

She nodded. "Look at the way you misinterpreted this coffee incident. How you overreacted. I prefer tea, but you never bothered to ask, you ordered coffee for me and expected me to drink it. Naturally, I was annoyed by such high-handedness. Furthermore, I'm not used to being waited on. In the PD's office, everybody served themselves. But did you give me a chance to explain anything? No! You instantly assumed that I'm a conniving, greedy witch looking for a reason to fire you and sell this company. Didn't you?"

She advanced toward him in full cross-examination mode, her gaze piercing and intense. "Didn't you?" The sound of her own voice startled her. She'd used this tone in challenging murder suspects. It occurred to her that perhaps she was also overreacting.

"You drink tea." Cade stared at her. "You're in a snit because I didn't offer you a choice between coffee or tea?" His tone was as incredulous as his expression. "No doubt about it, you've taken the Brennan family irritability to new heights."

"I'm not in a snit. I'm trying to make a point that you don't seem to be getting. Whether it's intentional or not, I'm not quite sure. Is it?"

"Is it what? Is what it?" Cade ran his hand through his hair, tousling it. His head was spinning. "This is crazy." Or maybe he was headed that way.

He felt frazzled, completely befuddled. The Brennans had always driven Gene nuts. His late boss had long ago delegated dealing with them to Cade, who merely found them annoying, not insanity-inducing. But *this* Brennan...Kylie Brennan...

The two of them were practically standing toe-to-toe. Her aggressive advance had fallen into the category of physical intimidation—which she'd accused him of using!—and brought them very close. Not that Cade was feeling the least bit intimidated. He was feeling...aroused.

Everytime he inhaled, the scent of her perfume filled his nostrils. It was a subtle, spicy, sexy aroma, just like her, and it further clouded his thoughts. The urge to touch her was so overpowering that he would've given in to it had he not beaten a purposeful retreat to the window. A tactical victory for her, but at this point he was too disconcerted to care.

"I can't stress how strongly I disapprove of you treating Donna like a servant," Kylie scolded his back, which he'd turned toward her. "It's pure classism. I am also opposed to sexism, racism and ageism," she felt compelled to add, just for the record.

"Well, so am I!" Cade exclaimed. She was the defense attorney, but she had him on the defensive for sure. "BrenCo is an equal opportunity employer. We've won citations for our fair hiring practices."

"I'm very glad to hear that." Kylie was genuinely relieved. "It would be awkward to have to report BrenCo to the EEOC, although I wouldn't hesitate to do so if the situation warranted."

Cade turned to gape at her. "How did we get from you preferring tea to the EEOC?"

"Actually, I'm not sure." Kylie's blue eyes were troubled. She'd always prided herself on her talent for presenting her points in a coherent and lucid form in the courtroom. "My clients would've been toast if I made the sort of irrational leaps I seem to be making today. You—confuse me," she admitted, averting her gaze from him to Lake Erie on the horizon.

"Glad to hear it. The feeling happens to be mutual." Cade began to pace the office, back and forth, on edge and ready for action.

Kylie remembered a *National Geographic* special on TV featuring a leopard pacing his territory in a remarkably similar prowl. Keeping in mind the unlucky mammal who'd wandered into the leopard's line of vision, she took a few prudent steps out of Cade's path, just to be on the safe side.

"You confound me in a way I never thought a Brennan could," he growled. "Or anybody else, for that matter." The admission did not please him.

They stared uneasily at each other for a few long moments.

"We've gotten off to a bad start." Kylie was the first to speak.

"A perceptive observation," muttered Cade. He grabbed his coffee and took a large gulp. And nearly choked. The brew was so ghastly it made airline coffee taste like a gourmet specialty brand.

Kylie was watching him. "I think I'll definitely stick to tea," she murmured.

Their eyes met. Kylie caught her lower lip between her teeth in a nervous gesture she rarely resorted to anymore. But Cade Austin made her nervous, and in a way that was exciting, not threatening. Which made him all the more dangerous.

She drew a sharp breath. "Do you think we could start over?"

"We can do whatever you want, Kylie."

His sudden suggestive smile made her heart jump. She knew instinctively that he was quite aware of his own masculine appeal and wielded it when necessary. He'd decided to use it now, as an alternative maneuver.

Kylie realized just how susceptible she could be when he chose to disarm her with his charm. "I'm speaking professionally," she said quickly. "As a public defender, I'm accustomed to seeking common ground in my clients' best interests and in this case—"

"You're not a public defender anymore, Kylie. Thanks to the terms of Gene's will, you're a businesswoman and an important figure in this community. I don't know if you're fully aware of how dependent Port McClain is on BrenCo or the economic impact the company has on this town."

"You mean like in 'if BrenCo sneezes, Port McClain catches a cold'?" She paraphrased the old General Motors maxim.

His smile widened, and this time it was reflected in his eyes. "Exactly like that."

Kylie reminded herself to breathe. Maybe starting over on friendly terms wasn't such a good idea, after all. It was easier to keep her composure and her imagination in check if she was feeling hostile toward him. When he smiled at her in that particular way, she could feel herself melting inside. She wanted to please him, to do whatever it took to keep him smiling...A dangerous notion, indeed.

Get a grip, Kylie, she ordered herself. She was not here to please Cade Austin, and she was on a lot safer ground when he was scowling at her.

"I know it's my responsibility to learn everything about the company and its impact on the town. I was stunned when I heard that Uncle Gene had left controlling interest in BrenCo to me. No more than you were, probably," she added with a wry grimace.

"The contents of Gene's will turned out to be a surprise to a lot of people."

"The understatement of the year, no doubt. Well, I don't want to sound ungrateful, but owning any part of a toxic waste plant wasn't exactly my idea of a dream come true."

"BrenCo isn't simply a toxic waste plant, Kylie. We take environmental waste from all over the state—and other states, too—and properly dispose of it in a way that is not only safe but beneficial to the environment." Cade's hazel eyes gleamed. "I expect all your liberal cohorts in the Public Defender's office would deny such technology even exists. That crowd believes *no* waste is the only safe waste, a ridiculous, hopeless point of view. Even the fires of our cave ancestors released waste products into the air."

"I know. I—haven't mentioned my inheritance to anyone," she confessed, a little sheepishly.

"Afraid of being dubbed the Princess of Toxic Waste by all your green friends?"

Kylie tilted her head and gazed at him from under her lashes, the feminine signals elemental and unconscious. "Why do you assume that my cohorts and friends are all wild-eyed liberals?"

"It's a natural assumption. If there is such a thing as a conservative public defender, I'd bet my shares in BrenCo that he has a multiple personality disorder with each alter unaware of what the others are doing. You can imagine the mayhem that will ensue when the conflicting personalities finally collide in the poor sap's conscious mind."

Kylie laughed. "You surprise me," she admitted. "I wouldn't have thought you were capable of appreciating the absurd."

"I wouldn't have lasted eight minutes, let alone eight years, in this town filled with Brennans if I didn't have a healthy appreciation of the absurd."

"Brennans. You talk about them as if they're a separate species."

"Now you're catching on. Brennans fall somewhere between vampires and parasites, though precise classification has yet to be established."

He was kidding, displaying an even greater, healthier appreciation of the absurd. Wasn't he? "Gene excepted, of course," she interjected his usual disclaimer.

"Gene excepted, of course. And according to Gene, your dad would have to be excepted, too. Gene admired your father, he was very proud of him. He often boasted about his brother Wayne, the navy captain who commanded a battleship and lived all over the world. He was a fan of your big brother, too. Gene always referred to him as 'my-favorite-nephew-Devlin-the-doctor.'"

"Devlin is finishing his orthopedic surgical residency at the University of Michigan Medical Center in Ann Arbor," Kylie lapsed naturally into her role of proud sister and daughter. "Dad is retired now. He and Mom are living in Florida and still aren't sure how they'll adjust to staying in the same place for more than a few years."

"If they're like my folks, who are retired army, they'll end up buying an RV and trolling the interstates on endless trips. Occasionally, they swing by Port McClain to see me."

"In March, no doubt. After all, it's the perfect time to visit here. The lake-effect wind and all that snow are big draws."

"Touché." Cade raised his brows again in that particular way of his.

Kylie raised her eyebrows right back. "Maybe Bridget's antiski lodge will be packing in crowds on their next visit."

"You're really on a roll here, aren't you?" Cade's voice was deceptively mild as he studied her.

She was flirting with him. Or was she? Given their volatile interaction since she'd set foot in his office, there was always the chance she was expressing her antipathy to him. What a blunder it would be to mistake aversion for flirtation!

But Cade was a risk-taker by nature. He took one now and moved closer to her. Close enough to cup her chin in one hand and tilt her head a little.

Kylie felt the world career. He was going to kiss her; she

could read the hot sensual intent in his eyes. And she was going to let him. She wanted him to kiss her, she wanted it very much.

The realization stunned her. This kind of behavior was completely unlike her. She'd never been driven by sexual urges. She was too cerebral, governed by her head, not her body's impulses.

Yet here she was, melting against Cade Austin as he pulled her into his arms. Closing her eyes as his mouth lowered to hers. Parting her lips for the breathlessly anticipated impact of his...

Two

"Cade, I'm sorry to interrupt but Bobbie Brennan is on the phone," Donna's voice, loud and clear, sounded over the intercom.

Startled, Kylie and Cade jumped away from each other as if they'd been blasted apart by a bomb.

Kylie's heartbeat thundered in her ears. She'd come so close to kissing Cade Austin that she had felt the warmth of his breath on her face. She'd been in his arms, his body pressing into hers, the formidable length of him, hard and strong, revealing the force of his own desire. The intimate recall made her shake. Heat scorched her from the top of her head to the tips of her toes.

From the corner of her eye, she saw Cade sink into his desk chair. She walked unsteadily to the window and touched her forehead to the cool glass.

"Bobbie says it's an emergency and she must speak to you immediately," Donna stated.

"An emergency?" Kylie snapped to attention. She turned around, her eyes widened with alarm.

"Don't worry, it's probably nothing serious. Everything is

an emergency to Bobbie.'' Cade heaved a groan. ''The cornerstones of her personality are hysterics and vengeance, and one fuels the other.''

''I told Bobbie you were in an important conference and couldn't be interrupted but needless to say, she refuses to take 'no' for an answer,'' Donna continued. ''She threatened to come down and break into your office with a hatchet if she had to. I decided we'd better not risk it.''

''We've learned the hard way that ignoring Bobbie is not the way to go,'' Cade said tightly.

''Do you really think Aunt Bobbie would hatchet her way into your office?'' Kylie was incredulous.

''There is already a long list of outrageous things Bobbie has done, when thwarted. Taking a hatchet to my office door would not be a stretch for her.''

''Get ready, Cade,'' Donna warned. She sounded like a pilot announcing an emergency landing. ''I'm putting her call through on speaker phone right now.''

''Cade!'' Bobbie Brennan's shriek filled the office.

Nails on a chalkboard sounded euphonious in comparison. Kylie flinched.

''Brent is in jail!'' Bobbie screamed. ''They set bail at twenty-five thousand dollars! A fortune!''

''Remember that you pay a bail bondsman ten percent which is twenty-five hundred dollars, Bobbie,'' Cade reminded her.

''I don't have that kind of money for a bail bondsman. It may as well be twenty-five million! What are we going to do, Cade? Oh, this couldn't have come at a worse time! I'm all out of patience with Brent, this time he's gone too far!'' Bobbie's tone grew even more vitriolic. ''It's all Artie's fault, damn him! He's a terrible father, he's the cause of all Brent's problems.''

''Tell me why Brent is in jail, Bobbie. What are the charges against him?'' Cade had to ask three times before she stopped yelling long enough to hear him

''I wrote down what the cop said, but I'm crying too hard to read my writing.'' Bobbie sobbed noisily.

''Shall I call Artie and ask him?'' Cade asked.

''No! That loser is the reason Brent is in jail.'' Bobbie's

sobs instantly ceased. "Brent has been charged with second degree burglary. You see, Artie rented out the basement of his house to this nasty young couple—I *told* him not to do it!— and Brent put a video camera behind a two-way mirror with a hole in it so he could tape that couple in their bedroom."

"Tape them without their consent?" interrupted Cade.

"So they say." Bobbie gave a very audible sniff. "They claimed they noticed a light in the mirror and investigated it and found the hidden camera, then called the police."

"Did Brent say why he was taping this couple?" Cade asked, grimacing.

"He—Brent—said he was going to turn the tape into a movie." Bobbie's voice grew lower. "You know, like one of those art films."

"An art film," Cade echoed flatly. "Just a minute, Bobbie." He switched off the phone. "Well, this is a new one. Brent, with art film aspirations."

"More than likely, he planned to sell the tapes to one of those places that pays for privately made porn videos," Kylie murmured. "In Philadelphia, a copy could go for as high as five hundred dollars."

"Does Bobbie have her facts straight? Granted, what Brent did is sleazy and illegal but is it really *burglary?*"

"It sure is." Kylie nodded her assent. "We've tried similar cases. Second-degree burglary covers unauthorized filming of individuals."

"That sleazy little jerk has outdone himself this time." Cade's expression was equal parts disgust and impatience. He switched Bobbie back on. "Have you called an attorney for Brent, Bobbie?"

"Of course not!" she howled. "I called *you!* We have to get Brent out of jail right away, Cade. You know what can happen to a good-looking boy like him in a place like that!"

"You've seen too many prison movies, Bobbie. Nothing is going to happen to Brent in the Port McClain lockup." Cade's tone was both firm and reassuring. "Besides, he's spent time there before. Remember the last time he was arrested? We decided that sitting in that cell would be a good lesson for him. He spent a week there and it didn't hurt him a bit. In fact, he's stayed out of trouble until now, nearly two years later, and that's a record for him.''

"I hoped he was finally growing up. I was going to ask you to give him another chance at BrenCo." Bobbie began weeping again.

"Bobbie, you know what Gene said. No more chances for Brent at BrenCo. It was even written in his will. I won't hire Brent for a job here, no matter what," Cade added with absolute finality.

"Maybe you would if Brent got himself together," countered Bobbie, ignoring Cade's absolute finality. "Damn Artie! He had to go and rent out the basement! You can be sure we didn't see a dime of that couple's rent money, Artie kept it all for himself. Cade, I can't afford to bail out Brent and I don't know if Artie will do it or not."

"Then Brent can stay in jail till his hearing, Bobbie. He's not a child, and he shouldn't expect his parents to bail him out—literally—every time he gets into trouble." Cade caught Kylie's eye. She nodded her agreement.

"Whose side are you on?" Bobbie swung from sorrow to rage. "Artie's? He doesn't care if Brent rots in jail, either!" In the next breath, her tone turned whiney. "Did you remember that Brenda and I have to take Starr Lynn to the regional novice competition in Detroit next week? We'll have expenses—food and gas and the motel. And Starr Lynn needs an extra special skating costume. We found one that is absolutely perfect for her. It costs six hundred fifty dollars, plus tax.''

"Six hundred fifty dollars for an ice-skating costume for a twelve-year-old is ridiculous, Bobbie," Cade said calmly.

"It's not unreasonable, some of the girls have costumes that cost nine hundred fifty. Are you going to help us or not, Cade?" demanded Bobbie. "I can always send Brenda over to your place tonight to—"

"No, not Brenda!" Cade said so fervently that Kylie was instantly on alert. She studied him even more closely. "Look, Bobbie, let me make a few phone calls about Brent. Meanwhile, promise me you'll at least look for another costume for Starr Lynn. You have a week till the competition."

"We'll look, but I doubt that we'll find anything else so

perfect for Starr Lynn. And she deserves the best, Cade. Even *you* know that. Call me tonight about Brent.'' Bobbie hung up abruptly and with such force that the sound of the receiver slamming echoed throughout the office.

"Good Lord!" breathed Kylie.

"Don't drag Him into it," Cade said dryly. "Well, Ms. Public Defender, feel like taking your cousin's case?"

"I'm not a member of the Ohio Bar. I can't practice law in this state unless I'm granted reciprocity."

"Which you haven't even applied for?" guessed Cade. "Smart move on your part. Defending your cousin Brent would be as thankless a job as your last one."

Kylie ignored the dig. "Why did Aunt Bobbie dump Brent's arrest on you?" she asked curiously. "What are you supposed to do about it? And what's all this about a six-hundred-dollar skating costume?"

"Six-fifty, plus tax." Cade rubbed the back of his neck, then heaved a resigned sigh. "Even though you aren't licensed to practice here, you fire questions like a professional inquisitor."

"Maybe you wouldn't mind answering them?" she prompted.

"Let me tell you a little about the Brennans of Port McClain, Kylie. At any given time, one of them is either feuding with another or feels miffed or snubbed or cheated in some way. They've made a life-style of backstabbing and bickering."

"And being thrown in jail?"

"So far, jail has been the sole province of your cousin Brent, a fact for which we can all be grateful. The reason I'm so knowledgeable about the Brennans and why my number is programmed into Bobbie's phone is because your uncle Gene annointed me Alpha Male of the clan. Gene's brothers and their wives and kids were always trying to drag him into their civil wars, and it bothered him so much that he delegated his patriarch position to me. Gene was very good at delegating," he added wryly.

"So you not only run BrenCo, you also mediate family feuds?"

"I've had far more success managing the company than I've

had trying to keep peace among the Brennans. Reaching a consensus among that group is harder than getting a unanimous vote in the UN General Assembly."

"I know that Uncle Artie and Aunt Bobbie's divorce was very bitter," Kylie murmured. "That's really all I know about it."

The Brennan extended family had played only a minor role in the lives of her very mobile, very nuclear family—which made it both strange *and* awkward that she was now involved via Uncle Gene's will.

"Wish I could say the same," growled Cade. "Well, let me bring you up to date. Artie and Bobbie have been divorced fifteen—or is it sixteen?—years but are still deeply entrenched in each other's lives. They are one of those tiresome couples who are eternally obsessed with each other."

"Obsessed with making each other miserable?"

Cade nodded. "They're masters of the art. I suppose you could say that Brent's problems are the result of his dysfunctional family but he's no longer a troubled teen, he's twenty-seven years old. I consider him to be fully responsible for his own actions."

"I agree," said Kylie.

He looked surprised. "I thought a bleeding heart type like you would drag out the crying towel and use Brent's unhappy childhood and his battling parents to excuse him."

"Maybe I would, if I were defending him in court. But since I'm not…" Kylie's voice trailed off, leaving the obvious unsaid. "I haven't seen Brent in years. But I do have an indelible memory of him from when we were kids. He lured me into the attic of Uncle Gene's house by telling me that our grandmother had a trunk filled with dolls there. When I looked into the trunk, he shoved me in and locked it. I don't think he had any intention of ever letting me out."

"Ah, Brennan family fun." Cade smiled sardonically. "See what you missed by not growing up here in Port McClain with the rest of the tribe? How did you get out of the trunk, by the way?"

"Lucky for me, my brother noticed I wasn't around and figured that Brent had something to do with it. Devlin *persuaded* Brent to admit it and lead him to me."

"Dare I ask how Devlin persuaded Brent?"

"He, uh, punched Brent in the nose," Kylie confessed sheepishly. "And broke it."

"Ah, bullying. As I mentioned earlier, it works well with certain Brennans. And I like the irony of Devlin's progression from breaking bones to setting bones as his life's work. That little bit of family history does explain why both Artie and Bobbie refer to your brother as 'that thug.' It's one of the few things they agree on."

"My mom and dad refer to Brent as 'that monster.' After the trunk incident, whenever we came to visit in Port McClain our parents kept Dev and me away from Brent. And after Uncle Artie and Aunt Bobbie's divorce, we didn't see much of Brenda or Bridget, either."

"What about your other cousins, Guy and Lauretta's kids? Did you spend much time with them?"

"No. Todd and Polly were a lot younger than Dev and me. And Ian—"

"Was an obnoxious creep?" suggested Cade. "He still is. Surprisingly enough, Todd and Polly are okay. Even likable, a fact that continually takes me by surprise."

"Maybe they were somehow switched at birth?" Kylie suggested drolly.

"Maybe they were." Cade grinned, then grew serious once again. "Your cousin Todd is in his junior year at Ohio State, majoring in business and Polly will graduate from Port McClain High in June. She has a scholarship to OSU and wants to study engineering. Both kids want to work for BrenCo someday and I think they'll be assets to the company. BrenCo should be here for them to return to, Kylie. It is Gene's legacy to his family and to this town," he added, willing her to meet his gaze.

Kylie averted her eyes from the pull of his. She'd been warned by her uncles that Cade would apply strong pressure to sway her to his point of view—which was to keep BrenCo a privately held company with him at the head. Asking her to consider the future of the younger Brennans seemed to be yet another strategy.

She couldn't immediately choose sides, Kylie reminded herself. She had to be like a judge and listen to all the arguments, to weigh all the evidence and information before rendering a decision. Keep the company in its current state or sell it to one of the giant firms that would merge BrenCo into their conglomerate? Her uncles, aided by cousin Ian, had invited an industry agent to town to explain the advantages of a sale and merger. She had to hear him out. Her decision was too vital to be rushed.

"Tell me why Aunt Bobbie wants to buy Starr Lynn a six-hundred-fifty-dollar ice-skating costume," she asked lightly, in a deliberate change of subject. "Plus tax."

She could tell by Cade's expression that he wasn't pleased with her blatant stall. She watched him assessing her—perhaps debating what tactic to take with this latest backstabbing, bickering Brennan who'd been inflicted upon him? Bullying, maybe? Kylie braced herself, prepared to fight back.

Instead, Cade returned to the coffee table and this time drained his cup of the dark murky brew.

"Your cousin Brenda's daughter Starr Lynn wants to be a figure skater. I guess you could say she already is one. She's been taking ice-skating lessons since she was four. The kid is definitely talented. She's won a number of novice competitions—that is the level just below the juniors which is just below the seniors—and she's being considered for admission to one of the top programs in the country at the Winterhurst Ice Rink in Lakewood. Bobbie and Brenda see Olympic gold in her future, and given Starr Lynn's talent and drive, it's not a totally unwarranted dream."

"You sound vaguely fond of Starr Lynn." Kylie settled into the charcoal gray leather chair across from Cade's, her thoughts centering on Starr Lynn Brennan, aged twelve.

She hadn't seen Brenda's child in years, though she remembered when Starr Lynn had been born. Vividly. Brenda, seventeen at the time, hadn't been married and it had been something of a family scandal, even for the Wayne Brennans living on a naval base in Europe, far from Port McClain.

"Starr Lynn *is* amazing out there on the ice." Cade's voice tore Kylie from her reverie. "She works so hard, getting up at dawn to practice, going to school and then putting in more hours of practice. Then there's her skating and dancing lessons and all the competitions. The kid is a real trouper," he added gruffly.

"You *are* fond of her!" Kylie marveled. Her eyes narrowed a bit. "What about her mother? I haven't seen much of Brenda in the past several years but she's always been pretty...and sexy."

She was horrified by the acerbic note that had slipped into her voice and hoped that Cade wouldn't notice.

A vain hope. He smiled, a smug cat-who'd-chowed-down-the-canary grin. "Brenda is still pretty and still sexy in that flashy bad girl way of hers." He leaned back in his chair and met Kylie's eyes. "Every now and then, Brenda decides that I would be a good match for her. I have never agreed. You can believe it when I say that Brenda Brennan holds all the appeal of a rattlesnake for me. Make that a rattlesnake about to strike and me without an antivenom kit."

"So that's why you panicked when Aunt Bobbie suggested sending Brenda over to your place tonight?"

"I did not panic!"

"Yes, you did." Kylie was aware that she was entirely too elated by his rejection of her cousin Brenda.

The feeling disconcerted her. How petty, how unlike her. She was not jealous of Brenda! Yet she couldn't deny the relief—the thrill?—of listening to Cade compare her cousin to a rattlesnake. Did she possess some long dormant Brennan vs. Brennan tendencies, which suddenly had been activated?

Cade Austin would undoubtedly think so. She saw the way he was watching her and blushed. Suddenly, an escape from his probing hazel eyes was essential.

"I've taken up enough of your time." Kylie jumped to her feet and headed toward the door. "I should have called first and made an appointment. I—I'm sure you have things to do and I'm keeping you from them."

"As president of BrenCo, I always have things to do." Cade followed her to the door, then moved in front of it. "But I always have time for our major stockholder, of course. You don't need to make an appointment, you have a standing one with me, Kylie. Whenever you want it."

His back was against the door, blocking it. "Would you like a tour of the plant? Perhaps an overview of company

policy? A look at our financial records and written long-range
goals?'' While his words were strictly business, his tone and
his expression conveyed an entirely different message.

Kylie interpreted the subtext, but not quickly enough. Before she could speak, move or even breathe, Cade's hands
were on her waist, pulling her to him.

No one had ever been so physical with her. The men in her
world were talkers who used words, not actions. Kylie could
match any man verbally—even best them—but dealing on a
tactile level was a very different playing field for her. Just as
Cade Austin was very different from the men she knew. He
acted first, without explanation or warning or eloquent dis-
course.

Kylie felt the warmth of his hard frame suffuse her. His big
hands slid to her hips and settled her against his masculine
strength. Instinctively her legs parted, letting her feel the full
burgeoning force of his manhood.

The effect on Kylie was electrifying. The rampant sexuality
of their position abruptly short-circuited the rational workings
of her brain. Instead of thinking things through and behaving
rationally, she ceded to the elemental craving he'd elicited
deep within her. For the first time in her careful, well-
organized life, she impulsively acted on what she was feeling—and that was a powerful, hungry need that demanded to
be assuaged.

His mouth came down on hers, taking her lips and parting
them in a kiss that was unlike any she'd ever known. This
was no idle or tentative getting-to-know-you kiss. Cade kissed
her as if he already knew her very well, as if he knew all
about her secret yearnings and would fulfill them whenever he
chose.

His kiss was hard and deep and intimate, demanding and
receiving her body's most primitive, passionate response. It
was a kiss outside the realm of her experience, beyond the
constraints her mind persisted in placing on her emotions.

But there were no constraints now, not with Cade. He'd
somehow slipped past her usual defenses and circumvented
her control.

Her arms were around his neck and she was clinging to
him, her anchor in the wild unfamiliar sea of sensuality. She

gasped a shuddering breath when he boldly covered her breast with his hand. It was too much too fast, Kylie knew it. She'd spent years fending off unwanted intimacies, usually more bored than angered by such attempts.

But she was neither bored nor angry now. And the too-soon intimacy that Cade was taking was not unwanted. Far from it. Kylie felt the heat of his palm cupping her, felt his long fingers begin a slow massage, and she loved it. A little whimper escaped from her throat and she quivered with sensual pleasure.

Through the soft silk of her blouse, through the lace of her bra, he rubbed her nipple with his thumb. The tight bud was achingly sensitive, and she pressed against his hand, encouraging him, needing more. An erotic barrage of hot little sparks burned in the most secret, feminine part of her.

He was hard and virile and continued to press boldly against her, evoking a syrupy warmth that flowed through her. She felt soft and weak and pliant. When his hands cupped her buttocks to lift her higher and harder against him, Kylie clung tighter to him, moist and swollen with desire.

The intensity of her response shocked and excited her. She'd never experienced such fiery sensuality before, she had begun to believe she was one of those strictly analytical types whose passion could only be expressed in her work. A cool, methodical woman whose thrills came from the mental gymnastics required in preparing or presenting a case in a courtroom, not from a man's kisses and caresses.

Cade Austin was proving her very wrong. He wasn't simply a man, he was *the* man, and he was shattering all those myths she'd held about herself. In his arms, she'd become a passionate woman. The wild and wanton thoughts tumbling through her mind were as new and as stimulating as the feelings surging through her. And it seemed that Cade could read them all...

He scooped her up in his arms. Another first for her. She couldn't remember ever being carried, though presumably it was her mode of transport before she'd learned to walk.

She was totally unprepared for and completely defenseless against the tantalizing sensation of being lifted in a man's arms and held against his chest as he strode across the office.

Kylie—the stable, dependable defender of the less fortunate—suddenly felt seductive and intensely feminine, like a character out of one of those romance novels she never had the time or inclination to read. Cade was so big, so strong. He handled her with ease, laying her down on the charcoal gray leather sofa and then coming down on top of her.

Her head was spinning, her eyelids felt extraordinarily heavy. It took too much energy and effort to keep them open so she allowed them to close, plunging her into a dark world of pure sensation.

He kissed her again, and she wrapped her arms around him, savoring the hard warm weight of him. The taste of him, the feel of him was exactly what she wanted, what she needed. She slipped her hands under the jacket of his suit to knead the muscular length of his back. The cloth barrier of his shirt frustrated her; she wanted to feel his bare skin beneath her fingers. She tugged at the material tucked into the waistband of his trousers, trying to get it out of her way.

Before she could succeed, Cade pushed aside her jacket and opened her blouse. Kylie felt his fingers deftly unfasten the front clasp of her bra. She knew she was exposed to him but instead of trying to cover herself, she arched upward, yielding greater access to him.

The touch of his hands on her bare breasts unleased piercing shards of desire deeply within her, too pleasurable to even consider ending. He fondled her, stroking and caressing, making her desperate for more.

"Cade, please!" She hardly recognized that desperate, husky cry as her own voice.

"I know, sweetie, I know." His voice was thick and raspy. "Me, too."

Kylie reached up to touch the hard, shaven skin of his cheek. She was charmed by his inarticulate mutter. She needed no translation, she knew exactly what he was saying. That he was as wonderfully out of control as she was. That he wanted her in the same fierce way that she wanted him.

Then his mouth was on the soft skin of her breast, kissing a sensuous path to its taut center that was tingling with arousal. She held her breath as his lips closed over her nipple to gently suckle her, then moaned as flames of desire licked through her. She hadn't known that a man's mouth on her breasts could affect her like this. The sensation was so intense, it was exquisite pleasure bordering on acute need.

His fingers slipped beneath the layers of her panty hose and white cotton panties to caress the soft, bare flesh of her belly. She felt him trace her navel, and she reflexively sucked in her stomach to provide him easier access. He dipped his thumb into the small hollow and kindled a wildfire that streaked directly to the pulsing heart of her femininity.

Kylie squirmed, trying to clench her legs together to ease the consuming ache there. Cade moved his thigh higher between hers, pressing against her. It helped but not enough. She wanted, she needed...

"Yes?" Cade murmured.

Through the dizzying fog of sensuality, Kylie realized that he was seeking her permission to continue. She wondered why he'd bothered; he didn't have to ask. Stopping him was the farthest thing from her mind. She wanted him with an urgency that bordered on desperation.

"Yes," she whispered.

She had no sooner spoken the word when Donna's voice boomed into the office once again, irrevocably shattering their private sensual cocoon. "Cade, Noah is here for your lunch meeting with the mayor."

Cade muttered an oath. Kylie's eyes flew open.

He was kneeling on one knee above her, in the process of sliding her panties and panty hose over her hips. Kylie gasped as the reality of the situation struck her with the force of an anvil. *She was on the verge of having sex with a man she hardly knew!*

"Kylie, I know this interruption isn't what either of us wanted to happen, but—"

"Get away from me!" she ordered, her voice little more than a raspy whisper.

She was horrified. *Sex on the sofa in Cade Austin's office?* What had she been thinking?

The answer, of course, was that she hadn't been thinking at all.

"I completely forgot that Noah and I are to have lunch with the mayor today. That's Noah Wyckoff, our senior vice president of operations." Cade caressed her midriff, seemingly mesmerized by the contrast of his tanned fingers against the snowy whiteness of her skin.

"I don't care who he is or who you're having lunch with." Kylie slapped his hands away and tried to sit up, a difficult feat with him hovering over her. "Let me go right now!"

Instead, he stunned her by picking her up again and carrying her toward a door at the far end of his office. His movements were so sudden, so unexpected that Kylie had no time to rally a protest. He'd opened the door and put her on her feet before she could utter a sound.

Kylie glanced around her. She was standing in a well-appointed bathroom—the executive washroom?—and Cade had reclosed the door, leaving her alone to repair her hair, makeup and clothing.

"Kylie, you'll need this." Cade rapped lightly on the door, then handed her purse to her.

Kylie snatched it with shaking fingers and swiftly slammed the door shut. He was so cool, so self-possessed! How had he recovered his wits and his composure so quickly, while she was still a shivering, quivering, unable-to-think-straight mess?

She forced herself to face the painful truth. Obviously, Cade hadn't been as sensually enthralled as she'd been. It was a devastating conclusion, both insulting and humiliating, but Kylie had never been one to hide behind the walls of denial.

One quick glance in the mirror made her groan aloud. Her mouth was moist and swollen and looked well-kissed, her lipstick was missing in action. And her hair...Kylie winced. It was in tousled disarray. She looked like she'd been doing exactly what she had been doing—indulging in a hot sexual tryst on the office sofa!

Moments later, she heard voices in the office, Cade's and another man's, presumably Noah Wyckoff, whose untimely appearance had interrupted the most impassioned episode in her life. The *stupidest* episode in her life, Kylie silently amended, reassessing the encounter through a critical, analytical eye.

Though she had been swept away, Cade had not been overpowered by that same wild abandon. And now, viewed in retrospect, his passionate advances seemed calculated, his recovery too quick and complete.

Kylie trembled. It hurt that his seemingly spontaneous burst of passion had actually been premeditated, a means of controlling her. He had seen her attraction to him and decided to use it to his advantage. Seducing BrenCo's major stockholder would be a real coup for the company president, bent on using her to further his own aims.

Her cheeks flamed. It was difficult enough to admit that she had lost her self-control and been ready to surrender—*aching to surrender!*—to a man she'd known less than an hour. But acknowledging that he had been playing sexual games with her, that she had been alone on that passion-drugged cloud, carried her to new heights of mortification. And outrage.

Her uncles had warned her that Cade Austin was ruthless and would stop at nothing to get his own way. It seemed that they were telling the truth.

Determinedly, Kylie worked on putting herself together until the mirror showed the reflection of an immaculately groomed woman, as cool and untouched by passion as she'd always believed herself to be. She pulled open the bathroom door and entered Cade's office.

The tall, wiry, bearded man talking to Cade started visibly at the sight of her. "I—didn't realize you had company, Cade," Noah Wyckoff murmured, glancing from Cade to Kylie, then back again.

"Ms. Brennan isn't company, Noah. She owns the company," Cade said. "I'd like you to meet—our boss." He completed the introductions.

Kylie noted sourly that unlike herself, Cade hadn't required a sojourn in the bathroom to eliminate any telltale evidence of their hot little interlude. She had needed a mirror, makeup, a comb and a vital rearrangement of her clothing to look as unruffled and undisturbed as he did—after no ablutions at all!

"Noah and I go back a long way," Cade said smoothly, filling in what could have been an awkward silence. "We were college roommates at MIT, three years in the dorms, one in an apartment that almost got condemned by the health department."

Noah chuckled at the memory. "Those were the days."

"How very interesting," Kylie managed to choke. She was seething. Cade spoke with the easy assurance of a host making small talk at a cocktail party. Another strike against him, for she was still too rattled to carry off a semblance of conversational patter.

She decided Cade Austin was as slick as an oil spill, which brought her to the unhappy conclusion that she had almost succumbed to the practiced charms of a smooth operator. Another appalling realization in a day that seemed to be filled with them. And it was only lunchtime!

The tension in the office was palpable. Noah cleared his throat. "Will you be joining us for lunch, Ms. Brennan?" he asked politely.

"No," Kylie said, more sharply than she'd intended. She had nothing against Noah Wyckoff but the prospect of spending another moment in Cade's company was intolerable.

"I have an appointment." She swept from the office without looking back.

"I'll be in touch, Kylie." Cade's voice followed her into the corridor.

A promise or a threat? Kylie mused cynically, deciding it must be the latter. Well, he was in for a surprise the next time he got *in touch* with her because she was prepared for him now. She knew the lengths to which he'd go to influence her, to control her. All her defenses were on alert and ready for their next encounter.

She could hardly wait.

Three

"**T**hat one is an entirely new Brennan prototype, one we haven't seen before," Noah remarked after Kylie's departure. "The Ice Queen. I swear the room temperature in here rose twenty degrees the moment she walked out."

"You think she's cold?" Cade gritted through his teeth, staring at the door through which Kylie had just exited.

"You think she's not?" Noah gave a short laugh. "With her around we won't need to build an autoclave to dispose of medical waste, she can freeze it with a single glance." He flopped down onto the sofa and sighed. "Of course, we won't be building anything if she sells BrenCo."

"Which Artie and Guy Brennan are desperate for her to do."

"She won't listen to *them*, will she?"

"I have no idea what Kylie Brennan will do." Cade stared sightlessly at the intricate patterns of the Oriental carpet at his feet. He felt disoriented, as if he'd been flung from a whirling carousel. Yet he was supposed to stand here, still and steady, without displaying a trace of the disequilibrium that had him reeling.

Though Kylie had left the office, she remained so firmly ensconced in his head that the images running before his mind's eye seemed more real than Noah's actual presence. Cade pictured her face, softened with passion. He could taste the sweetness of her mouth and feel the sultry heat of her body pressed to his.

He couldn't remember the last time he'd been so affected, so *consumed* by a kiss. He had learned early on that a kiss was simply a preliminary, a means to the climactic end. But kissing Kylie had been so exciting, so arousing, it was an end in itself.

And then he pictured her breasts, so round and full and milky white, the nipples a dark dusky rose. He remembered the way she had responded to him, how she'd clung to him, moaning her pleasure as his mouth closed over those sensitive little buds.

It had been so good and he wanted more, much more. They had barely begun when they'd had to stop, and now his body was tense and throbbing with all those unmet needs she'd aroused in him.

Cade groaned.

"We have to think positively," Noah said, misinterpreting the cause, though not the source, of his old friend's apparent agony. "Gene named her his heir, so he must've seen something in her that set her apart from the rest of the clan. I mean, imagine what we'd be facing if he'd left Guy those shares! BrenCo would be sold as fast as you can say 'Lauretta wants an in-ground swimming pool, a fur coat and a fancy vacation to brag about.'"

"She said she had an appointment." Cade began to pace the office. "Who with? One of the uncles?"

"I got the impression she just said that to blow us off," Noah said frankly. "She seemed like she was in a big hurry to get out of here."

"Yeah," Cade agreed, frowning. "She couldn't wait to get away."

From him. That rankled. He remembered the way Kylie had looked at him when she'd emerged from the bathroom, appearing as perfect and untouched as a porcelain doll that had never been removed from its box. He'd had to exert considerable willpower to keep from snatching her into his arms and transforming her back into that passion-mussed creature who had lain beneath him, warm and soft and hungry for him.

But the cold disdain in her blue eyes had served as an effective restraint. She'd glared at him as if he were some kind of unspeakable substance she'd accidentally stepped in. Cade read her loud and clear...she didn't want him to come anywhere near her.

He knew if they had been alone, he would have handled things differently. He would've tried to convince her that not only did she want him near, but she wanted him deep inside her. And judging by her explosive response to him earlier, he could have succeeded.

But Noah's presence halted any such attempt. What had gone on between Kylie and himself was intensely private; Cade wanted no third-party involvement, not even his best friend's. So he'd allowed Kylie to sweep out like the Ice Queen Noah believed her to be, rather than acting on those primitive possessive urges rushing through him. They were still rushing through him.

"Did you hear the latest breaking news on the Brennan front?" Noah asked, drawing a pensive Cade's attention. "Brent has been arrested and is in jail. Get this, he'd set up a videocam—"

"I heard. Bobbie called in full-blown hysterics. Did you know that unauthorized filming of individuals is a burglary charge?"

"I do now."

"How did you hear about Brent so quickly? From Bridget? I guess Bobbie must've called her here and—"

"Actually, it was Brenda who called and told me, a short while ago."

"Brenda?" Cade gaped at him. "Why would Brenda call you?"

"It seems I'm her new best friend." Noah shrugged nonchalantly, but Cade noticed that the other man did not meet his eyes.

He felt an ominous stirring. "How did that happen? And when?"

Noah shrugged again and gazed intently at the lake view,

as if bent on observing every rise and swell of the water. "I saw her at The Corner Grill about three weeks ago and we ended up having coffee there after her shift ended. I've heard from her almost every day since. She either phones or drops by my place with a question or with something she's whipped up in the kitchen. She's, uh, a pretty good cook."

"You've been seeing her every day for nearly a month?" Cade's voice rose in apprehension.

"Nothing's happened between us. As I said, we're just friends."

"You sound sorry about that. Does that mean you're thinking about—taking things further with her? God, man, be careful!"

"You sound so alarmed, like I'm about to take a dive into a vat of Agent Orange." Noah grinned, clearly amused. "What are you worried about, that Brenda is set on having her wicked way with me?"

"I'm worried because she is Brenda Brennan, who is manipulative and conniving and the first woman I've heard you mention since Janice left Port McClain two and a half years ago."

"I've spent the past two and a half years exactly the way you have, working sixteen-hour days to implement our ideas and bring this company to the industry's cutting edge." Noah was defensive. "I haven't been pining over Janice or avoiding women, I've been focusing all my attention and energy on BrenCo."

Cade laid a hand on Noah's shoulder. "Look, I know how hard you took the divorce and I don't want to see you get mixed up with a—"

"I appreciate your concern, but we're not nineteen anymore, Cade, you don't have to look out for me. I've been married and divorced, remember? You've done neither. Doesn't that make me the more experienced one? The one who should be giving the advice?"

"No. Not when Brenda Brennan is involved." Or any other woman, Cade added silently.

Despite Noah's marriage and divorce, Cade believed his friend to be as naive about women as he'd been during their college years. Back then Cade, a worldly army brat with a wealth of experience, had felt protective toward the shy, brilliant Noah who'd led a quiet sheltered life of privilege and private schools. He still felt that way.

Cade decided that now was not the time to remind Noah how he'd advised him against marrying Janice in the first place, that he had seen the divorce coming on their wedding day when he'd been cast as best man and had to pretend to be happy for the woefully mismatched pair.

"Cade, I know you're the expert on the Brennans but you're wrong about Brenda," Noah exclaimed earnestly. "I've gotten to know her pretty well these past few weeks. She is bright and sensitive and vulnerable."

"I've never seen that side of her," Cade muttered sardonically.

Lord, what a day this was turning into! First, he'd been blindsided by his attraction to Kylie Brennan, now he was faced with the alarming revelation that his best friend and the number two man at BrenCo was on the verge of being bamboozled by Brenda Brennan.

His eyes flicked to his desk calendar and he noted the date for the first time that day. March 15. "Beware the Ides of March," he quoted grimly. "An applicable bit of advice."

"Don't let the mayor hear you say that. Not on the day we're to convince him that supporting our zoning permit to build an infectious waste autoclave is a great idea." Chuckling, Noah glanced at his watch. "And speaking of the mayor, if we don't leave now, we'll be late for our meeting with him. A bad move. You know how His Honor reveres punctuality."

Cade stifled the urge to issue one more warning about the insidious wiles of Brenda Brennan. Noah didn't want to hear it, he'd made that clear. Worse, Cade found himself challenging his own expertise in matters dealing with the opposite sex. His previously resolute confidence was not quite so resolute.

This morning's encounter with Kylie Brennan had done that to him. He'd always considered himself to be unshakable, but she shook him up, all right. She just might be the most dangerous Brennan of all—smart and alluring and a completely unknown entity. He vowed to be on his guard—on full-alert status!—during their next encounter.

It worried him that he was already looking forward to it.

* * *

The old Brennan homestead was a stately though dilapidated Victorian-style house built in the late 1800s in Port McClain's oldest neighborhood. The spacious lots were landscaped with towering trees, tall hedges and flower gardens. Gene had bought the house for his parents years ago and lived there with them until they died, then stayed on alone until his own death last year.

Wearing jeans, boots and a thick cerulean blue sweater, Kylie sat on a weather-beaten wooden glider on the deep front porch. She'd driven her rental car to the house to oversee the flurry of activity initiated by her morning phone calls.

She stared out at the long, spacious front yard extending to the deserted tree-lined street and remembered summer visits when her grandparents were alive, when the yard was green and bright with color from Grandma's prized gardens. Now it looked as desolate and untended as the inside of the house, where currently a trio of maids from the cleaning service were working hard to make the place livable once again.

A crumpled paper bag held the remains of her lunch, a takeout order from The Corner Grill, a short walk from BrenCo headquarters. Kylie shivered as a chilly breeze rustled the bare branches of the trees. She debated whether to go inside or stay out here. The electricity and water had been turned on, but she didn't want to get in the way of the busy cleaning crew. Unfortunately, she couldn't leave yet, she was still awaiting gas, telephone and cable TV service.

Kylie swung back and forth on the glider, bored and growing colder by the minute. An old-fashioned front porch like this conjured up images of warm summer nights, gentle breezes and tall glasses of lemonade. Instead, the wind was picking up and the sky was darkening. Before long, she wouldn't have to swing herself on the glider, the force of the wind would provide the necessary momentum all on its own.

A tan-colored minivan, filthy and streaked with road salt, pulled into the long gravel driveway and drove right up to the stone path leading to the porch. Kylie tensed as her cousin Brenda climbed out and headed toward her.

She was struck by Brenda's resemblance to her. While they

weren't the "identical cousins" of TV sitcom land, they looked enough alike to be easily identified as family members.

There were some differences, of course. Brenda's hair was longer and pulled high on her head in a ponytail. She wore darker, heavier eyeliner and a dramatic shade of red lipstick, contrasting sharply to Kylie's muted, natural-look makeup. Brenda was several inches shorter than Kylie, and her figure was more voluptuous, her curves lushly revealed by her short tight black sweater and even tighter black jeans. She wore a black leather jacket, which couldn't have provided much protection against the cold wind.

Kylie pulled the zipper of her fleecy blue coat higher as she walked to meet her cousin. "Hello, Brenda. It's nice to see you again." The good manners her mother had instilled in her down through the years automatically kicked in.

"I figured you'd be here," Brenda greeted her without preamble. "I heard you bought lunch-to-go at The Corner Grill. I'm a waitress there, but I'm off today," she added.

Kylie nodded, for lack of a better response. She tried to remember the last time she'd had a conversation with Brenda and couldn't. The few times she had seen her cousin in the past years they'd been surrounded by other Brennans and barely had the time or opportunity to exchange hellos.

Well, there was nobody around now. Perhaps for the first time ever, the two cousins were alone together. They stood on the wide flat stone just below the three wooden stairs leading to the porch.

"How long are you planning to stay here?" Brenda asked bluntly.

"I'm not really sure," murmured Kylie with a small smile. No one could accuse Brenda of not coming immediately to the point.

"Are you here to sell the company and Uncle Gene's house like my father and Uncle Guy said?" Before Kylie had a chance to say a word, Brenda forged ahead. "They brought this big shot to town from Cleveland to convince you to sell BrenCo. His name is Axel Dodge. Have you met him yet? Ian was the one who hooked him up with Dad and Uncle Guy. A bad sign, right there. Ian is nastier than air pollution...he's human toxic waste. Too bad BrenCo can't dispose of *him* through one of their environmentally friendly processes.''

''Axel Dodge?'' Kylie chose to ignore the slur to their mutual cousin and tried for a tactful diversion. ''That sounds more like a car dealership than a person's name.''

Brenda's lips twitched, as if she were on the verge of a smile. She immediately suppressed the urge and scowled instead. ''If you're as smart as Uncle Gene seemed to think, you'll tell Axel Dodge to get lost. Then you'll tell Ian, Uncle Guy and my father to butt out of BrenCo for good. They're greedy, and it's made them stupid. So are you if you listen to them.''

Kylie thought of Cade's comment about the bickering, backstabbing Brennans. Now here was Brenda, bashing three members of the clan and indirectly Kylie herself, right to her face.

Nor had Brenda finished her tirade. ''Dad and Ian and Uncle Guy don't care about the business, they don't care about the people in town who'll lose their jobs if the company is sold. All they want is to get their hands on some quick easy money to throw around.''

''You sound exactly like Cade,'' Kylie blurted out.

''I heard you saw him today.'' Brenda's deep blue eyes seemed to bore into her. ''Bridget told me you showed up at BrenCo and Cade took you into his office. She said he was looking at you the way our cat watches the fish in Starr Lynn's aquarium.''

Every now and then, Brenda decides that I would be a good match for her. Cade's voice seemed to be echoing in Kylie's head. The intensity of her cousin's stare unnerved her. Was Brenda jealous of the time she'd spent with Cade? She couldn't tell, but remembering her own ignoble reaction to the thought of a Cade and Brenda coupling brought a rush of color to Kylie's cheeks.

Brenda noticed. ''Did Cade put the moves on you?''

''Brenda!'' Kylie made a strangled protest.

''You're actually blushing! He did hit on you, just like Bridget said he would!'' Brenda exclaimed gleefully. ''How far did you get? Did you do The Nasty right there in his office?''

"Certainly not!" Kylie was aghast. She remembered the way Cade had kissed her, had touched her, had carried her in his arms. Her blush deepened. "I—I'd really rather not discuss this, Brenda."

"Are you mad at Cade? Did he come on too strong? You can't blame him for trying to get next to you, Kylie. Why, he'd be crazy not to," Brenda stated baldly. "You're the major stockholder and Cade wants full control of the company. He should've had it, too. Everybody knows that Cade intended to buy out Uncle Gene's shares."

"Why didn't Uncle Gene leave the shares to Cade or make some arrangement in the will for him to buy them?" Kylie quizzed, hoping to divert her.

"My mama says Uncle Gene was so arrogant he thought he was immortal. He lived his life like he was gonna live forever but he didn't, and now BrenCo is at risk. Which would kill him if he weren't dead already," Brenda added with relish. "Uncle Gene loved the company more than anything or anybody in the whole world. I bet the threat of BrenCo being sold has that nasty old grouch spinning like a top in his fancy mausoleum."

Her outspoken cousin did not hold back when it came to other Brennans, Kylie noted, which fit Cade's description of the inner workings of the family. However, Brenda's staunch defense of Cade took her completely by surprise.

"You seem to be very loyal to Cade Austin," Kylie murmured, trying to sound casual.

"And you're wondering why." This time Brenda did smile. "No, you're way past wondering, you're *dying* to know why."

Kylie stared at her, transfixed. There was a sweetness about Brenda when she smiled. She looked younger, the hard weariness erased from her face.

"I think Cade's hot, I admit it." Brenda's smile widened and her blue eyes sparkled, making her very pretty indeed. "I mean, what's not to like? He's big and strong and good-looking, not to mention single. He's got that macho, take-charge attitude that women find irresistible, even fem-lib types like you, I'll bet. He has lots of admirers in town but he usually goes into Cleveland for his, uh, social life. It's less than an hour down the interstate and there's a lot more to do there than here.''

"So he leaves town to play swinging bachelor in the city?" Kylie's heartbeat was pounding in her ears.

"I heard he's dating a lady dentist there. Can you imagine dating a *dentist?* They put their hands in peoples' mouths!" Brenda shuddered her distaste. "Anyway, I made it pretty obvious to Cade that I was interested in him but he never took me up on it. Mama says that's why she trusts him, because he could've used me but he didn't. Plus, he's been very good to Starr Lynn. BrenCo has this special fund to support local athletics—the high school teams and Little League and Girls Softball—and Cade put Starr Lynn on the list. Uncle Gene was opposed, he said figure skating was too individualistic and elitist to qualify for his community sports aid. That mean old coot didn't want to give my baby a cent, but Cade made sure Starr Lynn gets money for her training every year from that fund.''

A lady dentist? Kylie didn't hear a word about Cade's valiant support of young Starr Lynn's endeavors. A slow burn kindled within her. *He was involved with a lady dentist from Cleveland?* Yet he'd made a heavy pass at her this morning anyway.

Well, as Brenda had so succinctly stated, why wouldn't he? Seducing a woman in order to control her was a course of action dating back to the last millennium, probably even before. Nor were Cade's intentions anything she hadn't already figured out herself, but hearing Brenda announce it, learning about the existence of another woman…

Kylie swallowed and found it painful. There was a hard lump lodged in her throat.

"You can have him if you want him, you know."

Brenda's voice sounded above the cacophony going on in her head. Kylie looked up to meet her cousin's gaze. She was disconcerted to find Brenda studying her, practically dissecting her with those glittering Brennan-blue eyes of hers.

"Why would I want a man who has no qualms about using me, despite his involvement with another woman? Who is only interested in my shares of BrenCo?"

"My guess is that your BrenCo shares aren't the only thing

about you that interests him,'' Brenda said, giving her another embarrassingly thorough once-over. ''You're beautiful. Classy. And smart. I bet you could beat out any dentist with a flick of your pinky.''

Kylie smiled in spite of herself. ''Maybe Cade doesn't share your aversion to dentists, Brenda.''

''Lady Drill-bit hasn't landed him yet,'' Brenda pointed out. ''I think it would be cool if you and Cade got together, Kylie. In fact, I'll help you nail him if you want.''

Having heard Cade rant against the Brennans, Kylie doubted that Brenda's assistance would be of much use, even if she wanted help *nailing* Cade. Which she most certainly did not because she didn't want any man who was unscrupulous and avaricious, qualities Cade Austin possessed in spades! Still, she was oddly touched by Brenda's offer. Her display of cousinly solidarity was heartwarming. According to Cade, that self-appointed Brennan-ologist, her cousin should have been venal and vengeful toward her.

''Thank you, Brenda,'' Kylie said quietly. ''I appreciate your offer, but I don't want Cade Austin.''

Brenda mulled this over. ''Are you interested in another man? Some guy back in Philadelphia?''

Kylie shook her head.

''Would you help me?'' Brenda asked suddenly.

Kylie was back on her guard. ''Help you to, er, nail Cade? To lure him away from Madame Root Canal in Cleveland?'' she tried to make a joke, though she didn't feel at all like laughing.

''No, I've given up on Cade. There is somebody else, a man who's different from any other man I've ever known.'' Brenda's voice filled with emotion. ''He doesn't treat me like I'm some kind of cheap, stupid nobody. He—acts as if he actually likes talking to me.'' She paused, seemingly staggered by the notion.

Kylie watched and listened carefully. At this particular moment, Brenda put her in mind of countless clients she'd defended, women who had no faith in their own abilities or appeal. Women who had been used by men and who considered themselves worthless. Most of those women weren't lucky enough to find a man different from any others they had known, a man who actually considered what they had to say to be worth listening to. But it seemed her cousin had.

Kylie made her decision on the spot. "I'll be glad to help you any way I can, Brenda."

"Do you really mean it?" Brenda's face lit up. "I can hardly believe it! Who would've ever thought that *you* would help me?"

"I can imagine the kinds of things you've heard about me," Kylie said dryly. Especially after Uncle Gene's will was read. "But, truly, I'm neither a fiend nor a demon."

"We thought you were a—well, never mind. When I came out here today to warn you about Axel Dodge, Mama said it was hopeless, that you'd never listen to me. But I thought I had to try, for BrenCo's sake."

Kylie pondered the alliances within the family and the company. And politics was supposed to make strange bedfellows! "I haven't met Axel Dodge but—"

"You will," Brenda cut in, frowning. "We heard that Dad and Uncle Guy are going to call you tonight and set up a meeting for tomorrow. Axel Dodge will be there. Probably Aunt Lauretta, too." Brenda's voice lowered, becoming hushed and confidential in tone. "I can't stand her! She puts on phony airs, just because she's married to the editor of the *Port McClain Post*—as if that crummy little rag is the *New York Times* or something! Anyway, everybody knows Uncle Gene bought Uncle Guy that position of editor with all the money he gave to the paper."

"I hadn't heard that," Kylie murmured, both drawn in and repelled by the family gossip.

"Oh, there's lots you haven't heard, but I'll fill you in. For instance, did you know that Aunt Lauretta calls herself a *socialite?* Can you believe it, a Port McClain socialite? That's good for a laugh."

"It does seem like something of an oxymoron," Kylie murmured.

"Yeah!" Brenda exclaimed so fervently that Kylie wondered how her cousin had interpreted her remark. She didn't want to stir up a Brennan vs. Brennan feud with herself in the middle and felt obliged to add, "Aunt Lauretta has always been very nice to me, every time I've seen her."

"Don't be fooled, she hates you," Brenda warned, her eyes flashing. "She hates your mother and dad and brother, too. She says the four of you think you're superior to everybody here and that you turned Uncle Gene against the rest of the family so he'd leave you the most in his will. Uncle Guy and Ian feel the same way. You should hear the awful things they say about you and your family!"

Kylie felt a blind rush of anger surge through her. If it was Brenda's intention to turn her against the Guy Brennan branch of the family, her salvo had been quite effective. Kylie caught herself right before she retaliated with a crack about small town snobs and their petty jealousies. She took a deep breath, willing herself to remain rational and in control.

"You know, Bridget and I have always loved your mom and dad!" Brenda exclaimed enthusiastically. "They're our favorite aunt and uncle. We treasure the dolls Uncle Wayne and Aunt Connie sent us from all over the world when we were kids. And now Starr Lynn loves to look at them. She knows they'll be hers someday."

Kylie's sense of humor asserted itself. Brenda was laying it on awfully thick. It appeared she was attempting, without a trace of subtlety, to claim most-favored Brennan status. If nothing else, Cade had made a legitimate point about the family backstabbing. This was an anecdote she might've shared with him—if she didn't despise him as a conniving user.

The cousins' attention was drawn to the street, where a dark green Buick was turning into the driveway.

"That's Cade's car," Brenda announced. "Bridget, Brent and me think Cade should drive something sexy and super-expensive, like a Porsche or a Ferrari. I mean, a Buick seems so staid and no fun. So very Port McClain. Uncle Gene drove a Buick, so did Grandpa Brennan."

"Maybe Cade keeps a flashy sports car stashed in Cleveland to use when he's playing smooth operator," Kylie said cattily.

"You think so?" Brenda suddenly clasped her hands to her face, her blue eyes huge. "Oh, Kylie, Noah is in the car with him!"

"Noah Wyckoff?"

"You know him?" Brenda seemed to be having trouble breathing. "How?"

"I met him today in Cade's office." Kylie noticed her cousin's loss of composure and reached an immediate conclusion. "Brenda, is Noah Wyckoff the man you told me about?"

Brenda nodded her head. "He's such a nice guy. But he's shy. I've been encouraging him—Mama says I'm chasing him—but he hasn't made a single move on me. He hasn't even held my hand yet! I know he likes me but I'm getting desperate."

Cade parked his maligned Buick directly behind Brenda's minivan, which was behind Kylie's car, a sparkling clean white compact. One of her stops this morning had been to the car wash to remove the grime from her long drive from Philadelphia.

The two men walked toward the cousins, their stride leisurely and unhurried—as if they were merely paying a casual visit, as if they were not on a mission of pressure and manipulation. But Kylie wasn't fooled. She seethed.

"Mama says I should play it cool," Brenda whispered urgently. "She says I'm acting too available and Noah will lose interest in me if I keep it up. But he *needs* encouragement, Kylie. If I play hard to get, he might decide not to try to get me."

Kylie watched Cade and Noah approach them, her heart beating far faster than it should. Not from nervous excitement, she insisted. From anger. From sheer disgust. She would not be used by that snake Cade Austin again!

She wanted to order him off the premises and would have done so, but for her promise to help Brenda *nail* Noah Wyckoff. As one who hadn't conspired in a female entrapment plot since junior high, Kylie wondered how useful she would be to her cousin's cause. But she had promised to try. She cast a quick glance at the visibly nervous Brenda.

"One thing I've learned is that mothers often have a way of being right," Kylie murmured. "It came as a distinct surprise to me because as a teenager, I thought my mom was fairly clueless. But the older I get, the more I realize that mothers usually know what they're talking about."

"Meaning I should play it cool like Mama says?" Brenda was skeptical.

"If Noah is shy, you don't want to scare him off by coming

on too strong." Kylie had a feeling that Brenda unleashed might fall into the category of downright unnerving.

"Then *you'll* have to do something to keep him around. Like—like ask us to have dinner with you tonight," Brenda whispered urgently. "Insist on it!"

Cade and Noah came to a halt a foot or two away from them.

"Well, this is a surprise." Brenda's voice lowered to a sultry purr and she shot Noah the hottest come-hither look Kylie had ever seen directed at anyone. So much for playing it cool.

A dull flush spread from Noah's neck to his forehead. "Hello, Brenda," he mumbled, then glanced uneasily at Cade.

"We didn't expect to see you two here, especially during working hours. That's very unBrenCo of you." Brenda took a few steps closer to Noah. "But we're thrilled you're here, aren't we, Kyle?"

"Incredibly thrilled," Kylie echoed, deadpan.

She saw Cade clench his jaw as he observed Brenda's come-on and Noah's reaction. Kylie instantly intuited his disapproval. Cade did not like the idea of a Brenda-Noah match, not at all. She watched as his frown became a full-fledged glower, and a naughty thrill shot through her. Why, Cade positively *hated* Brenda's fledgling relationship with his friend.

All of a sudden, her promise to her cousin became a pleasure to fulfill.

"What are you doing here, Brenda?" Cade demanded, in a parole-officer-to-recalcitrant-parolee tone of voice.

"Brenda and I have been catching up on family gossip," Kylie replied breezily. "In fact, we have so much to talk about we're having dinner together tonight." She turned to Noah. "I'm sorry I had to rush off this morning, I hope I didn't seem rude."

Noah shifted uneasily. "Er, not at all, Miss Brennan."

"Kylie," she corrected with a dazzling smile. "You're kind to overlook it, Noah, but I'm afraid I really was rude. As a way of making amends, I'd like to invite you to join Bren and me for dinner tonight."

"Kyle and Bren?" Cade gritted through his teeth.

"I—I would very much like to have dinner with you.

Both." Noah's eyes were locked with Brenda's and his breathing had accelerated.

"That's wonderful!" Brenda cooed. She moved so close to Noah that their bodies were a hairsbreadth from touching.

Cade scowled. "What time and where are we eating?"

"You're not invited," Kylie snapped. "It's just the three of us."

She'd already formulated her plan, which included pleading a migraine headache, ideally before the soup was served, and then going home, leaving the couple to finish the meal and the evening alone.

"Kylie's mad at you, she thinks you're a two-timing pig," Brenda said succinctly.

"What?" Cade gasped.

"Well, what do you expect her to think?" Brenda demanded. "You made a big play for her in your office this morning and you already have a girlfriend, um, stashed in Cleveland. With your sports car."

"Brenda!" Kylie groaned. As an ally, her cousin had a long way to go.

"What kind of tales have you been telling?" Cade was outraged.

Kylie wasn't sure if the question was directed at her or Brenda, or maybe both of them.

Noah stared at the ground, his shoulders shaking oddly. Cade realized he was laughing. "This isn't funny!" he snarled.

"Probably not," Noah agreed. But he didn't stop laughing.

Brenda laughed, too. "Did you know his girlfriend is a *dentist?* Who knows what kind of kinky stuff they do with all that weird dental equip—"

"Shut up, Brenda!" Cade's eyes smoldered. "Kylie, I want to talk to you. Right now."

He caught her arm and dragged her up the stairs and onto the porch, out of earshot of Brenda and Noah who were now chatting easily together. Their shared laughter had proven an effective icebreaker.

Kylie did not go quietly, she protested all the way. "Stop manhandling me! I don't want to talk to you. Unless we're discussing BrenCo, we have nothing to say to each other."

She tried to pull away from him but he had an iron grip on her arm and propelled her alongside him. It was a strange sensation, having her feet move when she didn't want to walk. Once again, Cade's size and strength had proven superior to her will. Kylie fumed. Despite Brenda's assumption, she did not find his macho, take-charge attitude irresistible. More like infuriating.

"Let me go!" she ordered.

Cade responded by ignoring her command and reinforcing his grasp, taking hold of her shoulders with both hands. He held her firmly in place, mere inches in front of him. "Just to set the record straight, I do not have a girlfriend stashed in Cleveland. Or a sports car."

"You're claiming that Brenda invented the lady dentist?" Kylie instantly regretted her reply.

She shouldn't have said a word, she should have frozen him out with icy silence. But she was curious. Would he lie about the woman in Cleveland? She half hoped he would, then she could brand him a liar and be done with him forever. There was nothing she despised more than a calculating liar.

"I assume Brenda is referring to Anne Woodley," Cade said tightly. "Anne is a dentist in Cleveland and we dated a while, but stopped seeing each other well over a year ago. To be more accurate, it was several months before Gene's death and no, there wasn't a big dramatic breakup scene. We didn't have that kind of relationship. Anne and I mutually decided to end it and we've remained on good terms."

"How civilized. And how convenient to remain on good terms with your dentist friend. Does that mean you commute to Cleveland for regular checkups?" The words were out before she could think not to say them. Kylie was horrified with herself. She seemed to be acquiring the Brennan cousin habit of blurting out whatever crossed her mind.

"You don't owe me any explanations," she added quickly, striving for damage control. "I don't care if—"

"Telling Brenda that I'm a two-timing pig implies that you do care." Cade's temper was dissolving, his angry expression swiftly transforming into one of dawning male satisfaction. A slow smile crossed his face.

Kylie was determined to wipe it off. "I never said that. The words—and the sentiment behind them—are strictly Brenda's own."

His smile widened. "Well, just to set the record straight and to keep the facts current, John Paul Vukovich here in Port McClain is my dentist. He's first-rate. I highly recommend him if you're in need of any dental work while you're in town."

Kylie swallowed. This was definitely an area to avoid. Sometimes in court an inflammatory loser of a topic was introduced. With disaster pending, the smartest course was to drop it quickly and move onto something else.

"What are you doing here?" she demanded brusquely. The old tried-and-true adage "the best defense is a good offense" was tried-and-true because it worked.

"Noah and I wanted to fill you in on our plans for BrenCo's future. We had a very rewarding lunch meeting with the mayor and thought you should be informed." Cade was still holding her and his fingers began to knead her shoulders. "And I wanted to see how things were going out here at Gene's place. If you've had any problems, I'll—"

"I haven't had any problems. Everything is progressing very well here." Kylie knew she should step away from him. There was no reason for her to stand here, letting him hold her.

Except she liked his touch too much to make him stop. Alarm bells sounded in her head. The lady dentist might've been relegated to footnote status in his personal history but there were other reasons for keeping Cade Austin at arm's length. First and foremost was her fifty-one percent stock ownership in BrenCo. *That* was what Cade Austin found most appealing about her. Not her body or her mind. She could look like a troglodyte and have the personality of a stone and it wouldn't matter, he would still attempt to seduce her.

He wanted to control her, to sweet-talk her into doing his bidding so he could retain control of BrenCo. Her pride demanded that she resist him. What woman wanted to be wanted for her shares in a toxic waste plant?

You can't blame him for trying to get next to you, Kylie. Why, he'd be crazy not to. You're the major stockholder and Cade wants full control of the company. Brenda had neatly summed up the situation.

Kylie lifted her eyes and met his. He was watching her, his gaze piercing. Assessing. Planning his next move? He considered himself an expert in the art of dealing with Brennans, and she was one of them.

The wind whistled around them and she shivered. Cade rubbed his hands up and down her arms to warm her. "It's too cold to stand around out here," he said softly. "Why don't we go inside and—"

The sound of car doors slamming, immediately followed by the roar of a car engine broke the silence. Cade and Kylie both turned to see Brenda drive her minivan over the frozen yard, going around Cade's car, which was blocking the driveway. Noah was in the front seat beside her.

"Hey!" Cade shouted and bolted down the porch stairs. "Brenda! Noah! Come back here!"

Brenda gave the horn a jaunty honk, then steered the van back onto the driveway. Within seconds, she'd peeled out and was on the street, heading away from the house.

You go, girl. Kylie grinned as she offered her silent support to her cousin. Mother's wisdom aside, playing it cool simply wasn't Brenda's style. Wasn't it better to simply be yourself in a relationship, without resorting to wiles and games?

She watched Cade standing at the foot of the stairs, his arms folded in front of his chest. She wondered what he was thinking; she could guess, but wondering and guessing weren't enough. Kylie left the porch to go stand beside him. For a few moments, the two of them stared at the trail of exhaust lingering in the air, the last traces of the getaway van and its occupants.

"I forgot all about them." Cade appeared stunned by his memory lapse.

"Poor Cade. So much to do, so little time," Kylie mocked. "You were concentrating so hard on trying to charm me on behalf of my BrenCo stock that you couldn't properly chaperone Brenda and Noah. Personally, I'm glad they escaped," she added tartly.

"Escape, ha! It's more like a kidnapping. Brenda lured poor Noah into—"

"You're lying to yourself, if you believe that. Noah looked thrilled to see Brenda. He was practically breathless with excitement. No, this was definitely a mutual escape from the condemning eyes of Big Brother. That's you,'' she stated, just in case he chose not to get her point.

"You're enjoying this immensely, aren't you?'' Cade asked, his expression as dry as his tone.

That surprised Kylie. She'd expected him to be jumping up and down shrieking his frustration, à la Rumpelstiltskin. Well, perhaps her next statement would drive him over the edge. "I think Noah is good for Brenda. I've gotten the impression that she hasn't been very well treated by men. He seems to be a wonderful change for her. I'm going to do whatever I can to help them get together.''

"That save-the-world streak of yours is rearing its ugly head, I see.'' Cade rolled his eyes. "You've been in Port McClain less than twenty-four hours and you're already on a crusade.''

Still, he wasn't ranting and raving. Kylie's eyes narrowed. "You're not angry?''

He shrugged. "I don't waste my energy on something I can do nothing about, and right now there is nothing I can do about Brenda and Noah.'' He smiled at her, that heart-stopping smile that had wreaked havoc on her self-control and her common sense earlier that day. "I'd rather concentrate on you.''

Four

"**D**on't you have a company to run?" Kylie took a step away from him, then another. Cade surprised her by dropping his hands and letting her move out of his reach. She hadn't expected him to acquiesce, and she was aware of a vague disappointment, which unsettled her. Had she wanted him to turn caveman and yank her against him?

Definitely not, Kylie assured herself. Reflexively, her eyes flew to his face to find him watching her, his mouth curved into an enigmatic smile.

"Are you telling me to get back to work, Boss Lady?"

"Of course not. It's just—I just— There is really no need for you to be wasting your valuable time here. I have everything under control." Everything except herself. She felt edgy and off balance, not to mention maddeningly conflicted. Kylie admitted the unholy truth to herself—she wanted him to stay as much as she wanted him to leave.

"I'm sure you do. And I'll give you a reprieve from me...but only on one condition." His smile had changed and this time it wasn't hard to read—it was elemental and pure male and stirred Kylie's already heightened senses.

"What condition would that be? Turning over my BrenCo shares to you?"

She hoped that she looked and sounded sufficiently cool and cynical. She certainly didn't feel it. Inside, she was as nervous as a schoolgirl, churning with a dangerous mix of confusion and excitement.

"If and when I buy those shares from you, there will be no conditions attached." Cade was serious now, the glimmer of humor in his eyes completely gone. "The decision to keep or to sell your shares in BrenCo is yours alone to make, Kylie. But it must be an informed decision."

"And you just happen to be the one to inform me?" she suggested wryly.

She suspected the facts he presented would lead to only one inevitable choice: to maintain the status quo at BrenCo. No doubt her uncles had facts to support the opposite decision, to sell BrenCo. Kylie stifled a sigh, and wished she were back in a courtroom in Philadelphia with a judge and a jury to make the informed decisions.

"Yes, I'm going to *inform* you, Kylie." He flashed a wicked pirate's grin.

How had he managed to make that innocuous verb sound titillating and filled with lusty promise? A veiled substitute for a specific, vigorous act. Kylie felt her cheeks flush with heat, even though the icy wind was whipping around them.

"If you have time now, I brought all the necessary information with me for a full presentation." Cade's voice, once more firm and serious, broke into the chaos swirling in her head.

Kylie stared at him. He was all business, not a trace of the seductive grin or the suggestive note evident in his voice. He could've been addressing the State Chamber of Commerce, so sober and professional was his mien. Had her fevered imagination conjured up that sexual innuendo? she wondered nervously. It was so unlike her. Why, her imagination had never before come close to being fevered!

'We can go inside the house or return to my office, if you prefer," Cade continued in his BrenCo chief executive tone.

"And, um, is that the condition you mentioned? To listen

to your presentation?'' She was guiltily aware that her mind had been drifting too far and too fast.

Worse, she was flooded with images of this morning's sojourn in Cade's office. The big gray leather sofa...his mouth, hard and demanding on hers...herself flushed and breathless and out of control as she writhed against him.

Kylie swallowed. If his presentation included a repeat of this morning's sensual blitz, she would do well to remain on her own turf where she was in command.

''I prefer to go into the house,'' she said decisively. ''We'll have to keep out of the cleaning crew's way, which might mean moving from room to room, but that shouldn't be more than a minor inconvenience.''

The trio's presence would also serve to deflect any possible physical encounters between her and Cade—not that she was encouraging any such thing! After this morning's embarrassing, too-revealing fiasco, she was determined to relegate the relationship between her and Cade Austin to a strictly professional basis.

''Whatever.'' Cade accepted her declaration with a shrug of nonchalance. ''I'll get my briefcase from the car.''

Kylie waited for him in the foyer of the front hall. The kitchen, living room and dining room each had a cleaning crew member hard at work so the pair chose the only unoccupied downstairs room. They entered Gene Brennan's study, which already had been vacuumed, polished, dusted and scrubbed.

Cade walked around the room, glancing at the books that lined the shelves, at the vast walnut desktop that was gleaming and bare except for a Lucite pen holder containing an assortment of ballpoint pens, the kind sold in packs at discount drugstores.

He sat down in Gene's chair behind the desk. When he leaned back, it creaked and bobbed precariously. ''Same rickety old chair. Gene refused to get it fixed or buy himself a new one. He hated spending money on himself. He wanted almost every penny to go back into the business.''

Kylie walked to the window and looked out. From the broken desk chair, the view was of four dented old metal garbage cans lined against the side of the house surrounded by the remains of frozen weeds. In the immediate foreground was the rotting wooden door that opened into the old-fashioned, un-used coal bin in the cellar. The visual effect was that of a seedy back alley.

"This must've been a particularly unappealing sight right before garbage pickup day, with the cans overflowing and all," Kylie mused aloud. "And in warm weather if the win-dow was open, the incomparable aroma of rotting garbage would fill the air."

She shook her head, puzzled. "Of all the rooms in this house, with so many of them overlooking the front or back-yards with those big beautiful trees and flower beds, why did Uncle Gene choose this one for his office at home? Let's face it, it's hardly a room with a view."

"A nice view didn't matter to him. I doubt that Gene ever glanced out the window. Your uncle was very single-minded, Kylie. If he was doing his paperwork in here, that would be his sole focus. Period. And keep in mind that Gene didn't find garbage offensive. BrenCo started out as a household waste disposal firm, remember?"

"Please don't make that awful 'garbage was his bread and butter' joke!" Kylie held up her hand, as if to ward it off. "I remember my grandfather and my uncles each saying it about ten times every time we visited. And my mom would always nudge me to remind me to be polite and laugh."

"Bad jokes aren't part of my presentation," Cade promised. "I want to tell you how——"

"I know the basic facts," Kylie cut in. Cade Austin's wildly successful stewardship at BrenCo was a familiar part of Bren-nan lore. "Uncle Gene hired you away from the SaniTech Corporation eight years ago and gave you free rein at the com-pany. You have an environmental engineering degree and an M.B.A., and you built BrenCo into a leading industry giant in the field of universal waste disposal."

"Gene allowed me to implement my ideas and choose my own team," agreed Cade. "I brought in Noah Wyckoff, among others. We built up BrenCo and you inherited it. That makes you a player in the field, too, Kylie."

Kylie winced. Her friends tended to equate waste disposal with Chernobyl, and she well remembered the jokes she and her brother used to make about BrenCo—that the color of the waters flowing in McClain Creek was an unnatural neon chartreuse, that workers at the plant glowed in the dark. Not true, of course. Just jokes.

But now she was a player in the field she'd mocked for years.

"Don't flinch." Cade was scowling. Since he couldn't keep his eyes off her, he observed her every reaction, no matter how brief or subtle. "Come on, Kylie, as a public defender you've dealt with all kinds of felonies but you don't flinch and wince or shudder at murder, grand larceny, armed robbery or assault, do you? Well, BrenCo's disposal of toxic waste is both safe and legal yet you seem determined to cast it as a repulsive and unseemly crime against—"

"That is sophistry, and if we were in court, I'd be all over you for it."

"I think it's a pretty good point," he drawled. "And even though we're not in court, I wouldn't mind having you all over me."

"Now there's a line worthy of either Beavis or Butthead." Kylie turned away from him to stare out the window again.

Once again, Cade read her loud and clear. She would rather contemplate the ugly view of the garbage cans than waste her eyesight looking at a crude, regressed adolescent like him.

He frowned. What a lousy time for her to shift into humorless feminist gear! Was she expecting an apology from him? He railed against it. Apologize for what? He'd made a little joke, and being the prickly Brennan that she was, she had been quick and eager to take offense.

For a few long minutes, neither of them spoke.

"Gene's office here at his home looks exactly like it did when he was alive. It's as if he just stepped out for a minute or two." Cade was the first to break the silence. After all, he was used to dealing with Brennans, and she was merely another one.

He stared moodily at Kylie as she gazed out the window. Who was he kidding? She was so much more than a troublesome Brennan and his pursuit of her was not solely motivated by BrenCo. Cade faced the uneasy truth. She was the woman who'd seized his imagination—and other more tangible parts of him—as no other woman before her.

He studied her profile, the smooth ivory skin and the soft pink of her cheeks, the graceful curve of her neck. He watched her tuck several loose strands of her dark brown hair behind her ear, drawing his attention to her delicately shaped earlobes, pierced with small gold studs. Out of her professional garb, wearing jeans and a sweater, she looked very young, relaxed and informal...but twice as lovely and sexy as hell.

As if on cue, he felt his sex stir, growing heavier and thicker as he continued his perusal of her. Though her sweater was comfortably oversize—certainly nothing like the second skin garments favored by her cousins Brenda and Bridget—he could see the outlined curves of her breasts. The subtlety, the private secrets of what lay beneath the thick fabric both teased and tantalized him because he *knew* what was so discreetly concealed.

The sensual memory of Kylie Brennan lying on his couch, her eyes closed, her lips parted, her lush, naked breasts in his hands struck him hard. Literally. Cade leaned forward in the broken chair and nearly groaned aloud.

"Nothing has been taken out of Uncle Gene's study since he died?" Kylie's voice drifted through the erotic haze encompassing him. "It's always looked like this, so sparse and impersonal?"

She turned to gaze around the office. "There are no pictures or certificates on the walls, not even a diploma. Nothing to break up the plain old beige wallpaper. And the desk and the tabletops are bare. There is almost a kind of monastic feel to the place."

Cade, who was far from feeling remotely monastic, merely grunted a nonreply.

"This is the first time I've ever been in Uncle Gene's office," Kylie continued softly, walking along the length of the bookshelves, glancing at the titles stored there. Engineering textbooks by the dozens. Bound thick copies of environmental studies. A dictionary. Several biographies, all of military officers. It appeared that light reading to Gene Brennan meant the voluminous editions chronicling the lives of Pershing, MacArthur and Patton, among others.

"When we visited here as kids, this door was always closed and I used to wonder what was inside," Kylie confessed. "Dad told Devlin and me that Uncle Gene's office was strictly off-limits." She smiled at the memory. "As born-and-bred military offspring, we knew that meant to keep out, no questions asked."

"So you never even tried to sneak in here? Not once?" Cade recalled his own days as a born-and-bred military offspring. He knew he would've made it inside the off-limits territory at least once or been busted trying.

The difference between officers' kids and noncoms' kids? Between navy and army brats? Or simply the basic differences between rule-conscious Kylie and risk-taking Cade?

"Never, not once," Kylie affirmed earnestly.

"Such obedient angels!" Cade laughed. "No wonder Gene preferred you and your brother to his hometown nieces and nephews. Apparently, that gang had no respect for the rule not to enter his Holy of Holies. Right up until he died, Gene would become irate telling how Brenda, Brent and Ian would sneak into his office whenever they were at the house visiting their grandparents."

"Weren't they just children at the time?"

"Of course. But Gene was convinced they were treacherous little connivers and he never changed his view of them. After your grandparents died, he wouldn't let them into the house. He said there was no reason for them to be there, that he'd only tolerated their presence in his house because his mother and father insisted on inviting their grandchildren over."

"That's awfully cold." Kylie thought of the way Brenda had referred to their uncle Gene. Mean old coot. Nasty old grouch. Apparently, she had some justifiable grounds for those sentiments. "He—he didn't have a very strong sense of family, did he?"

But Uncle Gene had supported his parents, he'd adored her dad and he'd left controlling interest in his successful company to her. Kylie felt both guilty and disloyal for judging him harshly.

"Gene wasn't a doting uncle and he never pretended to be. Your younger cousins didn't irritate him as much as the older ones, but at best he was indifferent to them." Cade shrugged.

"As for Gene's sense of family—he felt he couldn't escape his family. He considered them to be the proverbial millstone around his neck."

Kylie eyed him shrewdly. "And now the Brennans are *your* proverbial millstone?"

"Millstone? Ha! Try concrete abutment."

He had a flat, droll way of delivering certain lines that made her unsure if he was kidding or not. Kylie gave an uncertain little laugh. "I guess you must've gone ballistic when the will was read. I inherited the shares in BrenCo and you got the concrete abutment. Makes you wonder if Uncle Gene was of sound mind."

Their eyes met.

"He was," Cade affirmed. "And as Noah often reminds me, things could've been a lot worse. If Artie and Guy had those shares, BrenCo would already be on the block."

"I just don't know why Uncle Gene left them to me." Kylie stared at Cade, bewildered. "Why not my father or my brother?"

"I admit I've wondered that myself," he murmured.

He didn't mention that he'd also lamented the fact that Gene had bypassed Wayne and Devlin Brennan in favor of Kylie. He'd talked to both men by telephone and knew that either of them would've left all decisions regarding BrenCo to him. Neither one would have allowed any other Brennan to make a pitch at selling the company because Cade would've nixed it first. But Kylie "let's-give-all-sides-a-fair-hearing-just-like-we-do-in-court" Brennan was a wild card.

And the wild card happened to be the heiress.

He gave her a brooding stare. What a helluva dilemma Gene had set up for him! He resented Kylie but he wanted her, too. And the balance was perpetually shifting. When he was in her presence desire won out, but apart from her the scales tipped in favor of resentment.

Kylie felt his eyes on her. "I—I know this can't be easy for you, but I hope you understand my position. I have to be fair. And I'd like to weigh all the—"

"What was Brenda really doing here this afternoon?" Cade broke in, frowning. "Skip the catching-up-with-family-news excuse, we both know it's bogus. Was she trying to turn you against me? Telling you that I was involved with—''

"You have Brenda all wrong." It was Kylie's turn to interrupt. She did *not* care to delve into another rehash of Cade's relationship with the lady dentist from Cleveland. Imagining him with another woman—kissing her, caressing her, smiling into her eyes—made her stomach churn with flulike intensity. Best to get this discussion back to BrenCo.

"The reason Brenda came by was to warn me that her father and Uncle Guy would be calling me today to set up a meeting with them and their consultant, a man named Axel Dodge. Brenda and Bobbie are solidly behind you, Cade. Or else they're solidly against Artie and Guy, I'm not quite sure which cause is stronger."

"Axel Dodge?" Cade didn't look at all pleased. "So Guy and Artie are conspiring with that weasel?" He heaved a sigh of disgust. "It figures."

"You know him?"

"His reputation—and it's not a good one—precedes him. Dodge is based in Cleveland and acts as something of an independent agent, a business headhunter of sorts, pointing out the acquisition value of smaller companies to larger ones. Then, if there is a successful buyout or takeover, Dodge gets a commission fee."

"Sort of like a real estate agent?"

"More like a remora." Cade stood up and crossed the office to stand in front of her. "Don't listen to him, Kylie. Dodge will attempt to snow you with half-truths and bits and pieces of information taken out of context and if that doesn't work, he'll throw in some blatant lies. And your uncles will be willing dupes, going along with whatever he says so they can get some quick money for their BrenCo shares. I'm telling you now, Kylie, I won't let that happen."

He moved closer, and the purposeful sexual intent burning in his eyes told her something else. That he was going to make something happen right now. That he was going to touch her again, to kiss her again. Because he really wanted her or because he knew his lovemaking successfully blocked out her capacity for reasoning and judgment?

Kylie backed away from him. Cade's agenda and his fierce

opposition to the possible sale of BrenCo was well-known to her, but she still hadn't heard the other side. Should she assume that Cade was also willing to snow her with half-truths, with bits and pieces of information taken out of context or even blatant lies? And Cade had a powerful advantage that she feared he wouldn't hesitate to use—her explosive attraction to him.

She wanted him badly and he had to know it. She was afraid of the lengths to which she might go because she'd never been in a comparable situation before. She had never ached to be in a man's arms the way she was aching to be held by Cade right now. She'd never hungered for a man's kiss the way she desperately longed for Cade's mouth to open over hers this very minute.

Shaken by the force of her emotions, Kylie scurried from the study. She'd taken two steps into the hall when his arm snaked out and pulled her back inside, closing the door behind her. He pressed her back against it and leaned heavily into her.

Before she could say a word, he bent his head and kissed her, long and slow and deep. Kylie felt herself sinking luxuriously into the dark seas of sensuality as he moved his hands over her, caressing her breasts and hips and thighs. As if he had every right to do it, as if she already belonged to him. As if he were irrevocably branding her with his touch.

Trembling, Kylie raised her hands to his shoulders to cling to him and kissed him back with a sweet, searing fire all her own. She couldn't believe this was happening to her, she'd never dreamed desire and need could burn so hotly within her. He was making her want him in a way she'd never wanted a man before, and the urgency, the desperation, was staggering.

Their tongues met and teased in a seductive mating ritual, an erotic simulation of what was to come. Kylie felt the heaviness of his arousal against her, she smoothed her hands over the broad expanse of his back and combed her fingers through the springy thickness of his hair.

She'd never been the possessive type; she had always considered herself to be too fair-minded and egalitarian for that, but as she caressed him, as she kissed him, Kylie knew a primal yearning to make Cade Austin completely her own. To mark him off-limits to every other woman forever.

At long last, they simultaneously broke the kiss, though their lips remained only centimeters apart as they held each other, gasping and light-headed from the twin forces of passion and lack of air.

Her eyes closed, Kylie rested her head against Cade's shoulder as he rubbed her nape. "Let's go to bed." His voice was a raspy growl that sent shivers of longing rippling through her.

She wanted to, Kylie admitted achingly to herself. Right now, in the middle of the afternoon with the cleaning crew very much present in Uncle Gene's mausoleum of a house, she wanted to slip upstairs to one of the dusty old bedrooms and make love with a man she'd known for far too short a time. A man who might very well be using her sexually for his own ends... And according to her own cousin, who could blame him?

Kylie knew the answer to that. To her, the act of physical love was an act of commitment based on trust and emotional intimacy. It was what she'd been taught, what she firmly believed.

And even though she was in Cade's arms shaking with desire for him, she wasn't sure if she trusted him. As for emotional intimacy, how could it exist between two people who barely knew each other?

"We can't, Cade." Her voice seemed to be reverberating in her head. It sounded more like a miserable wail than the firm statement of intent she'd meant to deliver.

And Cade misinterpreted her completely. "I know, baby. Not here. We'll go to my place. Come on." He hooked his arm around her waist and pulled open the door, moving into the hall with her.

Kylie remembered how easily he'd swept her onto the porch earlier, how she'd walked right along with him though her mind was issuing the opposite orders to her legs. She knew a repeat performance was about to occur—this time with her ending up in his Buick on the way to his bed—unless she made herself unmistakably clear.

"Cade!" she cried desperately, her voice almost beseeching.

Cade didn't even slow down. That breathless little whimper was less a protest, more a plea. He couldn't be faulted for not knowing what she was pleading for, Kylie acknowledged grimly. Try again.

"Cade, no. I'm not going with you. You are leaving and I'm staying here." This time she sounded as if she meant it.

Cade stopped in his tracks, bringing her to a halt as well. This time he had heard what she'd said. Perhaps the appearance of a maid at the same time that the heavy brass door knocker sounded served to aid his comprehension.

He stared down at Kylie, watching her lovely face transpose into a mask of determination. "Don't say no, Kylie," he growled.

"You know it's too soon, Cade."

"I know you think it's too soon." He arched his dark brows in the way that already had become so familiar to her. "But waiting isn't going to change anything and you know it. We want each other—hell, we're *burning* for each other—and we are going to—"

"The cable man is here, Miss Brennan," the maid announced.

Kylie and Cade started visibly. They'd been so absorbed in their sexually-charged exchange, they had forgotten both the maid and the rapping at the door. But the maid hadn't been distracted; she'd answered the knock and admitted a uniformed cable installer.

"First time in Port McClain history that the cable guy shows up when he's supposed to, and it has to be today," Cade grumbled. His eyes narrowed, and he caught Kylie's wrist, halting her. "You must be planning to stay around for a while if you're getting cable."

Having the house cleaned and the utilities turned on were basic necessities for even the shortest stay. But having cable TV installed...that was not a short-term necessity—it was an action that implied longevity.

"I haven't decided how long I'm staying in Port McClain," Kylie murmured. She used her other hand to pry his fingers from her wrist. "I told you that in the note I sent."

"Where's your TV set, sir?" asked the cable installer. He'd grown impatient waiting for the couple to acknowledge him and had taken matters in his own hands, addressing Cade.

"It's her TV set," said Cade. "It's her house."

And *her* company, added a devil's voice in his head. For an eerie moment, he almost felt Gene Brennan's presence right there in the hall, and his old boss was laughing uproariously at the perverse joke.

"Right this way." Kylie headed down the hall toward the kitchen, where she knew one of the two TV sets in the house was located. The installer followed her.

Cade debated whether to stay or leave. Traipsing after Kylie struck him as a tactical error. She'd already said no to him, and he didn't want to play stalker. Nor did he wish to appear overeager, pathetically hanging around for whatever crumbs of attention she might bestow on him. Better to withdraw and establish his—

"It's gone!" Kylie's cry of dismay echoed throughout the first floor.

Automatically, Cade rushed to the kitchen, his strategic planning session forgotten.

Kylie, the cable man and one of the cleaning crew were standing there, looking at the empty space where Gene's twenty-inch-screen television set had been.

"There was no TV here when I came in," the maid stated unequivocally.

Kylie's eyes met Cade's, then flicked to the cable installer. "I guess I should've checked first. I didn't think that Uncle Gene might've given the set away," she murmured apologetically.

"Gene didn't give it away," said Cade. "Your father inherited this house and everything in it and when your folks left after the funeral, they took only some books and photographs with them. Everything else was left intact and the place was locked up. It's supposedly been locked ever since."

"Maybe there's been a burglary," suggested the maid, her interest piqued. "Is there anything else missing?"

"Like maybe another TV?" prompted the cable man. "Because if there aren't any sets here, I'm wasting my time. I do have some other stops to make, you know."

"Gene kept a smaller TV set in his bedroom," said Cade. "We may as well go up and see if it's still there."

He and Kylie, accompanied by the entire cleaning crew and

the cable installer trooped upstairs to Gene Brennan's bedroom. Where there was no TV set.

"Well, I'm outta here." The cable installer departed in a flash.

"Maybe you'd better see what else is missing," suggested one of the cleaning crew. "None of us has cleaned upstairs and we don't want to go into a room and be blamed for—"

"Nobody is blaming you," Cade interrupted. "I have a very good idea who has been helping himself around here. Go on back to work, and Kylie and I will go through the rooms and see what else he's taken."

The crew headed back downstairs, leaving Kylie and Cade alone.

"He?" Kylie repeated as they walked around her uncle's bedroom. She had no idea what to look for, which belongings might be gone. Uncle Gene's bedroom had not been declared off-limits during her childhood visits but she couldn't remember ever setting foot in this room. "Who do you have in mind?"

"Your light-fingered cousin Brent, who else? I should've guessed he would pull something like this. I *would've* guessed if I'd given it any thought, but I haven't been out here since your folks left."

"Cade, you really have no evidence to support your accusations."

"Oh, please! Spare me the innocent-until-proven-guilty rhetoric. I'm not the district attorney and I don't need evidence to build a case, and you're not Brent's attorney so you don't have to mount a defense. Let's just use logic and common sense. Brent has a track record as a thief and things are missing from his relatives' house. He took those two TV sets and probably more. I'd bet the zoning permit to build our new infectious waste autoclave on that."

Kylie grimaced at the imagery. "Whatever happened to betting the farm? And what on earth is an infectious waste autoclave? Not that I really want to know."

"You ought to know, boss. It's your business to know." Cade sat down on Gene's bed. The ancient box spring and frame squeaked ominously, as if protesting the unwelcome burden. "BrenCo has a zoning permit to build a two-million-dollar autoclave, which is like an industrial-size pressure cooker. By the end of the year, we'll be handling ninety tons of medical waste a day.''

"Does that means BrenCo will be importing medical waste into Port McClain?'' Kylie was incredulous.

"Correct. BrenCo will be taking medical waste from in and out of state, drawing from hospitals and clinics, veterinarians' offices, dentists' offices and mortuaries.''

Cade's face was alight with an enthusiasm Kylie couldn't comprehend. Had her parents and brother felt this way when she had tried to explain why she'd defended the criminals she had been assigned?

"Medical waste consists of gowns and needles exposed to infectious patients as well as blood and body tissues,'' Cade continued, eager to school her in what appeared to be a favorite subject of his. "Since an autoclave sterilizes infectious waste with heat and pressure instead of burning, it doesn't produce air or water pollution like regular hospital incinerators. They spew large amounts of dioxin and mercury into the air. After treatment in our autoclave, the sterilized waste will be able to be sent to a municipal landfill.''

"And that's good?''

"Of course. It's good for everybody, especially Port McClain.''

"Does the community know how very lucky it is?'' Kylie asked sardonically. Tons of imported medical waste did not strike her as good fortune, even if it was slated to be sterilized. "Or have you kept your plans a secret, to be sprung on an unsuspecting town after the dirty deal has already been signed, sealed and delivered?''

"You sound as if you're making a closing argument to the jury.'' Cade lay back on Gene's bed. At least three springs in the mattress stabbed him and he switched positions, trying to avoid being impaled. How had Gene managed to sleep on this lumpy torture rack night after night?

"There is no nefarious secret deal, Kylie.'' He raised himself on his elbow and propped his head on his hand. "BrenCo presented the plans in a town meeting shortly before Gene's death and explained all about the autoclave and its functions, just like I explained it to you. We had a videotape presentation and a question and answer session, we encouraged citizen participation, then scheduled another meeting for a vote on the project.''

''You did?'' Kylie was taken by surprise. She didn't expect corporations to invite citizen input.

Cade nodded. Her obvious amazement amused him. ''I minored in industrial psychology, Kylie. I know about the importance of maintaining excellent community relations. BrenCo's PR department is a model for others in the field. Anyway, the bottom line is that the autoclave will bring at least a hundred new jobs into Port McClain, the process is superior to any existing ones, and we even received a recommendation from the EPA. The town's support for the project was overwhelming. We have the zoning permit and building will begin—''

He broke off abruptly. If BrenCo were sold, he didn't know when or if the autoclave would be built, or if he would even be part of the company. Cade rejected the possibility outright. It was definitely time to take another tack.

''When will building begin?'' asked Kylie.

''Come over here and I'll tell you.''

She shot him a quick glance. He was smiling the kind of smugly arrogant male smile that made a woman itch to erase it. Challenge glittered in his eyes. Kylie heaved an exasperated sigh. So they were back to playing those games again?

''Do you honestly believe that the sight of you lying on a bed is so irresistible that if I come any closer, I won't be able to stop myself from jumping you?''

''Well, I wouldn't recommend jumping on this bed. It's liable to collapse. Just sit down on the edge. Slowly and carefully.''

''No, Cade. I told you that I will not—''

''We have a lot to talk about, Kylie. Our autoclave discussion sidetracked us from the problem of Brent who's undoubtedly been robbing this place blind since Gene's funeral.'' Cade lay flat on his back and raised his hands behind his head, to pillow it. ''We may as well be comfortable during our little chat, hmm? Really, *really* comfortable.''

She recognized at that moment that he was kidding. He'd

been teasing her and by taking him seriously she had not only leaped at the bait, but she'd also swallowed it whole.

"Congratulations. You tricked me into sounding like a testy old prude. I hope you have a good laugh over it."

Cade swung his legs over the side of the bed, then stood up. "Actually, I was hoping things would go the other way— that the sight of me on the bed would prove to be so irresistible that you wouldn't be able to stop yourself from jumping me."

"Don't bother, Cade." She tilted her head, looking up at him from beneath her lashes. "It won't work twice."

"That's the trouble with smart women," Cade pretended to complain. "They're always one step ahead."

She folded her arms and eyed him assessingly. "I have a feeling that the day *anyone* gets one step ahead of you has yet to dawn."

"If that's a compliment, thank you. If it's an insult, consider it duly noted."

She left her uncle's bedroom and walked down the hall, Cade at her side. He reached for her hand. She swung it away from him, tucking both into the front pockets of her jeans.

"Okay, I get it. You don't want to hold hands. Am I allowed to put my arm around you?"

This time she didn't miss the needling note in his voice. "No," she said sweetly.

"Too soon for that, huh?"

She caught his reference to their little scene downstairs, and an embarrassing flood of color heated her cheeks. "As far as I'm concerned, forever is too soon for—"

"Careful, sweetie. You're on the verge of sounding like a testy old prude again."

"I know you're trying to provoke me, Cade, but it's not going to work."

"If I really wanted to provoke you, you'd be provoked, Kylie. Instantly."

"You're that irritating? That obnoxious? That confident of your ability to be infuriating?"

"All of that and more."

"No doubt you honed your talents by associating with the Brennan family for the past eight years?"

"No doubt," he agreed.

He sounded the way her brother used to, back in those days when teasing her was their sibling way of life. Kylie cast a quick covert glance at Cade. What was it about him that made her feel so off balance? How could she feel like his kid sister one minute, then feel like she could fall madly in love with him the next, only to want to smack him the moment after that?

"Where are we going now?" Cade asked, sauntering along-side her, close enough to touch her if he chose.

Kylie waited for him to do it, but he chose not to. She told herself that she was relieved. Perhaps, he'd finally gotten her hands-off message. "I'm going to my grandparents' room."

She swerved to the right, accidentally brushing against him. Every erogenous zone in her body clamored for her to do it again—and to prolong the contact. She restrained herself. "Although I can't remember if there was anything worth stealing in their room."

"Well, if there was, Brent has already swiped it, you can count on that."

"Cade, it really isn't fair to—"

"Wearing your public defender hat again? All right, coun-selor, I'll keep my unsubstantiated speculations to myself— for now." He paused on the threshold of her grandparents' bedroom. "Were you really planning on having dinner tonight with Brenda and Noah?"

She stepped inside the room. "Yes, but I think that's off now. It seems unlikely they'll come back for me. In fact, I hope they don't. I've never relished being the third wheel."

"You won't be. You're having dinner with me tonight. I'll pick you up here at seven...unless you're planning to stay another night at the Port McClain Hotel? If that's the case, I'll pick you up there."

"I checked out of the hotel but—"

"Good. I'll be here then. Seven o'clock." He took off down the hall, breaking into a run.

Kylie hurried to the wooden railing that lined the upstairs hall, overlooking the staircase. Cade was already bounding down the steps, two at a time. "I didn't agree to have dinner with you," she called as he reached the bottom step.

He didn't look up, he didn't stop, he left the house without responding to her protest. She didn't know if he'd pretended not to hear her or if he really couldn't—after all, two vacuum cleaners were whirring loudly downstairs.

As things now stood, he would be arriving back here at seven o'clock to take her to dinner.

Kylie decided she was annoyed at his high-handedness. She had never appreciated macho displays of dominance...not that she'd been subjected to many. There was something about her—her no-nonsense demeanor? her ability to argue?—that caused males to treat her as a genderless equal. Professionally, that worked to her advantage. On a personal level, being genderless did not garner a whole lot of dates.

Kylie hadn't really minded. She was very much the captain of her own ship and always had been, to use one of her father's favorite navy metaphors.

But to use another one...Cade Austin was the admiral of the entire fleet.

Five

The Creek View restaurant was aptly named because it was built along the banks of Port McClain Creek, and a wall of windows provided a panoramic view. The decor of the place provided an odd contrast, the stone fireplace and wood-paneled walls suggesting the rustic atmosphere of a cabin, while the snowy white linen tablecloths, three-taper candelabras and gold-edged china place settings on each table were distinctly formal.

As a hostess seated Kylie and Cade in a private little alcove beside the window, rain began to fall, hitting the glass with increasing force. Kylie glanced outside at the fast-moving waters. It wouldn't take much more water for the rough wide creek to overflow its banks.

Cade followed her gaze. "Worrying about the possibilities of a flood?"

"Not quite worrying. Wondering," she amended. "Does it happen often?"

"Too often. But none of the businesses along the creek want to move. They claim that a waterfront location is too valuable to leave, so they simply clean up after every flood and persevere. Your cousin Bridget's favorite hangout, Club Reek, got its name because certain flood aromas lingered."

"And nobody minds?"

"Nobody minds."

"Just the sort of hardy, undaunted souls to welcome infectious waste with genuine enthusiasm," Kylie murmured. "You knew what you were doing when you chose to expand BrenCo here in Port McClain."

"I sense a backhanded compliment, but thank you all the same. And in case you're wondering why I brought you to a restaurant on a flood plain in the middle of a rainstorm, you mentioned earlier that you liked fish. This place serves the best in Port McClain."

"Along with everything else, it seems." Kylie leafed through the thick menu. "Italian, Mexican, Chinese, French, Thai, Greek and good old American dishes, too. Kind of an international extravaganza."

"I recommend the trout," Cade said dryly. "It's fresh, grilled or broiled, and always good. A wholesale place that sells frozen entrées to restaurants provides the international extravaganza. The microwave does the rest."

"Still, the thought of traveling the world frozen course by course is kind of intriguing." Kylie smiled across the table at him. "Think of the possibilities—an appetizer from Italy, a salad from Mexico, the vegetable course from China, the meat course from—"

"Sounds like one of the dinners my mother used to make. She picked up new recipes from every country we lived in and saw no reason not to mix them up. We had some harrowing meals."

"One of the hazards of being a military brat," Kylie agreed with a laugh. "What countries did you live in?"

"We were stationed at posts in Japan, Germany, and Italy, plus in five different states. We sometimes mixed with air force kids because there were air bases in the vicinity, but there were no navy families around."

"Dad had a tour of duty in Italy, but not near the army. We also lived in Spain, England, the Philippines and four states."

Military kids had their own versions of war stories about

living in foreign places and transferring to school after school, and Kylie and Cade swapped them, laughing.

"And your dad was a high ranking officer, a captain." Cade studied her. "The army's equivalent of a colonel, am I right?"

"Something like that," she agreed.

He couldn't seem to drag his eyes away from her. She looked cool and lovely and serene. Her simple navy blue dress might have appeared plain—even severe—on anyone else, but on her it was as classy and elegant as the pearl necklace encircling her neck. He guessed she could wear torn dirty rags and make them look tasteful. And sexy.

He noticed that the top two buttons of her dress were undone—a casually stylish touch, not meant to be titillating—but he was aroused by the modest exposure of her skin. He wished she would unfasten another button so he could see more; he wanted to undo each and every button on her proper little dress...

With great effort, Cade dragged his mind from *that* path. He cleared his throat. "I bet you were the model navy captain's daughter. Good manners, good grades, good looks. The perfect little princess."

"No, the highest ranking officer's daughter would be the princess. That's an admiral's daughter in the navy. In the army, she'd be the general's daughter."

"Hmm. I used to know one of those."

"Was she a perfect little princess?" Kylie was curious. She'd never known a general's daughter, though she'd met admirals' daughters from time to time. They did tend to be princesses of perfection.

"Leslie was neither perfect nor princesslike." Cade chuckled, as if he was enjoying a private joke. "She was—how can I describe her? Born to be Wild. Always looking for adventure."

"And you were happy to accommodate her, uh, quest?" Kylie asked drolly.

"Sure. Wasn't there some restless son of a seaman eager to seek adventure with Captain Brennan's darling daughter?"

"I don't have an adventurous streak. I still don't. I was Born to be Dull, I guess."

"Oh, I don't know about that. Defending criminals for a

lousy state paycheck could be interpreted as rebellious by some.''

"My mom and dad did consider my work in the Public Defender's office to be a phase, one I would hopefully outgrow.''

"I bet your folks felt like writing the governor a thank-you note for making those budget cuts. To be honest, I don't like the idea of you associating with felons and prisoners, either.''

"You'd rather that I be here, associating with BrenCo and my relatives?'' she countered archly.

"I don't mind having you here associating with me, Kylie. I think we're going to be very, very close.''

He gave her a slow sexy smile as he stretched his legs under the table, inadvertently brushing against hers. Well, not quite inadvertently, he admitted. Quite deliberately, in fact. He positioned his calves on either side of hers and left them there.

Frissons of heat emanated from their point of contact and shot through Kylie's entire body, centralizing in her deepest most secret part. "Behave, Cade," she warned.

Her voice was embarrassingly shaky. Why, she'd sounded more commanding and in control as a first year law student nervously arguing her first moot court competition!

"Do I have to?'' Cade reached across the table and laid his hand over hers.

"Yes.'' She knew that taking action—withdrawing her hand from his and tucking her legs tightly beneath her chair out of his reach—would add more credibility to her order. But a sensual lethargy was fast suffusing her. Her legs felt too weak to move, her hand felt too good in the firm clasp of his. Kylie left them exactly where they were.

However, in case he misread her body language she felt obliged to inform him, "And to avoid any misunderstandings right from the start, after dinner we're going our separate ways. I'm going back to Uncle Gene's house and you're going to your own home.''

He lifted her hand to his lips and gently nibbled on her fingertips. "Consider me forewarned.''

She watched him through a fast-blinding haze of sensuality. Her body felt languid and limp. If he could affect her so profoundly with such a simple caress, her declaration of how this evening must end might have to be revised...

Kylie gave her head a shake, as if to dislodge that traitorous thought. Though she knew Cade Austin better than she had this morning when they'd ended up on his sofa together, she still didn't know him well enough to sleep with him tonight, she reminded herself sternly. It was time for her to set limits, to redirect the course of action.

"Where do you live? Near Uncle Gene's place?" she asked crisply as she yanked her hand away from him. She nearly knocked over the candelabra in the process.

Cade was quick to steady it. His smile told her he knew all about the riot going on inside her, but he politely answered her question. "I have a house on the outskirts of town, in the McClain Woods development. A nice neighborhood, fairly new compared to Gene's part of town. Your uncle Guy and aunt Lauretta bought a house there about seven years ago."

"So you're neighbors?" Her heart was still racing. Was it possible to will it back to its regular rate?

"Not exactly. They live about eight blocks from me, too far to walk to borrow a cup of sugar or to drop in for a cup of coffee. Thank God."

"You're not the neighborly type? Or just not neighborly to anyone named Brennan?"

"My neighbors seem to think I'm okay. Draw your own conclusions."

"Oh, I will. I am."

She gave a sudden gasp. Cade had reached under the table and lifted her foot onto his lap. She felt his fingers caress her ankle then slip inside the soft navy leather of her pumps to begin a sensuous massage of her instep.

Kylie was shocked. No one had ever touched her foot like this. She'd never imagined such a thing! Yet she was feeling the effects of his provocative caress all through her body, in every intimate place...

She jerked upright in her chair, dragging her foot away from his exquisitely pleasurable, wicked touch. "Don't, Cade." Her breath caught in her throat. "We decided to forgo the seduction, remember?"

"No, I have no recollection of that." He pretended to look

puzzled. "Was this a mutual decision or one of your unilateral decrees?"

"I don't issue decrees. I—strive for consensus whenever it's humanly possible."

"Maybe back in Philly you do, but not here. I think you're on a Port McClain power trip, relishing your position as BrenCo's biggest cheese."

He was clearly teasing her but his words stung anyway. What was that old saw about there being truth in jest? Troubled, Kylie pondered her behavior. "Have I really been acting that way?"

"I've been hearing a lot of 'Cade, no' and 'Cade, don't' and 'Cade, we can't' and 'Cade, we shouldn't.' Very repressive, boss. Definitely symptoms of a power trip."

"That isn't what I meant. I was discussing business, not sex, and you know it." She was turning out to be an incredibly easy target, she acknowledged wryly; Cade got her every time he took aim.

A waiter arrived and Cade gave their orders. Trout for both of them. The moment he left, Cade turned his attention back to Kylie. "Was I being chauvinistic and overbearing again, ordering for you?" His eyes gleamed.

She knew he was trying to rile her, expecting a repeat of her earlier coffee-tea fuss. Kylie balked at playing the sour straight man to his comic foil; she was neither prim nor humorless.

"I don't object to a man ordering for me although I do think the concept is more than a little retro." She settled back in her chair and folded her arms, unconsciously assuming a classic defensive posture. And went on the offensive. "Did your lady dentist friend from Cleveland enjoy such quaint—"

"Remind me to thank Brenda for spreading irrelevant gossip and pointless speculation," Cade growled. "I repeat what I said earlier, I have not seen Anne Woodley in nearly a year and a half and I have no plans to see her in the future. Case closed."

"I thought you said you two remained on good terms." Kylie was enjoying the cross examination. If they were in court, she'd be the one scoring the points with the jury. "Is no contact at all your idea of good terms?"

Cade shifted uncomfortably. "Look, it's not like we were in love or anything ridiculous like that. Anne kept talking about her biological clock running out. She made it quite clear that she wanted a sperm donor, not a relationship. I have to admit the whole scenario gave me the creeps and I bailed out."

"I can relate to that. There's something very unappealing about being used, whether it's for your sperm or your shares in BrenCo."

Their eyes met. "I could deny that I'm not using you but you wouldn't believe me, so what's the point?"

Kylie was disheartened. She'd never heard such a lackluster denial. Even so, she knew she was susceptible to him, to being used by him. Her mind clouded when he looked at her in that particular way and her senses rioted at his simplest touch. It was a humbling admission, and one that stirred her ire.

Reflexively, Kylie struck back and she knew exactly where to aim. "Did I tell you that I finally have phone service? Guess who was my first caller?"

"It was either Guy or Artie," Cade surmised grimly. "Calling for the purpose of setting up your meeting with Axel Dodge."

She nodded.

"Are you going to tell me where and when it will be held?"

"They specifically asked that you not be included in the meeting, Cade. And that I not reveal any information about it."

"I expected that of them. I suppose I was foolish to expect something more from you."

Was that *hurt* resonating in his voice? Kylie was taken aback. Or was he merely acting, and doing a stellar job of it?

But suppose he was genuinely disappointed in her? Kylie hated letting people down. She'd set out to needle Cade not to crush him. Remorse flooded her. "Cade, I want you to understand that I can't—"

"You don't owe me any explanations, Kylie," he interrupted coldly. Tension seemed to visibly emanate from him. "You're free to do as you please, to see whoever you want, whenever you want. I have no intention of interfering."

The waiter arrived with a basket of rolls and Cade examined

the contents, taking a long time to select his choice. Kylie stirred uneasily, watching him. He seemed so remote and withdrawn. And though she had halted his attempted seduction and tried to squelch his teasing, she found herself missing the camaraderie between them. If that's what it was.

"Cade?" Whatever it was, she wanted it back. She didn't like the cool distance between them and sought to end it. "I— You—" she faltered a little when he made no response whatsoever. "You know all about my family but I don't know a thing about yours, except that your folks are retired army who still like to travel. Do—do you have any sisters or brothers?"

Cade, who was meticulously buttering a piece of his chosen hard roll, looked up and grimaced. "Oh God, this sounds suspiciously like banal first date conversational filler. What's next, trading astrological signs?"

Kylie was undeterred. "I'm a Libra. You know, the scales. Weighing both sides."

"That certainly fits. Of course, you take it to extremes."

She let that one pass. "And you are?" she prompted.

"Tired of this conversation."

"All right. We can sit here in silence while you sulk, if that's what you prefer." Kylie took her turn delving into the breadbasket. "It won't bother me."

Cade said nothing. He continued to spread the butter on his roll with a concentration that set her nerves on edge. Surely Michelangelo hadn't put as much effort into painting the Sistine Chapel as Cade was expending on buttering that damn roll!

She looked around her. The restaurant was filling up, nearly every table was taken. And at every table, the diners were talking and laughing and looking convivial. Except at theirs, of course, where dour silence reigned supreme. The sound of the rain against the window seemed to magnify, and she watched it for a while.

When she finally glanced back at Cade, she found him staring at her.

Kylie met his gaze, only to find that she couldn't look away. The flames from the candles seemed to blaze in his eyes, accentuating the green flecks there. Hazel eyes flecked with green. They were the most captivating, fascinating eyes she'd ever seen.

Her mouth felt dry and she grasped her water glass. Cade reached across the table and took it from her, replacing it with a glass of chilled red wine.

"Try this," he instructed. "It's a vintage catawba wine from the Meiers Wine Cellars in Sandusky, Ohio. I know fish is supposed to be served with white wine but we'll disregard that decree. You ought to try a local product while you're here."

"I didn't know there were any vineyards in Ohio." Bemused, Kylie looked at the wine bottle. She couldn't remember the waiter placing it on the table, she had no recollection of him opening it. It was unnerving to realize that when she was in Cade's presence, she seemed to focus solely on him, vitally attuned to his every move, look and nuance. Anything or anyone else hovered on the periphery of her awareness.

Cade touched his own wineglass against hers. "To the future of BrenCo," he proposed the toast. "I think we can agree to drink to that, can't we?"

Kylie took a sip of the wine, then another. "It's not bad," she admitted. "In fact, it's pretty good."

He smiled. "It's only a matter of time before Sandusky takes its rightful place among the wine capitals of the world."

"And deservedly so." The more wine Kylie sipped, the more she appreciated its flavor and bouquet. She drained her glass before Cade was half-finished with his, and he quickly gave her a refill.

"You're not planning on getting me drunk, are you?" She frowned her disapproval at the very idea.

"Give me credit for some style, Kylie. Getting a woman drunk is sleazy and obvious, and I've never aspired to either."

"If I did get drunk, would you take advantage of my diminished capacity?"

"Not even if you begged me to." A flash of humor shone in his eyes. "Oh, before I forget—my sign is Taurus."

She knew it was his version of the peace-seeking olive branch and accepted it gratefully. "That would be the bull. Stubborn, single-minded, aggressive. A description of you?"

"Possibly," he conceded. "You're really into this astrology stuff, hmm?"

"No, but my grandmother—my mom's mother—is. I picked up a lot of information from her without even trying."

"Sort of absorbed it through osmosis? That happened to me with dog breeds. My sister raises weimaraners and talks about dogs incessantly. After spending an hour with her, I was able to hold my own in a detailed discussion about the declining popularity of poodles."

"The popularity of poodles is declining?"

"You don't want to know."

"So you do have a sister?" Kylie latched onto the nugget of personal information. She didn't really want to discuss poodles, anyway.

"I have four sisters—one thirteen months older than me, she's the weimaraner nut—and three younger. I also have two younger brothers."

"Wow! Seven kids!" Kylie's eyes widened. Having just one sibling, she found the number of Austins staggering. "Was it fun growing up with all those sisters and brothers? Moving around so often from army post to post must've really been a challenge with—"

"Fun and challenging doesn't quite describe it," Cade interjected. "It was really hard on my mother because my father was gone so much of the time. Dad always volunteered for unaccompanied assignments—it meant more money for the family, but sometimes I think he just wanted to escape from the nonstop commotion at home. My mother was overwhelmed by all the responsibility, she was dependent and passive and needed someone around to take charge and make decisions..."

His voice trailed off. "I don't know why I'm boring you with ancient history. All the Austin kids managed to grow up and are on their own, and my mother is thrilled to have my dad retired and with her full-time. End of story."

Kylie eyed him thoughtfully. "Would I be wrong in assuming that the someone who was in charge and made the decisions while your dad was away on all those remote tours of duty was you?"

"It was me," he confirmed her hunch. "And there were

many times when I wasn't a patient, understanding John-Boy Walton type of big brother. My sisters and brothers claim I was a tyrant, although they're becoming more forgiving now, especially the ones with kids of their own.''

"No wonder Uncle Gene found it so easy to dump the Brennans and their problems on you. You were a natural when it came to taking charge of a family," Kylie observed.

Cade shrugged noncommittally.

Being burdened too early with too many familial responsibilities could also explain his single status at thirty-five, Kylie mused. When it came to family life, he probably had a "been-there, done-that" mentality and was in no rush to take it all on again. Witness his lady dentist friend whose ticking biological clock had sent him on his way.

"Has your immersion in the Austin and Brennan clans made you rule out having a family of your own?" she asked lightly, trying to ignore the peculiar sinking sensation in her chest.

"No, I intend to have kids someday but I admit that so far, it hasn't been my top priority."

"BrenCo tops your priority list," she said knowledgeably and Cade nodded his agreement. "Well, if you want to have a big family you'd better not put it off too much longer," she felt obligated to advise. "After all, that ticking biological clock is—"

"Not quite ready to strike," Cade assured her. "And I have no intention of fathering a whole tribe, two children will suit me just fine." He toyed idly with the salt shaker. "I can still remember watching those two-child families when I was a kid and feeling acute envy."

"Envy?"

"With only two kids, each one could sit by the window in the car." He smiled wryly. "In the Austin family car, we didn't even get our own seat, we had to pile in on top of each other. Try riding cross-country like that. We did, four times. It was literally hell on wheels."

"Our family drove from Virginia to San Diego once, and Dev and I each sat by the window in the back seat," Kylie recalled.

"Which would've been my idea of paradise, no matter how monotonous the drive." Cade chuckled. "You probably each had your own bedroom, too. Those three-bedroom houses on post or base were great for a family of four, but cramming a family of nine into one of them made for miserably close quarters. It was always the same—our parents in one bedroom, the three boys in another, the four girls in the other. Growing up, I viewed the prospect of having a bedroom all to myself as an inconceivable luxury.''

''Which you have now achieved,'' she reminded him.

''True. But now I don't mind sharing my bed or my room— under certain circumstances.'' He arched his brows suggestively.

She didn't dare to follow that lead; it conjured up too much internal heat. ''Well, as a veteran of one of your idealized two kid families, I always wanted my family to be bigger.'' Kylie opted for a safer topic. Maybe she really was Born to be Dull? ''My cousins had three kids each in their families and I felt cheated there was only Devlin and me in ours. I promised myself that I would have at least three children of my own.''

''And do you still want three or has sanity prevailed?''

''I still want three children. They can be all boys or all girls or mixed but I definitely want three.''

''Three.'' Cade considered it. ''Okay, I guess I could live with that. But no more after the third baby. If you want something else to mother, I'm sure my sister will be happy to supply a weimaraner puppy.''

''Are you proposing to me?'' Kylie asked playfully.

Cade choked on his wine.

''I'll take that as a no.'' She laughed at his expression. ''Does this mean our three kids will be born out of wedlock? And what about our dog?''

Cade felt as if his skin were on fire. ''This is what happens when you drink Meiers incomparable catawba on an empty stomach. It goes straight to your head.'' He managed a weak, sheepish smile.

''I'm not trying to get you drunk,'' Kylie promised. ''It's too sleazy and obvious. And don't worry, I have no intention of taking advantage of your diminished capacity, not even if you beg me to.''

The waiter arrived with their dinners at that moment, and Cade vowed to double his tip in homage to the impeccable timing. He desperately needed intervention, for try as he may, he couldn't come up with the requisite glib comeback to counter the effects of that three-kids-and-a-dog exchange with Kylie.

He was thoroughly disconcerted. Because for the first time, the prospect of giving up his cherished privacy, of ending the quiet solitude in his house, didn't send a foreboding chill through him. Because the idea of Kylie bearing his children— all *three* of them—seemed exciting and rewarding, not appalling. Even sharing a puppy with her held a certain appeal. He had always liked dogs and kids; he just wasn't in a hurry to live with them again.

Now he felt amenable to the possibility—if Kylie Brennan were a part of it all.

He gripped his fork as he watched her sample her first bite of trout. She tasted it and smiled her approval. Cade wondered if it were possible to implode from the force of unslaked desire. If so, he was in prime danger of it.

He wanted Kylie desperately, and he was experienced enough to know that she wanted him, too, though she was trying hard to fight her attraction. Because she didn't trust him. Her fifty-one percent ownership of BrenCo stock stood between them as solidly as a concrete wall. Whatever decision she made concerning her shares would impact on their relationship, for better or for worse.

Cade consumed his trout, without really tasting it. Worse was not a prospect he cared to consider, but he knew that Better was far from assured. Kylie had that meeting tomorrow with her uncles and their imported nuisance named Axel Dodge. What if they managed to convince her to sell her shares?

"Have you heard from Noah since he and Brenda took off this afternoon?"

Kylie's voice filtered through the fog of gloom that was swiftly encompassing him.

"No." Somewhere out there, his defenseless best friend was at the mercy of Brenda's potent wiles. Cade groaned. "Not a word from him—or her."

"I haven't, either. I guess they're too absorbed in each other to give us a thought," Kylie replied with a bright smile.

Or was it a taunting smile? Cade wasn't sure. Not only were the Brennans deft at backstabbing, but they also enjoyed twisting the knife. Kylie could be doing exactly that. "Absorbed in each other," he repeated cynically. "Is that what they're calling it these days?"

"Why are you so negative? It's possible that Brenda and Noah care deeply for each other."

"I'll grant that landing Noah would be a major coup for Brenda. He's got a nice house, a good job, plenty of money and—"

"He treats her well, they enjoy each other's company." Kylie came to her cousin's defense. "They could be very good for each other."

"Brenda is about as good for him as Delilah was for Samson, and we all know how that turned out," Cade intoned darkly. "And as long as we're on the dismal subject of your cousins, did you find out what else Brent took from Gene's house, besides the two TV sets?"

"Cade, I know you think the U.S. Constitution doesn't apply to my cousin Brent, but he is entitled to be considered innocent until it's proven otherwise."

"I noticed that the piano was still in the living room and the big crystal chandelier was still hanging in the dining room. Brent would need help getting them out so that means he is working alone," Cade speculated, ignoring her concise explanation of criminal law. "What else was missing after your inventory this afternoon?"

Kylie sighed. "It wasn't a very thorough inventory. I had a hard time remembering what was in each room. I know there was an antique tea cart in the living room that isn't there anymore. I remembered a few distinctive pieces, like Grandma's writing desk and a gilded pagoda-shaped mirror, but I truly don't know when I last saw them. It's possible that Uncle Gene could've given them away or sold them after Grandma died."

"I doubt it. More than likely, Brent hauled the stuff to an antiques dealer who paid him a quarter of what it was actually worth. But as long as he got some quick cash in his hands, Brent wouldn't care about the true value. Do you see a correlation here, Kylie? Your uncles want to do the same with—"

"Did Aunt Bobbie call you again about Brent's bail?" Kylie quickly attempted to divert his incipient BrenCo diatribe.

Cade frowned. He was being about as subtle as a thermonuclear weapon. For BrenCo's sake, he *had* to rein himself in. It wasn't easy. "I talked to Bobbie again and we decided that being in a jail cell for a time would give Brent the opportunity to reflect on what he'd done. Maybe even to regret it, although I'm not holding my breath on that one."

"And Aunt Bobbie went along with that?" Kylie asked skeptically, remembering her aunt's earlier reaction to the same plan.

"Yes, with a remarkable lack of hysterics. We ended the conversation on excellent terms, for a change."

"Because you agreed to advance her the cash for Starr Lynn's ice-skating costume!" Kylie exclaimed at once. Her deduction skills had always been first-rate. "You also promised that the money for their trip to the novice competition in Detroit would come out of BrenCo's community athletic fund." She grinned at his look of surprise. "Brenda told me about the fund. She also said you always made sure that Starr Lynn benefited from it, even though Uncle Gene was less than willing to include her."

"Brenda certainly talked a blue streak this afternoon," Cade grumbled.

"I think it's admirable that you took it upon yourself to help Starr Lynn. Brenda and Aunt Bobbie are both appreciative, though you'll probably deny it."

"I probably will."

Kylie laughed. "You try to act like such a gruff curmudgeon but deep down inside, you're—"

"Even gruffer. Ruthless. Autocratic, arrogant and stubborn. Those are only a few of the words that'll be used to describe me in that meeting tomorrow, Kylie."

"Let's not forget to add single-minded to the list," Kylie said dryly. "You turn every conversation back to BrenCo. And right now you're totally fixated on that meeting tomorrow, aren't you?"

"I'd be a fool not to be concerned, Kylie. Think about it. A secret meeting whose sole purpose is to undermine me while I'm given no opportunity to defend myself. Doesn't that strike you as unjust? Criminals, no matter what they've done, are given representation in a hearing but I'm to be shut out of—''

"Cade, tomorrow's meeting isn't a trial," Kylie said earnestly. "It's a—"

"It feels like a trial to me. In a kangaroo court. And here is my crime, Kylie. I've made BrenCo successful enough to stimulate your uncles' greed. You see, the way the company is run, the dividends are reinvested in the business, paying out only a small amount to the shareholders. Your uncle Gene and I agreed on that course of action, to plow most of the profits back into the business. It's one of the reasons why BrenCo is doing so well."

His voice was low and quiet but the intensity of his tone was reflected in his eyes, which held hers in a compelling gaze. Kylie couldn't look away; she didn't even try.

"Artie and Guy and a few other Brennans, Ian and Lauretta in particular, resent the small dividend checks," Cade continued tautly. "Never mind that the continuing growth of the company benefits them and will become even more lucrative for all later on. They would rather sell their shares for a quick, easy profit."

"Then why don't they? After all, nobody is forcing them to hold onto their stock."

"True. But between the two of them, Guy and Artie only own thirty-four percent of the stock. As long as you're the majority holder with me at the helm, our dividend policy holds, which doesn't make that bloodsucker Axel Dodge happy at all. Your uncles will get more money for their stock—substantially more—if you agree to sell, too. That would guarantee Dodge's potential buyer-client total control of BrenCo. They can sell or install new management who will raise the dividend payouts or do whatever they want. Now, do you understand exactly how important your decision is to them?"

"And to you," Kylie reminded him, in the name of fairness.

"They don't care about what effect the fate of the company will have on the town or even the rest of the Brennan family, Kylie. And I do."

Cade was relentless, Kylie acknowledged. His tenacity and drive both wearied and impressed her. He was strong and powerful and he wouldn't give up. "I'm glad you didn't go into law," she murmured. "You'd have been a terrifying force in the courtroom, whether prosecuting, defending or judging."

"I don't want to terrify you, honey." He reached across the table and took her hand in his. "And I don't want to badger you, either." The pad of his thumb stroked the delicate skin on the inside of her wrist. "I think you know what I do want, Kylie. I want you."

Hot excitement flared through her, and she marveled that he could arouse her so quickly, so wildly with merely a touch, a word, a look... And the promise of what was to come.

By the sexy gleam in his eye and the husky note in his voice, Cade Austin intended to fulfill that promise tonight. *The night before her crucial meeting.*

That nasty little reminder crept into her head, generating a quelling chill. "I know exactly what you want, Cade," she said quietly. If only he didn't view her as an adversary, if only she could believe that the passion he claimed to feel was as real to him as it was for her. If only she could trust him...if only he could trust *her.* If only. "You want complete control of BrenCo. That means controlling me, any way you can."

Cade dropped her hand, scowling his exasperation. "Just when I begin to forget you're a Brennan, you come out with a remark like that!"

"You mean, just when you think you have me duped, I wake up and smell the coffee."

Their waiter happened to be passing by and thought she was making a request. "Coffee, miss? I'll bring it right away."

"Bring it at your own risk," warned Cade. "She drinks tea and perceives any attempt to serve her another beverage as threatening and subversive."

The waiter looked alarmed. "I'll bring your tea right away, ma'am," he promised nervously, taking off.

"Did you have to scare the poor guy?" Kylie complained. "He looked at me like I'm a maniac in the throes of an attack of PMS."

"Are you? That would certainly explain a lot."

"I won't even dignify that with a response."

The dinner, which had begun on a tentative edgy note,

ended the same way. Cade pulled into the driveway of Gene Brennan's house and Kylie flung open the car door and hopped out before he could turn off the engine.

A gust of wind blew a stinging splatter of raindrops in her face. "Stay in the car," she insisted when she saw Cade prepare to get out, presumably to walk her to the front door. "No use both of us getting soaked."

The rain swirled around her as she raced to the porch and into the house.

It wasn't until she was standing in the foyer, shaking the raindrops from her coat, that she realized she'd simply pushed open the front door in her haste to get inside. The door had swung open, meaning it must have been slightly ajar.

She could distinctly remember locking the door when she'd left the house with Cade, and now it was unlocked.

The realization struck at the same moment she heard the sound of water running and splashing loudly within the house. Was the rain pouring in through a major leak in the roof?

Kylie followed the sound into the kitchen and gasped her dismay. The taps had been turned on, and water blasted out of the faucet into the overflowing sink, then spilled onto the floor, turning it into a giant puddle at least an inch deep. She sloshed through it to turn off the taps, only to notice that the water sounds had not ceased, though they were more muted without the torrent from the kitchen faucet.

She hurried into the downstairs powder room, located near the left side of the staircase. Water was gushing from that faucet and had already overflowed the sink to soak the floor. Uttering a particularly salty curse more suited to a sailor than a navy captain's well-brought-up daughter, Kylie quickly turned off the taps. Still, the sound of rushing water did not abate.

Kylie ran upstairs to check the two bathrooms there. After the deluge downstairs, she wasn't really surprised to find the water running in both sinks and both bathtubs, yet the sight dazed her anyway. Both bathrooms were badly flooded. She turned off the water, but it had already begun to seep into the adjoining rooms.

What should she do? Panicked, Kylie ran into her uncle's bedroom and grabbed the phone. Who should she call? The police? A plumber? The dilemma was instantly solved when she heard no dial tone. She would not be calling anyone. The phone was dead, though it had been in working order before she'd left the house to go to dinner with Cade.

Cade! Kylie ran downstairs and threw open the front door, just in time to see the lights of his car heading into the street, away from the house. She could shout but he wouldn't hear her, not from this distance with his car windows shut and the rain making such a racket.

She closed the door and leaned against it, shivering. It occurred to her that it was as cold inside the house as it was on the porch. Which shouldn't be the case. The gas had been turned on this afternoon, and she'd set the thermostat immediately afterward to a toasty seventy degrees. With an ominous foreboding, Kylie walked to the thermostat farther down the hall to find it turned off.

The astonishing yet indisputable facts struck her all over again. Someone had broken inside and in a deliberate act of sabotage, had turned off the heat and turned on every faucet in the house, flooding the place. The phone was dead, too. She would bet the zoning permit to build the new infectious waste autoclave that bit of bad luck wasn't merely coincidental.

Her shock began to lift, giving way to anger. Who had done this? And why? Fear kicked in. What would the perpetrator do next? She was here alone, without a phone to call for help.

Not for long! Her heart thudding, Kylie hurried up the stairs. She would grab the few things she needed for the night and get out of here. She didn't allow herself to consider that her car might have been tampered with. If someone was trying to drive her out of Uncle Gene's house, it wouldn't make sense to sabotage her means of escape. Unless there were other plans for her? Perhaps to get rid of her permanently?

She was in the small guest bedroom she'd always used during those long ago summer visits with her family, shoving some essentials into her overnight bag, when she heard the front door open. Quietly. Too quietly, as if whoever was opening it didn't want to be heard.

Kylie glanced wildly around her. There was nothing in this little room to use as a weapon. The most obvious choice, the lamp on the bedside table, looked too light and insubstantial to inflict even a bruise. If she'd been in the kitchen, she could've grabbed a knife although the thought of stabbing someone made her knees buckle. Or maybe it was the rampant terror coursing through her. She waited for a bolstering surge of adrenaline, equipping her for flight or fight.

But that particular internal mechanism seemed to be malfunctioning because she could barely stand, ruling out both battling and fleeing. All she wanted to do was to hide.

She heard the footsteps on the stairs. In just a few moments, the intruder would be here on the top floor—looking for her? Kylie reacted instinctively. She sneaked into the small bedroom closet and soundlessly closed the door behind her.

Six

"Kylie?" Cade's voice echoed in the upstairs hallway. "Kylie, where are you?"

Inside the closet, Kylie breathed in the pungent scent of mothballs—there must be hundreds stored in here to produce such an overwhelming odor—and pressed her body closer to the wall. A hanging garment bag swung gently against her and she jumped. Her nerves were truly shot.

She heard Cade calling her name again, his voice louder, his tone more urgent. Kylie remained frozen in the closet, her heart beating at triple time. She'd spent the evening with Cade, she reminded herself. She knew without a doubt he had not been the one who'd broken into the house. For a few tormenting moments, she entertained the notion that he'd hired some goons to do it and was now here to personally finish her off, then decided she was confusing reality with the spate of women-in-jeopardy TV movies she'd watched over the years.

Pride dictated that he not find her cowering in the closet. Kylie slipped out and crept into the hall. Cade was standing at one end, staring into the flooded bathroom.

"The water was running when I came in," she said. "Now

I know how the owners of those creekside places feel after a flood."

Cade whirled around, startled. "I've been calling you. Why didn't you answer me? What's going on here?" He sounded as agitated as she felt. "Kylie, are you all right?" He advanced toward her.

"I'm fine. Just a little wet and cold, that's all," she murmured, trying for insouciance. And failing. She was pale and shivering and Cade pulled her into his arms. She was only too glad to let him.

He held her tight and she leaned heavily against him, absorbing the strength and warmth he imparted, feeling protected and inordinately grateful for his strong, solid presence. She buried her face against his chest and closed her eyes as the tension that had gripped her every muscle slowly began to recede.

"I thought you'd gone," she whispered, her voice muffled by his coat. "When I looked out, your car was pulling away."

"I drove one block and turned around." His big hands moved over her back in long gentle strokes. "I didn't like the way the evening ended tonight, Kylie." His lips brushed her shiny dark hair. "I came back to change the ending."

He sniffed suddenly, his brow furrowed. "I think I smell— mothballs?" He took another sniff. "In your hair?"

"Don't worry, it's not the latest scented shampoo on the market." Kylie tried to be flippant.

Cade didn't buy her act. Instead, he deepened his embrace. "Honey, where have you been?"

Kylie thought of the dark acrid closet where she'd taken refuge, and shuddered. "I was scared, Cade," she said softly. She drew back a little and looked up at him. Her hands rested on his chest and he linked his arms around her waist.

He bent his head down and touched his forehead to hers. "Tell me exactly what happened here."

"Someone broke into the house tonight, Cade. Every faucet in the house was turned on and the heat was turned off. I was, uh, packing to spend the night somewhere else when you arrived. How did you get in?"

"The front door is unlocked. I just walked inside."

She'd left the door unlocked? Kylie was horrified by her

oversight. Her bulging case file back in Philadelphia offered tragic evidence that one careless mistake was all it took. Of course, she'd carefully locked the door earlier, for all the good that had done. Her bulging case file also offered proof that if someone was intent on committing a crime, precautions were merely a temporary nuisance.

Discouraged, she sagged against Cade. It felt good to let him support her.

"This bathroom is a waterlogged mess," he murmured, staring at the sight. "Are they all like this?"

Kylie nodded. "The kitchen, too. Cleaning up will be—"

"Don't think about a cleanup just yet, Kylie. I'm going to call the police and get them over here to see the damage. It will be useful to have a written police report on file for insurance purposes as well."

"The phone doesn't work," she said wearily. "I think that whoever broke in here did something to it."

"I'll call from my car phone. Come with me."

He took her hand and Kylie compliantly trotted along beside him. Staying inside the house alone, even for a very short while, was not an alternative she cared to consider. Those terror-filled moments in the closet had instilled a fear in her that even her scariest clients had not.

Officers Krajack and Pecoraro arrived and followed Kylie and Cade from one flooded room to another. A further investigation revealed that the phone wires had been cut. As Kylie watched the policemen taking pages of notes, she was struck by the gravity being accorded what actually was a rather minor bit of malicious mischief. She knew she would not have received this sort of attention for a similar incident in a city the size of Philadelphia.

At first she attributed the thoroughness to the dynamics of a small town where crime is rare and every citizen's call was considered important. Then she began to notice the officers' deference to Cade. Every time she supplied an answer to a question, they looked to Cade for confirmation and wrote down what he said. She didn't think any of them noticed when she stopped answering and let Cade do all the talking.

At some other time and place, the closed ranks might have offended her, but at this point she was still too shaken to feel anything but relief that she was safe and not cowering in that closet. Or worse.

"Do you have any ideas who might've done this, Mr. Austin?" asked Krajack.

Cade looked troubled. "Any other time I would swear it was Brent Brennan but I know you have him locked up so that eliminates him as a suspect."

"Brent Brennan isn't in jail," Pecoraro said. "He made bail this afternoon."

"Who posted it?" demanded Cade, and Krajack immediately headed out to the police car to radio for the information.

"Do you really think Brent would do this?" Kylie stared from Cade to Officer Pecoraro, her eyes darkening with apprehension. "Knowing I was here—"

"That would be the precise reason why he would do it." Cade clenched his teeth. "To scare you. To drive you out."

Innocent until proven guilty. Kylie silently repeated her mantra, but when Officer Krajack returned to report that Ian Brennan had posted the bail for his cousin, a wave of anxiety swept through her.

"Ian?" Cade wasn't anxious, he was furious. "Normally, Ian wouldn't give Cousin Brent the time of day, and now suddenly, he bails him out of jail? What's that little weasel doing here in town, anyway? He's supposed to be in law school in Columbus."

"Spring break?" Kylie murmured.

That drew a snicker from Pecoraro. "Sure, why go to some sunny place like Cancún for spring break when you can whoop it up right here in Port McClain?"

Cade's frown grew fiercer. "Would you mind paying a call on both Brent and Ian Brennan tonight?" he asked the officers. "See what either of them knows about what happened here?"

"Sure," Pecoraro agreed. "Krajack and I have our good-cop-bad-cop routine mastered to perfection. We'll get one of them to talk, I can promise you that. Should we call you afterward?"

"Call me in the morning at my office. I'm staying here tonight and you won't be able to reach me since the phone wires are cut," added Cade.

"You're staying here?" Kylie's voice rose in apprehension.

"Good idea." Krajack nodded his approval. "Just in case those little twerps decide to come back to play."

"You don't have to stay here tonight, honey," Cade said soothingly, as he slipped a comforting arm around Kylie's shoulders. "The officers will be glad to escort you to one of the motels out by the interstate exit and stick around till you've checked into a room."

Kylie began to emerge from the lethargy that was engulfing her. She decided that the situation warranted a certain rousing alarm. Cade was clearly directing the police investigation and in her view, the officers seemed to have given him tacit approval to do whatever he chose to "those little twerps" if they were to make another appearance here. Worse, all three believed those little twerps were her cousins!

She forced herself not to jump onto the anti-Brennan bandwagon. Her two years as a public defender had been an exercise in examining the facts of each case rationally and objectively, of not overreacting to circumstantial evidence. And there was not even a shred of that linking her cousins to tonight's antics.

If she were tucked away in some distant motel tonight, there would be no witness to any possible collusion... And collusion among Cade, Krajack and Pecoraro seemed quite possible indeed. "I—I'll stay here tonight," she heard herself say. "I want to start mopping up that water before it does permanent damage to the floors and to the ceiling."

She was prepared to insist on her right to stay, but nobody tried to dissuade her from her decision. The two officers left after a private conversation on the front porch with Cade, one that did not include Kylie. She changed into jeans and a sweatshirt and assembled an assortment of mops, buckets and faded old towels in the kitchen.

It could be worse, she reminded herself, wringing a mopful of water into a bucket. It wasn't as if the place had been flooded with raw sewage or infectious medical waste. The water from the faucets was clean and safe.

But there was so much of it! Too much. Kylie grimaced as water seeped through the leather of her shoes and sloshed over the tops of them, soaking her wool crew socks and the hem of her jeans.

She glanced up in surprise when Cade joined her in the kitchen wearing sneakers, dark blue running shorts and a T-shirt with the BrenCo logo on the front.

"I keep a gym bag in the trunk of my car," he explained his change of clothes as he reached for a mop. "Do you want me to help you here or start on the bathrooms?"

"You don't have to—"

"You'd rather I sit around and watch you work?"

Kylie considered that. "I'd probably end up dumping a bucket of water on you if you did," she admitted.

"I figured. I'll go upstairs and do the bathrooms. When we're finished, we're both going to want to take a shower without having to wade to it. There should be some hot water by then, since the heater is turned on again and working."

"I definitely need to wash the aroma of mothballs out of my hair." Kylie wrinkled her nose in disgust. "I think it's growing stronger rather than fading."

"It only adds to your allure, darling."

Kylie felt anger lash her, even as she tried to reason it away. Cade was kidding, she knew that. He was given to sarcasm, she knew that, too. At times, she admired his gift for the well-timed sardonic crack. But not now. Right now she wanted him to—to what?

She wanted him to cuddle and comfort her, as he'd done earlier. The realization hit her with the force of a raging flood. She wanted him to forget about mops and cleanup, to carry her upstairs and...

Her face flamed. She'd never been passive and dependent in her life and now she seemed to be succumbing to both states, a humiliating first. Brought on by the macho, take-charge domination of Cade Austin. *...that women find irresistible, even fem-lib types like you.* Brenda's words echoed in her head.

Kylie was appalled. She'd spent years proving to her big brother, Devlin, that anything he could do, she could, too—and maybe even do it better. Only to turn into a simpering wimp at the hands of Cade Austin? A man who wouldn't hesitate to use her weakness to his advantage at BrenCo?

That surge of adrenaline that had remained so elusive earlier, suddenly poured into her system like a blast from an open faucet. With it came some startlingly unexpected developments.

She found herself staring at Cade, at his powerfully muscled arms, bared by the short-sleeve T-shirt, at his long, iron-hard muscular thighs dusted with wiry dark hair. His gym shorts were too skimpy to hide the thick evidence of his virility. Her blood heated in her veins and throbbed in pulsing rhythm. She'd read of studies asserting that danger induced or heightened passion, but she'd never thought to experience the phenomenon personally.

She was definitely experiencing it now, and the unexpected attack of lust struck her hard. No, Kylie vowed. She would not give into it, she would not give in to him!

"We have work to do," she barked out the order.

"Sir, yes, sir!" Cade mimicked a lowly recruit hailing a superior officer, right down to the mock salute. He grabbed a mop and bucket. "I'm off to swab the latrines ASAP."

And though she'd practically demanded that he get to work, Kylie was furious that he was leaving her. Her eyes wild with frustration, she watched him walk out of the kitchen and into the narrow corridor leading to the front hall.

"Do you call all the shots in this town just like you do at BrenCo?" she shouted after him, her tone belligerent and deliberately provoking.

Cade paused and turned to face her. "Meaning?"

"Meaning Port McClain is a police state with you running the show. You don't bother with pesky things like evidence and trials and judges around here. You and your cop buddies have already tried and convicted my cousins. What comes next? The electric chair?"

Cade actually laughed. "Even tyrants like me and my faithful henchmen find that to be excessive punishment for turning on a few faucets. A life sentence without parole will do. Now, any other complaints or can I get started on my job?"

Without waiting for a reply, he headed to the stairs whistling an off-key rendition of "Whistle While You Work." The song playing in Kylie's head was "Town Without Pity."

Cade proved to be an incredibly efficient worker. Kylie was putting the final drying touches on the kitchen when he came back down, having finished both the upstairs bathrooms. He immediately started in on the downstairs powder room.

"Go on upstairs and take your shower," he said when she tried to join him with her mop and bucket a short while later. "It's too small in here for two. I'll take care of it."

Kylie stood on the threshold for a few moments, watching him work. He was as adept with a mop as he was at building a company and running it, she acknowledged silently. She felt the need to make amends for her earlier embarrassing outburst. Nearly ninety minutes worth of slopping cold water around had served to cool her frenzied emotional state.

"Thank you for staying and helping," she murmured. "You wield that mop like a pro."

"One of my many talents." He flashed a mocking grin. "I find manual labor relaxing after a long hard day ruling a police state."

"I admit I was out of line." She lowered her eyes. Playing humble supplicant was difficult. "But you have to admit, you and Officers Krajack and Pecoraro were awfully chummy." She rallied a little. "And they were very willing to do what you—"

"*Suggested* is the word I believe you want to use," Cade interrupted dryly. "Don't say 'commanded' or this paltry attempt at an apology will be all for naught."

She raised her eyes to meet his. "Suggested," she agreed.

"BrenCo contributes to the Port McClain Policemen's Benevolent Fund," Cade explained. "I'm a good friend of the chief's, and I'm personally acquainted with every officer on the force. Some of them have relatives who work at BrenCo. So although I have no authority with the Port McClain PD, I admit I probably do have a certain amount of influence."

"BrenCo maintains a fund for community youth sports programs and contributes to the police department's charity fund. Any other good works I should know about?"

"BrenCo also is an annual contributor to the Volunteer Fire Department, the Port McClain Hospital, and the community Little Theater. There might be a couple others."

"BrenCo is a regular font of benevolence. Your idea or Uncle Gene's? And no false modesty, Cade. Be honest."

"False modesty has never been my strong suit."

"But industrial psychology is. Every aspect of it."

"Let's just say I learned the principles well and applied them." Cade leaned against the doorjamb, his expression thoughtful. "To truly succeed, a company like BrenCo *must* foster goodwill and maintain excellent relations within the community. It took a while to convince Gene—I don't know if he ever really became a true believer—but he gave me a free hand with everything connected with the company, just like he'd promised. Toward the end, I think he came to enjoy the town benefactor reputation that came with BrenCo's pivotal role in Port McClain."

"And the rest of the family?"

"Resented every dime spent on anybody but themselves." Kylie winced. "I should've seen that one coming."

"You said you wanted honesty."

"Maybe I should've added objectivity, too. You are not objective on the subject of the Brennans, Cade."

"Point taken. Now, go take your shower and get ready for bed. You look ready to collapse and you still reek of mothballs." He eyed her curiously. "You never did say how that happened."

She had no intention of admitting she'd taken terrified refuge in that odoriferous closet. "You can have either Uncle Gene's or my grandparents' bedroom. I'm staying in the little room at the back of the house. I've always used it during my visits here."

"Since I've already sampled Gene's mattress—I think it might've seen torture duty in the Spanish Inquisition—I'll take your grandparents' bedroom. Are you sure you wouldn't rather have it? It's the best room in the house and I don't—"

"No, you can have it. Good night, Cade."

He calmly resumed his mopping. "Good night, Kylie."

Over two hours later, Kylie lay shivering in the narrow single bed in the back bedroom. Not only was this room the smallest in the house, but she was certain it was also the coldest. Though the radiator made a valiant attempt at hissing out heat, it stood no chance against the force of the wind that blew against the windows. The icy drafts seeping through each ancient window frame defeated any hope of raising the temperature a few more degrees.

Kylie pulled the bedcovers to her neck and curled up on her side in an attempt to conserve body heat, but the blanket and spread were ineffective against the cold. She briefly considered the two woolen blankets stored in the mothball-protected closet, but couldn't bear the thought of using them. Not after she'd finally washed away that throat-closing camphor scent from her hair and skin.

Furthermore, the chill in the room was not the only factor keeping her awake. She was wired and restless, her mind jumbled with images and words, most of them centered on Cade Austin. Who at this moment was lying in bed in a room right down the hall. He was probably sound asleep, Kylie decided resentfully. No doubt he'd conked out the moment his head had hit the pillow while she tossed and turned and grew colder and more wide-awake with each passing second.

The rain, which had let up in the past hour, suddenly intensified again. Kylie groaned. The sound of raindrops pattering against a windowpane was usually benign, even pleasant, but this storm was unlike any other. So were these windows. What were they made of, anyway? It sounded as if someone were tossing handful after handful of marbles against a metal sheet, loud, and thoroughly maddening. After a few minutes of listening to that infernal racket, she was even more keyed up.

And then she became aware of another sound, a peculiar noise that could have been the wind whipping through the bare branches of the trees surrounding the house. Unless it was something else altogether. An otherwordly moan, perhaps? Kylie shuddered. Involuntarily, she recalled some disturbing programs featuring paranormal phenomenon.

There was something about ghosts and cold spots in a room...

Kylie tried to remember what she'd been told about the history of this old house. It had already passed through a few generations of a Port McClain family before coming on the market at a bargain price, at which time Uncle Gene had bought it for himself and his parents. Kylie thought about that long-gone, forgotten family. Had anyone actually died in this house? Maybe in this very room? It was certainly chilly enough to be a ghostly cold spot.

She sat up in bed when an unidentified rattling noise seemed to grow louder. Thinking more practically, she ruled out spirits and considered the possibility of vandals returning to finish what they'd started tonight. Suppose they hadn't actually left the premises? The officers had gone into every room and shone their flashlights into the dark, dank cellar, but they hadn't conducted an exhaustive search of the place. No one had thought to climb through the crawl space to look into the attic. The criminals—perhaps crazed from crack?—could very well be there just waiting to strike!

Kylie hopped out of bed and raced into the hall. She noticed a stream of light coming from beneath the closed door of her grandparents' bedroom and unerringly headed to it.

Propped by pillows in the four-poster bed, Cade was trying to interest himself in a comprehensive biography of Dwight D. Eisenhower. And then he heard the light, tentative knock on the bedroom door. He set the book aside. "Come in."

Kylie opened the door halfway and stood there, barefoot in a long-sleeve plaid nightshirt that reached the tops of her knees. Cade smiled. "Can't sleep, either?"

"My room is too cold. And noisy and—creepy." She nervously tucked a strand of her hair behind her ear. "My imagination has been running riot tonight. I've gone from ghosts to burglars and was on the verge of conjuring up ax-murderers in the attic when I..." Her voice trailed off and she gave a self-mocking laugh. "No, I can't sleep."

In a flash, he'd crossed the room and stood in front of her, clad in white boxer briefs and a T-shirt. Kylie gulped. If he were to ever pose for an underwear ad, it would become an instant collector's item, gracing women's walls from coast to coast.

Cade scooped her up in his arms. "You're shivering and your teeth are chattering," he murmured as he carried her to the bed. "From the cold or from the possibility of a close encounter with clandestine ax-murderers?"

"Who are high on crack," Kylie added wryly. She linked her arms around his neck and held on tight.

"In Port McClain, they'd probably be high on a couple of

six-packs.'' Cade stood beside the bed and laid her down in the middle of it. ''You'll be warmer here,'' he said huskily, climbing in beside her and pulling the covers over them both.

Kylie wasn't sure who moved first, but an instant later, she was back in his arms. She clung to him, admitting the truth to herself at last. The reason she'd stayed in this house tonight had nothing to do with the necessity of mopping the flooded floors or keeping tabs on a possible conspiracy to frame her cousins. She was here because Cade was. Because she, too, wanted to change the ending of their evening.

She wanted the evening to end with the two of them together. Like this.

''Better?'' Cade gazed at her through heavy-lidded eyes.

He looked dangerous and sensual, and Kylie had to remind herself to breathe. But she nodded her head. She was exactly where she wanted to be.

His hand cupped her cheek, then moved over her shoulder, his fingers kneading and caressing. He lowered his palms to her breasts, which were taut and swollen against the fabric of her nightshirt. Kylie closed her eyes and uttered a soft moan.

And abruptly, without warning, he withdrew his hand and wrapped his arms around her, holding her tightly against him. ''I don't want to take advantage of you,'' he whispered, his lips brushing the top of her head. ''You've had a shock and a scare. You're exhausted and vulnerable and you need to sleep, not to—to—''

''I don't want to go to sleep,'' Kylie cut in, aware that she sounded slightly whiney. She was beyond caring.

Her arms were pinned to her sides by his. She felt as if she were strapped in a straitjacket, she couldn't free her hands. To caress him. To show him what she really wanted. ''And I'm not *vulnerable*. I'm insulted that you think I'm so timid and fragile that I can't handle a little vandalism. You said it yourself—turning on a few faucets is not that big a deal.''

''I never meant to imply it wasn't a serious situation,'' Cade protested. ''If you thought that, you're wrong, Kylie. I'm taking this very—''

''Oh, I know. If this were the military our status would be DEFCON One Alert.'' She wriggled against him, rather experimentally, testing the range of motion allowed to her. Her arms were immobilized but she was able to rub her breasts against his chest, to settle her hips more snugly against him.

Cade groaned. "Lie still or my noble sacrifice will be shot to hell."

Kylie managed to slip her leg between his and press her stomach against the enormous bulge throbbing against the cotton material of his boxers. In the process, her nightshirt slid up, baring her thighs. Their legs tangled, hers smooth and silky, his hard and brushed with wiry-thick hair.

"Your noble sacrifice is to protect me from my own exhausted, vulnerable impulses brought on by my shock and my scare?" She laughed. Taunting him, challenging him. Enticing him.

Cade wondered how she'd managed to convey all those things with a mere laugh. But she had. And now she was using her thigh to apply a gentle rhythmic pressure exactly where he wanted her to.

"I thought you would be tense and uptight," he heard himself say in a thick voice he hardly recognized as his own. "I thought getting you into bed would be as difficult and complicated as planning the North Africa campaign in World War II."

"Is that why you were reading about General Eisenhower, hoping he might offer some tips? He planned the D-Day invasion of Normandy, didn't he?"

Cade closed his eyes. The soft, warm feel of her body caused jolts of sensual lightning to flash through him. Hardly a situation conducive to rational conversation, but he gave it a try. "Kylie, I want you, obviously you know that, but—"

He broke off with a gasp. The fingers of her trapped hand had strayed to the front of his briefs.

"Just wanted to know how obviously you want me, Cade," she said, her eyes gleaming with devilish innocence.

"This is like a bedroom version of Ms. Jekyll and Ms. Hyde." Cade drew in a sharp breath. "As Jekyll, Female Barrister, you look so proper and starchy and you know all the standard rhetoric guaranteed to keep men on guard."

And now she was in bed with him, touching him in a way that heated his blood and scrambled his brains. He tried to remember why he wasn't letting her have free rein with his body, as she so clearly wanted to do.

"I plead guilty, you pegged me correctly, Cade." She stretched her neck to take a light, sexy bite of his earlobe. "I'm usually all those things you said—and maybe worse. I either keep men on guard or send them running."

She kept moving against him, using her body and her legs— he still had full control of her arms—to arouse him. She nibbled sensuously on his neck, along the line of his jaw. "But somehow I'm different with you."

"It's the circumstances that are different, Kylie." Cade laughed grimly, marveling at his own self-control even as he mocked himself for it. He was different with her, too, determined to protect her though the lady did not require or even want his protection.

Give it up and give in, he advised himself. It's what you both want. Definitely what you need.

"You got very little sleep last night in the Port McClain Hotel, you drank too much wine tonight and then came back here to find the place vandalized," he heard himself say instead. "This has not been your usual twenty-four hours, Kylie. It's bound to have had an, uh, unpredictable effect on you."

"You're very modest." She nuzzled her cheek against the raspy stubble on his jaw. "Not giving yourself any credit at all for making me want you."

Still he wouldn't release her arms. He wouldn't kiss her or caress her, either. Kylie might've despaired if she hadn't felt the indisputable proof of his arousal, warm and virile against her belly.

"Credit," he repeated softly. "What if tomorrow it's blame, Kylie?"

She touched her mouth to his, tracing his lips with the tip of her tongue. "I promise to respect you in the morning, darling."

Cade half laughed, half groaned. "I'm giving you one last chance to call this off, baby." His hands began to glide over her back in long, slow circular strokes. Up and down and around until his thumbs grazed the undersides of her breasts.

Kylie's nipples, already pointed and taut, tingled. She

whimpered. She wanted him to touch them, with his fingers, with his mouth.

"Speak now or forever hold your peace," Cade drawled. "Or words to that effect." His hands were under her night-shirt, smoothing over the warm bare skin of her midriff. When they slipped inside her panties, Kylie sucked in her breath, contracting her stomach, giving him easier access.

But instead of sliding lower, to touch her where she was hot and achy and swollen, where she most wanted him to touch her, Cade withdrew his hand. He rolled on his back, folding his arms outside the covers.

Kylie shuddered. "I didn't speak," she said raspily. "I didn't call this off." Had she ever felt so frustrated? Or so exasperated? Cade's restraint tonight was propelling her to new heights in both. "I didn't say no, Cade. So what part of *yes* don't you understand?"

"Those chaste, prim cotton panties of yours gave me an attack of conscience." Cade scowled. "They reminded me that you came in here because you were scared and cold, not to get laid. Instead, I hustled you into bed."

He felt like a rat, and he wanted to be the good guy. For her. Cade muttered an oath. Was he becoming unhinged? He'd always been uninhibited and bold, unencumbered by guilt in the bedroom. Except tonight. He was with the woman he wanted more than any other, and he was acting like some kind of idiotic white knight.

Chaste! Prim! Kylie's cheeks were burning. "You were expecting me to wear a—a black satin thong or something?"

"Or nothing at all," Cade amended grimly. "Then we could dispense with any possibility of ambivalence and ambiguity."

"I'm so sorry to disappoint you." Kylie was sarcastic. She sat up in bed and stared at the meticulously sewn pattern on the antique quilt that covered them. The variations of colors and prints seemed to dance before her eyes.

"Going to storm out of here in an outraged huff?" Cade watched her, his gaze hot and intense.

"I'm considering it." She thought of the icy little bedroom that awaited and decided to prolong her consideration a bit.

"Brennans love dramatic exits. I've seen a wide variety

over the years." His tone was baiting, his conscience swiftly clearing. He'd given her a choice and an out. Enough time had elapsed for cooler heads to prevail, and she was still here. Not because she was scared and vulnerable, but because she wanted to be. She wanted him. Cade grinned wolfishly.

"Then let's see how my dramatic exit compares to all those others you've seen." Kylie tossed back the covers.

Before she could make another move, Cade's fingers fastened around her wrist.

"I want you to stay." The sound of his voice, deep, husky and excitingly male, affected Kylie viscerally.

Not that she was going to let him know. Not yet. Even though his sexual reticence had been based on concern for her, his determined self-control had made a significant dent in her pride. Now it was time to recoup.

"Does that mean you finally resolved your ambivalence and ambiguity?" She sounded cooler than she felt, which bolstered her confidence. She gave her hand a slight tug but when he didn't release it, she made no further attempt to break free.

"*Mine?* You've got it all wrong, honey. I wasn't bothered by either one, but I wasn't sure about you," Cade retorted. "I wanted you to be clear about your motives before—" He paused to swallow, hard. His eyes were fixed on her and the longer he looked, the more aroused he became. Which amazed him because he was so hot and so hard already that he half expected to implode at any moment.

"Before?" Kylie prompted. The ardent intensity of his gaze was as potent as a caress. Her entire body hummed its response.

Cade's train of thought was as totally derailed as a commuter express that had jumped the tracks. He stared at her beautifully shaped mouth and remembered the taste of her lips. He lowered his eyes to her breasts that were swollen and trembling, the tight crests thrusting against the cloth of her nightshirt. The shirt was twisted to her waist, and he gazed lustily at her long bare legs. The V of her white cotton panties was visible at the tops of her thighs, and he decided that perhaps the garment wasn't as chaste and prim as he'd originally believed.

"Come here." He growled the sexy command.

Kylie managed to hold out long enough to taunt, "Aren't you worried I might hit you with a sexual harassment suit in the morning?"

"I'll countersue." He reached up and pulled her down to him.

Seven

His mouth possessed hers and she responded instantly, urgently to his ardent mastery. She felt his tongue thrust between her parted lips and probe deeply into the warm, moist hollow of her mouth. It was delicious and thrilling and everything she'd been wanting. Coherence and control skidded giddily away as she gave herself up to the wild, sweet pleasure of his lovemaking.

As if to make up for lost time, and his earlier restraint, he stripped her with a swift and dizzying expertise.

"You're so beautiful," he whispered roughly, his eyes taking in every inch of her naked body, which was flushed with desire and with need. For him.

"So are you," Kylie murmured, tugging at the hem of his T-shirt. He was quick to accommodate her and take it off. When she boldly slipped her hands beneath the elastic waistband of his briefs, he obligingly removed them, too.

She ran her hands over the bare muscular length of his body and sighed. He was so strong and powerful and wondrously male. "I've never felt this way before, Cade," she admitted achingly. "What have you done to me?"

"The same thing you've done to me." He cupped her breasts, filling his hands with them, fondling gently. "I'm hungry for you, Kylie," he said hoarsely as his lips closed over her nipple. "Like I've never been before."

Her body arched convulsively as a flash of heat seared her. Kylie surrendered to the intense yearning that pulsated within her. She clung to Cade, caressing him with increasing urgency, wanting to give and give to him. But to take as well. Her hand found him, smooth and hard and throbbing with virility. He moaned his pleasure, and her ability to please him thrilled her.

Cade was equally adept at pleasing and thrilling her. He circled one long finger around the secret bud concealed deep between her thighs, skimming, teasing, applying a gentle pressure yet holding back, until she was twisting helplessly with blind need.

"Oh please, Cade," she cried, tossing her head back and forth on the pillow, enveloped in a white-hot mist of wanting. The erotic tension was driving her out of her mind.

He began to lave her nipple with his tongue, then drew it deeper into his mouth to suck on it. She could feel the sensation spark deeply in her womb, as if a tiny wire were attached, providing an instant connection. Between her legs, his touch became concentrated and intense, and she opened to him as he found her warm wet center.

Kylie cried out, shivering as a fiery shaft of pure pleasure shot through her. Still, it wasn't enough. She wanted him inside her, deep, deep within. She was an empty ache craving to be filled, and only he could give her full completion. "Cade, now," she pleaded.

He raised his head and met her glazed eyes. "Are you okay or am I going to have to delve into my trusty gym bag for something?"

It took a full minute for her to comprehend his question. When she did, she blushed. Precautions had not occurred to her, not once, from the time she'd taken flight to his bedroom until this moment when she'd begged him to take her. For a compulsively careful, ever-cautious woman like her, it was a most telling lapse.

Cade watched her, his green eyes perceptive. She felt as if he were reading her mind, that he knew exactly how unusual her behavior was for her, exactly how powerfully he affected her. But all he said was, "I'll take care of it."

"Quite the Boy Scout, aren't you?" she noted with a touch of asperity as he pulled a foil-wrapped packet from his gym bag. "The living embodiment of their motto Be Prepared."

Once again, her total loss of control sharply contrasted with his ability to think things through, even in the heat of the moment. It seemed a disconcerting replay of their passionate scene earlier in his office. She frowned. "Are you *always* prepared? For *everything?*"

"Always," he agreed wryly, sheathing himself. "For everything."

She had to marvel at his dexterity, at his unshakable reliability but she resented it a little, too. "What else do you keep in that magic bag of yours? Road flares? Tourniquets? A Swiss Army knife? After all, one never knows what emergencies the King of BrenCo and Emperor of Port McClain might encounter in the course of a day."

"You do get irritable when the program isn't moving fast enough for you," Cade observed. He came down on top of her, nuzzling her neck. "I'll keep that in mind for the future."

Her fingers clenched on his shoulders. Whether to hold him or to push him away, she hadn't quite ascertained herself. "Don't patronize me, Cade."

"Uh-oh." Cade heaved a heavy sigh. "This is getting awfully close to the borderline. Why are you upset, honey? Because I didn't cast our fate to the winds and take a big, big chance?"

"I'm not upset!" she snapped, stung. "And I certainly wouldn't be mad about something like that!" Truth be told, he'd really nailed her on that one. It was embarrassing how clearly he read her.

"You think I one-upped you." He trapped her chin with his hand and forced her to meet his too-knowledgeable gaze. "Reconsider, Kylie. This isn't the courtroom and I'm not the prosecuting attorney out to rack up points against you."

He settled his body more fully against her, letting her feel the heavy strength of him. Kylie's muscles relaxed and she accepted the hard, warm weight of him; she savored it. Slowly, sensuously, she began to smooth her hands over his back.

"I guess I can be—competitive," she admitted huskily. Her skin was hot and tingling, every nerve ending jumping with anticipation. "It drives me kind of crazy that I was totally lost and you were completely competent, carefully planning ahead."

"It's something of a character flaw of mine. Don't hold it against me." He nibbled at her lips, his voice deep and raspy with an appealing combination of humor and passion. "That's not to say that my head wasn't spinning, honey. You have that effect on me."

"Is that a compliment or a complaint? From what I've heard, every Brennan makes your head spin. Uncle Gene excepted, of course."

Cade's eyes gleamed. "Consider yourself in a category all your own, Kylie." Before she could say another word, he slanted his mouth over hers, sealing them together in a rapacious and intimate kiss.

Kylie clung to him, running her hands over him, learning the virile textures of his body as he explored her own soft feminine secrets. His big hands cupped her bottom and lifted her, positioning her to receive him.

"Are you ready for me, sweetie?"

"Oh, yes, Cade, I'm ready. I feel as if I've been waiting forever," she added breathlessly.

In a blinding flash of insight she realized how long she really had been waiting; *she'd been waiting for him her entire life!* Waiting and hoping, but never expecting to find a man like him, a man who wasn't intimidated by her strength and her independence, a man who was capable of mastering her when she wanted to be mastered. And right now, in bed, she wanted to be feminine and vulnerable and open, all those things she could never be without the right man. Her heart and soul joined her body in acknowledging that Cade Austin was definitely the right man.

He thrust into her with a sure steady surge, stretching her, filling her, making her cry out his name. Her breathing was shallow and she trembled beneath him as her body softened, accommodating him in a melting flood of sheer pleasure.

Kylie closed her eyes and wrapped herself around him, holding on tight as he began to move in an erotically tantalizing rhythm. Hot ripples of rapture radiated through her body and she matched his pace, her liquid heat enveloping him as their shared pleasure built and grew, stunning them both with its force.

Passion and desire and need combined into a rushing force that swept them both into a vortex of dynamic tension so intense, so electrifying, that it took only moments for both of them to be swept away on wave after wave of pure ecstasy.

Finally, Cade collapsed against her, burying his head in the hollow of her shoulder. Kylie hugged him, feeling incredibly replete—and something much more.

Was she in love? She clung to him, dazed and wondrous. What she felt for Cade was unlike anything else she had ever experienced. And it was not just because he was good in bed—well, fabulous in bed, actually. No, she was too practical to be blinded by sheer sensuality, Kylie assured herself.

What were the lyrics to "I've Never Been in Love Before"? she mused dreamily. Her mother, a show tune fan, often played Broadway soundtracks and Kylie knew the titles and snatches from many a song. If falling in love was this unfamiliar yet enthralling emotional deluge that changed everything, especially herself, then she'd never truly been in love before.

She was in love with Cade Austin. Kylie tried out the words in her head. To her surprise, it didn't sound as strange or self-deluded as she might've thought.

Their bodies still joined, they lay languid and drowsy in the sweet aftermath, kissing and caressing and murmuring soft sexy things to each other. When they finally, reluctantly separated, he tucked her against his side, his arms wrapped around her, keeping her close.

"I have a confession to make." Kylie stretched luxuriously against the length of him. "I've never gone to bed on a first date before." It was important that he realize how much he meant to her, how many of her own rules she'd broken for him.

Cade smiled lazily. "Somehow I knew that. But this didn't feel like a first date, did it? I'm almost grateful to your terminally nitwitted cousins for their part in bringing us together tonight."

His fingers tangled in her dark, thick hair. He felt fantastic, on top of the world. And he'd been taken there by Kylie Brennan who could logically and legitimately qualify as his bona fide nemesis.

Kylie was in no mood to argue about anything with him, not even the alleged guilt or innocence of her cousins. "This was different from any first date I've ever had," she agreed happily. "We skipped that awkward getting-to-know-you stage and really bonded, Cade." She gazed at him, her eyes shining. It was as close to a declaration of love that she dared to make, to herself or to him.

"Oh, yeah!" Cade laughed softly. "We've bonded, baby."

Kylie turned to face him and lifted her mouth to kiss him with all the warmth and tender emotions flowing through her. He quickly took control of the kiss, deepening it into one of intimate possession. His hands moved over her supple curves, savoring their alluring rounded warmth and the creamy smoothness of her skin. Like a spark kindled to flashpoint, a vibrant passion quickly flared between them once more.

Her legs flexed and she lay open and vulnerable to him. Uttering a deep moan, he entered her, losing himself in her velvety softness. The stunning pleasure shredded what little was left of his control. He didn't think anything could be as good as his first time with her but incredibly, this unexpected, impulsive, way-too-soon second time more than equaled it.

He felt her intimate muscles clench him, felt her body suddenly convulse with ecstasy, and her climax triggered his in exquisitely attuned timing. A few moments later, he fell asleep in her arms, too satiated and passion-spent to stay awake and talk.

Kylie didn't mind. Her last coherent thought before she, too, dropped deeply and swiftly off to sleep was that if actions spoke louder than words—as that old tried-and-true adage claimed—they had no need for further conversation, anyway. Tonight, their bodies had told each other everything they needed to know.

Cade and Kylie sat across from each other at a table in The Corner Grill, studying their breakfast menus. Under the table, their legs were comfortably entwined. On top of it, Cade held Kylie's hand, his thumb absently stroking the inside of her wrist.

"I can't concentrate," Kylie admitted, closing her menu in defeat. There were too many new thoughts and images vying for priority and space in her mind to waste brain cells on something as prosaic as breakfast food. "I know the waitress is getting tired of waiting for us to make up our minds. Just order whatever you're having for me, too."

"You want me to order for you? That's more than a little retro, Kylie," Cade used her own quote to rib her.

"Just don't forget that I prefer tea," she added, trying and failing to sound stern.

"Oh, I'm not about to make that mistake again."

Their eyes met and they smiled at each other. They'd been doing a lot of gazing and smiling and touching since awakening earlier that morning. Kylie was amazed at how easy it was to wake up naked in bed with Cade, at how right it felt. She was particularly surprised at the lack of awkwardness and tension that one might assume would occur the morning-after-the-wild-night-before.

But there was no embarrassment or misgivings, no unease. They'd made love again and moved on to shower and dress as if they had done so many times. The intimacy felt natural, their camaraderie unforced.

Since there was no food in Gene's house, Cade suggested breakfast at The Corner Grill before he headed to the office. They'd stopped at his house first, so he could change into his office attire. His CEO power suit, Kylie had teased, watching him dress with admiring, possessive eyes.

She had opted for casual herself: jeans and a close-fitting, gray knit sweater that hugged her firm, rounded breasts and was short enough to reveal a glimpse of her smooth midriff if she moved in certain ways. He devised maneuvers that caused her to move in those ways so he could stare at that tempting band of skin.

Underneath, he knew she wore wine-red bikini panties—that were definitely *not* chaste or prim—and a matching lacy bra that he had personally fastened. Remembering sent frissons of heat through him. The image of her in that sexy lingerie seemed to be seared in his mind's eye and sent his pulses into overdrive everytime he called it up. Cade suppressed a groan. He felt like a sweat-palmed teen slavering over a *Victoria's Secret* catalog.

Their breakfasts arrived—The Corner Room's specialty, blueberry waffles—which Kylie immediately recognized as the supermarket frozen variety. She didn't care. What she ate was irrelevant. Sitting across from Cade, watching him, talking to him, touching him was all that mattered. Her heartbeat raced, her skin tingled. She wanted to be alone with him. The long hours of the day seemed to stretch interminably ahead, and she wanted them to be over so she and Cade could—

Kylie set down her fork in midthought. For the first time since she'd awakened this morning curled in Cade's arms, it occurred to her that he hadn't mentioned seeing her tonight. He'd suggested breakfast, not dinner. She had no idea when they would be together again after leaving The Corner Grill.

Until now, everything had seemed so simple. She was sure they'd skipped all that uncertainty, the does-he-care, how-far-and-how-fast-should-we-go hurdles that tended to plague new relationships. But here she sat, worrying and wondering and not so sure of anything at all.

Her mouth felt dry, her throat seemed to close, and anxiety roiled through her. The symptoms brought back that hideous period in junior high school when she'd been waiting and hoping to be asked to the Spring Dance. Adolescent insecurity was not a place she cared to revisit; for Cade Austin to take her there sent apprehension rippling through her. He had such power over her. It was little consolation that she had willingly granted it.

"Consider our Brennan-free respite officially at an end," Cade's voice intruded on her nervous reverie. "The Terrible Trio has just invaded the premises."

Kylie's gaze followed his to the door where her cousins Brenda, Brent, and Ian were entering the restaurant, already pulling off their coats. Brenda was dressed for work in her waitress uniform, a pink blouse and black slacks, her dark hair pulled high in a ponytail that brushed her collar. Brent wore ripped, faded jeans and a dark sweatshirt cut off at the shoulders, exposing an eye-popping array of tattoos up and down his arms. A ponytail like Brenda's would've benefited his appearance greatly, but his long unwashed hair hung in scraggly disarray to his shoulders. Ian was preppily clad in khaki trousers, a white oxford cloth shirt and a striped tie, his attire as traditional as his neatly cut hair.

"They're a somewhat, um, eclectic trio but they don't qualify as terrible," Kylie felt obliged to defend them. "Well, except maybe for Brent."

Cade was scowling fiercely at her cousins. If looks could kill, the three Brennans would certainly be headed for the embalming table. "For God's sake, don't make eye contact with any of them," he ordered, but it was too late. Kylie and Brenda had spotted each other, and Kylie gave a hesitant little wave.

Which was all the invitation the trio needed. As the three Brennans approached them, Kylie glanced anxiously from Cade to her cousins, wishing for a court-appointed intermediary to keep the peace, knowing that hapless task could very well fall to her. It was not a pleasant prospect.

The moment the threesome reached the table, Cade stood up, towering over them, his height and his expression intentionally, effectively intimidating. Kylie watched each of her cousins take quick defensive steps away from him.

"Your little trick last night was idiotic beyond imagining," Cade immediately launched his attack, dispensing with even the pretense of a friendly greeting.

"I don't know what you're talking about, Austin." Ian threw back his shoulders and puffed out his chest, presumably to give him greater presence, but he remained short and slim, the runt of the litter yipping at the heels of the pack's alpha male. Cade Austin.

"Yeah, right, Ian." Brenda laughed. "Like any of us are dumb enough to believe that."

"Shut up, Brenda!" Brent flexed his muscles, and shook a threatening fist at his sister. "Or I'll shut your mouth for you."

Kylie's eyes widened. Those tattoos of his did strange things when his skin rippled. Did he actually intend to hit Brenda? He certainly appeared to be capable of it. Automatically, Kylie rose to her feet ready to intervene on the other woman's behalf.

She didn't have to.

"You touch your sister and I'll wipe up the floor with you," Cade promised. He grabbed a fistful of Brent's sweatshirt and lifted him a few inches off the ground. His eyes bored into Brent's until the younger man looked away, sulkily staring at the ground. Only then did Cade speak again.

"Last night's brand of juvenile vandalism is exactly what I'd expect from a witless coward like you, Brent." Cade's tone was filled with such contempt that Kylie cringed.

She watched as Cade abruptly released Brent, dropping him to the floor. Her cousin stumbled backward, his shoulders slumping, his mouth twisting into a pout, but he didn't utter a sound. After his show of belligerence toward Brenda, Kylie was surprised by Brent's passivity. He certainly hadn't flexed a single tattooed muscle against Cade.

Kylie sat back down, feeling superfluous and uneasy. Wishing she'd taken Cade's advice and not made eye contact in the first place.

Cade next turned to Ian, who sidestepped behind a chair in an obvious move to escape Brent's fate.

Brenda noticed, and snickered. "Pick him up and throw him across the room, Cade," she urged gleefully.

"He's not worth the energy." Cade zeroed his laser gaze onto Ian. "I'm fully aware that you're a shortsighted, greedy little weasel, Ian, but I didn't think you were quite *that* stupid as to post Brent's bail so he could vandalize Gene's place. Did you enjoy your visit from the police last night?"

"They have no evidence connecting me to anything," Ian insisted. The fact that he appeared on the verge of panic did not add to his credibility.

Cade's glower heated to nuclear intensity. "That's not what I hear. The charges pending are almost too numerous to mention, but I'll list a few anyway. Burglary, breaking and entering, malicious mischief, for starters. Not to mention conspiracy and risking a catastrophe," he added with barely contained fury.

Kylie's jaw dropped. He had to be kidding, though her cousins didn't seem to get the joke.

"Can you make those charges stick?" Brenda was curious.

Not if the district attorney, defense attorney, or judge had graduated from law school, Kylie thought. She debated whether or not to inform her cousins that Cade was bluffing, that there was no evidence linking either Brent or Ian to the scene, let alone a shred of proof to indict for the more serious crimes Cade had cited.

But Cade answered Brenda's question with one of his own. "Can I make them stick?" he asked coldly. "What do you think?"

By the expressions on the faces of Brenda, Brent and Ian, they clearly thought Cade could and would.

"It wasn't my fault!" Brent exclaimed. Kylie recognized the tone. It was one she heard when a client was about to cut a deal on his own behalf and to hell with his accomplice.

Cade looked bored. "We'll talk about it later. Now get lost."

Brent and Ian left the restaurant, quarreling and nearly tripping over each other in their efforts to make a quick getaway.

Brenda shrugged and sat down in Cade's chair at the table across from Kylie. "Hey, how'd it go last night?" she asked in breezy girlfriend-to-girlfriend fashion, as if the altercation of the past few minutes had not occurred. "You wouldn't believe where Noah and I ended up, Kylie." Her voice lowered. "I have almost ten minutes till my shift starts. Come into the back with me and I'll tell you all—"

Cade slipped his hands under Brenda's armpits and lifted her bodily from the chair. He set her on her feet and glared at her. "I want you to tell me everything you know about the break-in at your uncle Gene's house last night, Brenda. And I mean *everything*. Because if you don't—"

"You'd better stop threatening me and start sweet-talking me into being your ally," Brenda retorted. "You're going to need one, you know."

Cade caught Kylie's eye. "Wasn't that what Stalin said to Roosevelt?"

Kylie almost smiled, but reconsidered and didn't. Cade had already bullied her cousins and seemed intent on continuing the behavior. It was conduct she could not reward, not even subtly, by smiling. Her instincts were to shield and defend the underdog, and right now that was certainly Brenda, not the almighty Cade Austin.

"I'd like to hear about your evening with Noah, Brenda."
Kylie turned purposefully to her cousin.

"That's my cue to leave." An impatient Cade glanced at
his watch. "I'll talk to you later, Kylie." He leaned down,
placed a quick proprietary kiss on her mouth and strode from
the restaurant.

"He kissed you!" Brenda gawked after him. "The last time
I saw you two together you were yelling at each other on
Uncle Gene's front porch. And now—wow! You're a fast
worker, Kylie. I want to hear all about *your* night!"

Kylie's cheeks were hot. Her lips tingled and throbbed; it
was as if she could actually feel the imprint of Cade's mouth
on them. The sensation recurred in her breasts and her nipples
tightened. She grew moist and swollen between her thighs,
where she still felt evidence of his passionate possession. Kylie
drew a sharp, shuddering breath.

"So how good is he in bed?" Brenda asked with real interest. "Four or five stars?"

"Brenda!" Kylie squeaked a protest.

"Should I go higher or lower?" Brenda pressed.

"Brenda, do you plan on working today or are you here as
a paying customer?" Another waitress, several years older and
at least three sizes bigger, arrived at their table to snarl at
Brenda. "Should I take *your* order or will you get moving and
wait on the Library Senior Women's committee over there by
the window?"

Kylie was relieved at the interruption, despite the older
woman's testiness. She simply couldn't confide anything about
last night to Brenda or anybody else. What was between herself and Cade was too private, too precious—and too confusing—to share with an outsider. And an outsider was anyone
but Cade and herself.

"I'm ready now, Dee." Brenda sighed and rose to her feet.
"I'll take the Senior Women's table." She nudged Kylie with
her elbow. "To be continued, huh, Kylie?"

Kylie smiled weakly. "I'm glad things worked out well for
you and Noah last night, Brenda."

"Obviously, not as well as they did for you and Cade 'cause
our date didn't continue through breakfast," Brenda said slyly.
Her face softened. "But, yeah, we had a good time. Noah took

me, Starr Lynn and my mother to dinner at The Panda House, if you can believe that. I've never had any date invite my mom and my kid to come along with us. Then we went to the rink and watched Starr Lynn practice for a while and ended up at home to watch a video. Noah helped Starr Lynn with her math homework. She actually understood it after he explained it to her." Brenda stared into space, in something of a daze. "He didn't even try to get me into bed, but he kissed me good-night. It *felt* like he wanted me, if you know what I mean, but when he didn't follow up..." She frowned worriedly. "What do you think?"

"I think Noah respects you and doesn't want to rush things." Kylie's reassurance to Brenda stoked her own anxiety. If not rushing things sexually was a measure of respect, ending her first date with Cade in bed placed her somewhere beyond the pale.

Brenda went to work, and a very preoccupied Kylie left the restaurant to walk to her car parked in the adjacent lot. When a strong hand seized her arm from behind, bringing her to an immediate unwilling halt, red-hot anger streaked through her, combined with an equally potent bolt of fear.

She reacted instinctively, letting the rage take over, knowing that acting afraid around the criminal element was an irrevocable mistake. "You're in enough trouble without adding assault to the list of charges, Brent!"

"Brent?" Cade's voice, deep with amusement, echoed in her ears. "An interesting conclusion, counselor. Whatever happened to your innocent until proven guilty mantra?"

He dropped her arm, and Kylie whirled around to face him. "Why did you sneak up on me? I thought I was being mugged!"

The relief flowing through her didn't dilute her anger. Instead, it seemed to exponentially increase, abetted by guilt. She'd automatically blamed Brent as her attacker...so much for her lofty proclamations!

"You're not the only one who imagined Brent jumping you out here in a fit of temper." Cade's eyebrows drew together. "Did you really think I'd go off and leave you if there was a possibility that the Dastardly Duo were still lurking around?"

"I thought you'd left for the office—which is what you said."

"Which is what you assumed," he amended. "I had to escape from listening to the torrid rendition of Brenda's night of passion with poor Noah. I've been waiting out here for you."

Kylie noticed his car parked near hers, exactly where he'd left it earlier when she had followed him in her car to The Corner Grill. Had she been less absorbed in wondering where she stood with Cade, she might've noticed him standing close by.

A cold breeze gusted around them, and she shivered. "There was no torrid rendition or no night of passion. They spent a wholesome family evening together."

"Do I detect an accusatory note in your voice?" Cade was smiling as he reached for her. His gaze fastened on her mouth and he pulled her closer, sliding his hands under her coat to mold her to the hard contours of his body. "Why? For not sticking around to chat with Brenda this morning? Or for by-passing wholesome family fare last night in favor of our adult evening alone?"

"Adult?" Kylie echoed. "That's a bland euphemism for how we spent the night."

Inspired by those sensual memories, her body arched against him, seeking the heat and the satisfaction she'd found with him. They were in a public parking lot, but she felt the hard ridge of his erection pressing insistently against the softness of her belly, her breasts were cushioned provocatively against his chest.

"Bland is not a term that could be used to describe the way we spent last night, honey." His voice reverberated in her ears as he kissed her neck.

Kylie ached with a sweet pain that could not be assuaged here—not unless she wanted to shock the Library Senior Women's committee, seated at their table by the window with an unparalleled view of the parking lot.

Cade, clearly on her wavelength, released her with a sigh of regret. "I'll see you at lunch," he said huskily. "We'll make it a long, long one. Come to my office around noon."

Kylie gave a dreamy nod. He took her keys from her hand

and opened her car door. She slipped inside, a syrupy warmth suffusing her. Noon. A glance at the car's clock told her that she had only a few more hours to wait.

And then she gripped the steering wheel, her eyes widening in dismay. "Cade, I can't."

He had closed her door, but opened it again at the sound of her near plaintive wail. "What's the matter, Kylie?"

"I'm meeting my uncles and Axel Dodge for lunch today,' Kylie blurted out. "I'm supposed to be at the restaurant by quarter to twelve."

A chill shuddered through her and she averted her eyes, unable to meet his. She felt like a dyed-in-the-wool traitor, the stereotypical backstabbing Brennan. What kind of a woman met with the enemy the very day after a passionate night with her lover?

But before she could formulate an answer, her equitability enabled her to see from her uncles' point of view. Artie and Guy would consider her night with Cade as sleeping with the enemy. To them, her alliance with Cade made her a dyed-in-the-wool traitor.

"I can't cancel, Cade. They're my dad's brothers. I owe them at least an hour for lunch."

Cade stared at her, taking careful note of her distress. "All right," he said after a few long moments. "You have to meet them for lunch."

Kylie was rigid with tension. "I—I did promise."

"Yes, you did."

He was agreeing, he hadn't tried to argue with her, but Kylie felt the barrier between them, as solid and impenetrable as the Berlin Wall once had been. Of course, that had come tumbling down…

"We could have dinner together tonight," she said, hoping she sounded diplomatic, not desperate. "I—I'll cook something at Uncle Gene's."

Cade gave a brief nod. "Call me later," he said briskly and started toward his car.

Kylie leaned out of hers. "Cade, I—you—you do understand why I can't tell you where we're meeting?" Her voice was a plea but she didn't care. "I promised that I'd—"

"Kylie, stop worrying," Cade called over his shoulder. "I understand."

She remembered a judge who'd used that same tone with her in the courtroom. Authoritative. Somewhat patronizing. Dictatorial mixed with a touch of indulgence. The feelings evoked within her were the same then as now, a combination of indignation and relief.

Kylie sat in her car and watched Cade drive away. She had a few hours to kill until that fateful meeting and wondered how to spend them. Returning to Uncle Gene's house where she would be immersed in memories of making love with Cade did not seem like a good idea, not when she needed her thinking to remain clear and impartial.

She began to tally the number of Brennan encounters she'd experienced since arriving in town. It was somewhat similar to comprising a witness list. She had already seen four of her cousins and would see her uncles at lunch. That left her two aunts, Lauretta and Bobbie, unvisited and unseen.

Impulsively, Kylie decided to visit Bobbie. Brenda's pronouncement that Lauretta hated the entire Wayne Brennan branch of the family, whether true or not, made her less than eager to drop in on Uncle Guy's socialite wife.

Bobbie greeted Kylie rather laconically and ushered her into the small frame house she shared with Bridget, Brenda and Starr Lynn in a tidy working-class neighborhood, not far from the BrenCo plant.

There were none of the effusive hugs and kisses Lauretta invariably bestowed, Kylie noted, remembering how thrilled her aunt always claimed to be when Wayne, Connie and the kids came to visit. *And all the while she was hating our guts.* The renegade thought slipped in and Kylie quickly sought to expunge it. Brenda had effectively implanted a subliminal stealth missile in her mind, and awareness of it did not lessen its efficiency.

"What brings you here?" Bobbie asked, seating Kylie at the kitchen table and pouring them each a cup of coffee. Kylie decided to make do and not ask for tea instead. Something about Bobbie, whether it was her dark, vivid blue-black hair— a startling shade that did not occur in nature—her hard unsmiling face, sharply assessing blue eyes, or wiry toughness, precluded special requests.

"I've seen Bridget and Brenda and, uh, Brent and I thought I'd drop by to say hello." Kylie spooned teaspoon after teaspoon of sugar into the dark brew, hoping to make it palatable.

"Before your lunch meeting with Artie and Guy and that slick Dodge character they dragged down from Cleveland?" Bobbie did not waste time making small talk, she got right to the point. "They want you to sell your shares and sell out BrenCo. They'll lie to you, say anything you want to hear, so you'll do it. Are you going to?"

Stalling, Kylie took a sip of her heavily sweetened coffee. Surprisingly enough, it wasn't bad, as far as coffee went. "I haven't made any decisions," she admitted. "I've heard Cade's side and I feel I should listen to theirs."

"Oh, yeah? And you told Cade that?"

Kylie nodded.

"Bet that went over big." Bobbie gave a snort of laughter.

"He said he understood," Kylie murmured.

"What's to understand? If you go along with those jerks, you're not the whiz kid Gene thought you were. You—hey, wait a minute!" Bobbie interrupted herself. "You said you saw Brent? When? Where? Did you go down to the jail? Who the hell told you to—"

"I saw him this morning at The Corner Grill," Kylie cut in quickly.

"He's out of jail?" Bobbie roared. She began firing questions at Kylie who answered to the best of her ability. None of the answers pleased Bobbie. She began to curse and pound the table and appeared ready to hurl the pot of coffee at some ready target.

Kylie hoped it wouldn't be her. She knew full well that the messenger of bad tidings was often blamed for them, a reaction dating all the way back to antiquity.

"It must've been Guy who gave Ian that money to bail out Brent!" Bobbie raged, after hearing about last night's break-in. "Where else would he have gotten it? That damn Artie never has a spare nickel on hand."

Kylie hadn't intended to tell all, but Bobbie's investigatory techniques—she'd perfected the dual roles of good-cop-bad-cop and played both herself—ferreted out all the facts. Except for one very personal one, that she'd spent the night in bed with Cade.

Kylie drained the rest of the coffee from her cup and poured another, seeking a bolstering jolt of caffeine. "Cade didn't mention Guy, but he does think Ian deliberately posted bail so Brent could..." Her voice trailed off and she left the obvious unsaid.

Bobbie said it for her. "So Brent could break into Gene's place and damage it. Wait until I see him, I'm going to slap him silly. And that jackass Artie was in on the plan, too, you can count on that!"

Kylie guessed that all four male Brennans were in danger of being slapped silly by Bobbie should they be reckless enough to cross her path.

"I'm calling Bridget right now!" Bobbie grabbed the phone. "When she hears how they used Brent, she'll think twice at letting herself be used! She'd better, or I'll brain her!"

Kylie felt an ominous stirring within her. "Aunt Bobbie, do they want Bridget to—to do something illegal?"

The unknowable, obscure *they*. Usually, Kylie avoided conspiracy theories but this time *they* seemed dishearteningly familiar—her uncles and her cousins Brent and Ian.

"God!" Bobbie seemed to be summoning the Almighty. She replaced the receiver in its cradle, then sank heavily onto the kitchen chair and lit a cigarette. "I can't smoke when Starr Lynn is around," she said, inhaling deeply. "It wouldn't be good for her to breathe smoke, she has to stay in top condition. But at times like this...Damn, why do my kids have to be so stupid? All three of them are idiots who let themselves get jerked around and talked into doing things that anyone with an ounce of common sense would know to run screaming away from."

Kylie studied this calmly pessimistic Bobbie and felt a deep pang of sympathy for her. "What do they want Bridget to do, Aunt Bobbie?" she asked quietly.

"To threaten Cade—and BrenCo—with a sexual harassment suit."

Eight

Kylie went still. "A sexual harassment suit?" The ugly words seemed to reverberate in her head.

"Yeah. Axel Dodge came up with the idea to discredit Cade. Artie and Guy aren't that creative, but they'd go along with any plan to bring down Cade. Bridget is supposed to say she'll file a claim against BrenCo accusing the company of sex discrimination and fostering an atmosphere of pervasive sexual harassment. Those are the exact words they used."

"And what would be the basis of this claim?" Kylie asked tersely.

"She's supposed to say management threatened retaliation against women employees who refused to have sex with them and male workers grabbed their female colleagues' intimate parts," Bobbie recited. "That there were leers and catcalls and dirty jokes and stuff like that happening every day and all of it was reported but nothing was done to stop it."

Kylie felt sick. "Is any of this true?"

"Bridget told me nobody's ever done anything to her. She's never heard any women at BrenCo complain, either, but Axel Dodge said if Bridget just threatens to file the claim, it'll give them leverage against Cade. Even though there's no proof of anything, he wouldn't want the trouble of a claim like that and to stop it, he'll do whatever they want, like raise the dividend payouts or something. That's what they hope, anyway.''

"So the allegations are completely false," Kylie said flatly.

Bobbie nodded. "I tried to tell Bridget it's a dumb plan, but I don't know if she believed me. You can never tell with her.''

"It's more than dumb, it constitutes fraud, abuse of process and probably civil conspiracy.'' Kylie clutched her head in her hands, contemplating the nightmarish case. "Why would Bridget even consider doing such a thing, Aunt Bobbie?''

"Her father doesn't have the time of day for Bridget. Never has.'' Bobbie sighed. "Brent is Artie's favorite and he tolerates Brenda because of Starr Lynn. He thinks Starr Lynn will be a rich and famous Olympic champion ice skater someday so he treats her nice. Bridget, he totally ignores. Except suddenly this plan comes up and Artie is Mr. Devoted Daddy, taking Bridget out to dinner and giving her money and stuff. Trying to bribe her into cooperating. I warned her about those Brennan men.'' Bobbie's eyes flashed. "User-slimeball-rats, every last one of them!''

Kylie winced. "I'm sorry for Bridget, Aunt Bobbie, but she can't be allowed to go through with filing a false claim. She'll end up in trouble beyond her wildest dreams.'' Impulsively, she laid her hand over the older woman's. "The charges I cited are the minimal ones. There are far more serious versions that can be brought against her, and they will be since her claims are patently false.''

"You're saying that Cade will fight back?'' Bobbie was glum.

Kylie thought of Cade's reaction to such a claim and shuddered. "I think you can safely predict that he will fight any false charges brought against BrenCo with the best attorneys and investigatory team that company money can buy. And since Bridget's claims are untrue, they will be unable to be proved.''

She tried to maintain the calm and matter-of-fact demeanor of an unbiased lawyer considering the facts of a hypothetical case. Riling the volatile Bobbie didn't seem to be in anyone's best interest. "Investigators for BrenCo will look for the motive behind the false claims and that will lead to the conspiracy, bringing in Artie and Guy and Axel Dodge."

"So Bridget won't be the only one in trouble?"

To Kylie's alarm, Bobbie seemed enthused by this prospect. "They'll all do jail time," she warned. "They'll also have to pay substantial fines. And after being cleared, BrenCo and Cade himself can sue for damages and libel, just to name a few possibilities. The entire plan is a disaster, Aunt Bobbie, but I think Bridget will be hurt worst of all."

Kylie was relieved to see that her tacked-on warning had its desired effect.

Bobbie's expression turned bleak once more. "Will you try to talk some sense into Bridget? If she won't listen to her mother, maybe she'll pay some mind to you. She thinks you're so pretty and so smart. She kind of admires you."

Kylie doubted that. "I'll talk to Bridget," she promised anyway.

"And if you have any luck getting through to her, you can tackle Brenda next," Bobbie intoned darkly. "She's in way over her head with Noah Wyckoff, that pal of Cade's. Which is exactly what Cade intended. It's part of his plan."

Kylie thought of Cade's reaction to the budding Brenda-Noah romance. "Oh, Aunt Bobbie, I really don't think so."

"It makes perfect sense," insisted Bobbie. "I see Noah using Brenda to get whatever information she hears about Artie and Guy's schemes and then passing it along to Cade. Oh, he's a smooth one, all right!"

Kylie cleared her throat. "Cade or Noah?"

"Both. They know that Noah isn't like the men Brenda's used to. I'm worried sick about her. I even tried some of that retropsychology, you know, when you say one thing to get somebody to do the exact opposite?"

"You mean reverse psychology."

"Yeah, that's it. I told Brenda to play it cool around Noah, thinking that she'd blow off my advice like she always does and would come on so strong she'd seem like a stalker. I figured, spy mission or not, that would scare him off. He'd tell Cade he couldn't stand it and to infiltrate the Brennans some other way."

"But your plan hasn't worked?"

"No. I can't figure it out. Last night Noah asked me and Starr Lynn to have dinner with them—and we had a great time. Yeah, he's a real slick one."

"Isn't it possible that Noah genuinely cares about Brenda and they don't need manipulation and strategies?" suggested Kylie.

"Oh, sure!" Bobbie gave a cynical snort of laughter. "I bet you think that Cade is just a tame pussycat instead of a man-eating tiger, too. Let me set you straight on that point, sugar. Cade Austin is ruthless. There isn't anything he wouldn't do for BrenCo, and you ought to think about that because you're the one standing in the way of his total control of the company. If he tries to sweet-talk you into bed, keep in mind that what he really wants from you is a helluva lot more than your body."

"You told Brenda that you trusted Cade," Kylie reminded her. Her hand shook a little as she set the coffee cup down, either a reaction from the double ingestion of caffeine or from the nerve Bobbie had so unerringly struck.

"Sure, I trust him not to use Brenda sexually. Cade Austin is too smart to be led around by his—" Bobbie glanced at Kylie and rephrased. "He isn't driven solely by sex. Anyway, he can get it from other women, so why bother to tick me off by messing around with Brenda?" She smiled slightly. "Cade doesn't like it when I get upset."

"But wouldn't that line of reasoning also apply to Noah Wyckoff?"

"Noah is a safe step removed from Cade. They thought I wouldn't catch on because Brenda hasn't. Ha!" Bobbie crushed the stub of her cigarette in a ceramic ashtray shaped like a skate.

"On one of the soaps I watch, somebody said 'being underestimated is a gift.' Well, it's true. I'm underestimated by certain people, but it works for me because they don't know how good I am at figuring things out. And since you're a sweet girl and I always liked you, even though Artie and Guy and Lauretta say you're a phony little nuisance, I'm going to talk to you like I talk to my own girls."

Kylie braced herself for the words of maternal wisdom.

"Watch yourself around Cade Austin." Bobbie lit another cigarette. "He knows that if you get pregnant, your father will insist that you get married. In fact, you'd probably insist on it yourself. Cade is counting on that."

"He's counting on, uh, making me pregnant?" Kylie dared to ask.

"And then making you marry him. That'll put him in the catbird seat once and for all. As your husband, Cade will control BrenCo lock, stock and barrel."

Kylie stared at the swirling stream of smoke. Bobbie had recited a plot straight from daytime television, one she should have found ludicrous, especially after last night. Cade's precautionary actions had thoroughly disputed her aunt's dire predictions. However much he wanted control of BrenCo, there were certain lines Cade wouldn't cross.

Would he? A niggling doubt began to nag at her.

"Look, I don't want BrenCo to be sold," Bobbie continued. "If it is, and Cade is replaced by somebody from some gigantic corporation who doesn't know us, my family loses the most. Cade pays Bridget more than the other receptionists at the company because she's Gene's niece. Starr Lynn gets a chunk of BrenCo community aid money for her training and competition expenses. I know some stranger would never do that for us, and I want Cade to stay in charge. But it's only fair that you have all the facts to protect yourself."

Viewed from Bobbie's dark perspective, Kylie knew that her aunt believed she was helping. Bobbie had nothing to gain and everything to lose if Cade was ousted yet she didn't want to see Kylie duped by him; she didn't want to see Brenda duped, either.

Kylie frowned thoughtfully. In Bobbie's world, obviously someone was always trying to put one over on someone else. It seemed a stressful way to live, remaining hypervigilant, always waiting for the next lie or deceitful trick.

Compassion stirred within her. "I appreciate your concern, Aunt Bobbie," Kylie said softly. "I'll be very careful."

"You really are a smart girl!" Bobbie seemed pleased. "Brenda and Bridget would yell at me and say I'm paranoid and trying to spoil things for them, but you understand."

She leaned forward in her chair, her eyes blazing with an

almost messianic fervor. "I know what it's like to be trapped in a lousy marriage, living with a jerk you hate, watching your kids get more screwed up every day. You don't deserve that, Kylie, even if Gene did leave you all the stock."

The plan was for Kylie to meet her uncles and Axel Dodge at a place called the Peach Tree Inn, halfway between Port McClain and Cleveland. Kylie followed the directions Uncle Guy had given her, exiting the interstate and driving along a seemingly endless two lane road.

Perhaps it was the result of her visit with Aunt Bobbie but suspicion began to gnaw at her. Why had they chosen a place so out of the way? There were certainly enough restaurants in Port McClain without traversing Ohio in search of one. The name of this place raised further distrust. Were there any peach trees in the state of Ohio? What if this so-called Peach Tree Inn didn't exist? Perhaps the idea was to lure her far from town and then...

Kylie felt perspiration bead on her brow. If paranoia was contagious, she'd caught a whopping case of it from Aunt Bobbie.

Doubts that should've occurred to her earlier suddenly struck her now in full force. Aunt Lauretta and Uncle Guy could have hosted this meeting in their house. Certainly, that would've been the easiest course of action, *unless their plans involved disposing a body—hers!* Naturally, they wouldn't want their own home to be the crime scene!

Kylie's heart pounded so ferociously she half expected it to explode from her chest. She was letting her imagination run away with her, she conceded, combining her knowledge of criminal intent and actions with all those programs extolling the despicable deeds family members perpetrate on each other. She was scaring herself silly, which she'd also done last night.

Except last night she had run to Cade and now he had no idea where she was. If only she'd told him! Maybe she should turn around right now and drive back to Port McClain, to BrenCo. It wasn't too late, she could—

A small sign reading Peach Tree Inn, 1 Mile, came into view.

Alone in her car, Kylie actually blushed. There really was a Peach Tree Inn, and she was suddenly quite certain that her uncles had not cooked up some sinister plot to arrange for her untimely demise. She breathed a thankful sigh that no one would ever know about her ridiculous fantasizing. It was the type of thing her supremely confident, never-a-fear brother Devlin would never let her live down!

As for Cade...Kylie grimaced. He would probably tell her she was on the right track, that Brennans were capable of anything.

Cade is ruthless. There isn't anything he wouldn't do for BrenCo, and you ought to think about that because you're the one standing in the way of his total control of the company. Bobbie's voice rang in her ears.

No wonder she was a nervous wreck, she was mired in a swamp of mistrust and suspicions. Cade versus the Brennans; various Brennans versus various others. And all of them versus her?

The Peach Tree Inn was centered in a grove of trees that Kylie supposed could be peach trees. In the bare starkness of mid-March, there were no flowers or fruits on the branches for identity purposes.

A plaque beside the door gave a brief history of the inn. It was a designated historical landmark and had been a working inn since the early 1800s, serving travelers, soldiers and westward-bound pioneers. The brick walls were covered with all sorts of antique memorabilia from old pitchers and pots to yellowed schoolgirl embroidery samplers. The waitresses wore long flowered dresses and aprons, reminiscent of nineteenth-century costumes.

"Kylie, darling!" Lauretta Brennan, wrapped in a fox fur coat, rushed forward to greet her and enveloped her in a hug. She wore a two-piece silk suit and heels, a distinct contrast to Kylie's jeans and sweater.

Kylie well remembered Uncle Guy telling her that "the place we're going is real casual so don't dress up." Was this Aunt Lauretta's casual wear?

"It is just wonderful to see you! Isn't this the most charming place? I do hope you think it was worth the drive," Lauretta chattered on. "The men wanted to meet in Port McClain

but I insisted that we have lunch someplace special. Guy and
I brought your mother and dad here for dinner a few years
ago, during one of their visits to Gene. They absolutely loved
it and you'll soon see why. The food is marvelous!''

Taking Kylie's arm, she led the way through a narrow corridor to a dining room far in the back. Kylie made no comments; none were required. Cutting into Lauretta's monologue
seemed awkward at best, rude at worst.

Uncles Guy and Artie and a tall gaunt silver-haired man,
who had to be Axel Dodge, were seated at a round table in
the center of the room, which was otherwise unoccupied. The
three men rose when Kylie and Lauretta entered.

Guy introduced Axel Dodge who proceeded to gaze raptly
at Kylie. ''Guy and Artie told me that their niece was beautiful, but I thought they were merely being loyal doting uncles.'' He took Kylie's hand between his own. ''Now that I've
met you, I can see that they didn't exaggerate at all. If anything, they've underestimated your loveliness.''

Kylie felt a perverse urge to giggle. Axel Dodge's over-
blown compliments struck her as hilarious. Surely, he didn't
expect to be taken seriously? ''Well, as that wise old saying
goes, being underestimated is a gift.'' She managed to keep a
straight face, though it took considerable effort.

''Oh, yes, I know that quote. Oliver Wendell Holmes, I
believe,'' Axel said pompously. ''Or perhaps it was Oliver
Hazard Perry. Yes, it was one or the other.''

Bobbie Brennan, quoting a soap opera character, Kylie
longed to reply but judiciously refrained from doing so.

''Kylie, you must fill us in on the latest family news!''
Lauretta enthused as they all took their seats. She slipped off
her fur coat, pausing to stroke the reddish-gold sleeve. ''How
are your mother and dad enjoying his retirement? And when
are they coming to Port McClain for another visit? We miss
them! And Devlin, that dear brilliant boy! How is our nephew,
the doctor?''

Kylie wondered if she would've bought Lauretta's act, even
if Brenda and Bobbie hadn't clued her into the woman's true
feelings. Lauretta certainly sounded interested and fond of
Wayne, Connie and Devlin. Kylie reflexively returned her
aunt's smile. Her uncles were beaming at her, too, though

lunching with "the phony little nuisance" must be galling to them all.

As soon as they'd given their orders to the waitress, Axel launched his pitch. He made every single point in favor of Kylie selling her BrenCo stock that Cade predicted he would make. None of them seemed credible to her, and Kylie found herself playing the devil's advocate, tossing out Cade's arguments against a sale.

"I'm concerned about the effects on Port McClain if BrenCo should be sold. Inevitably, there will be some sort of restructuring that will lead to job losses, especially if the headquarters is moved out of town." She glanced from her uncles to Axel Dodge. Only the latter met her gaze.

"There is no reason for a beautiful young woman like you to worry about jobs in Port McClain," Dodge said unctuously. "All you have to do is to think of ways to spend all that money you're going to get from the sale of your shares. You can take great trips, buy a fabulous car and jewelry and all the pretty clothes you want. Wouldn't you just love a fur coat like your aunt Lauretta's?"

Kylie was incredulous. "I'm supposed to go *shopping* after I've helped cripple the economy of an entire town?"

"We did mention that Kylie has a social conscience, Axel," Guy said, chuckling uneasily.

Kylie stared at her uncle. "What about Todd and Polly, Uncle Guy? They've both expressed an interest and a talent for coming to work at BrenCo when they're finished with school, but the company might not be around if it's sold. Don't you want them to have an opportunity to be part of the family business?"

"Dammit, Brent was right! Austin already got to her!" Artie blurted out. "You've been brainwashed and you don't even know it, missy."

"Artie, stop it!" Lauretta snapped a warning.

"Kylie, that particular argument of Cade's—keeping the family business intact for future Brennans—is disingenuous on his part," Axel inserted silkily. "Cade Austin plans to own BrenCo himself, he couldn't care less what any Brennan does or wants in the future."

"That's right," Guy seconded. "As Ian says—"

"Uncle Guy, why did Ian bail Brent out of jail?" Kylie interrupted. Had she been in a courtroom, opposing counsel would've howled an objection, but here at the Peach Tree Inn her question was met with dead silence.

"Ian bailed Brent out of jail?" Lauretta was the first to break it. "When?"

"I believe the more relevant questions are why and how?" Kylie replied quietly.

"Why shouldn't he?" Artie blustered. "Ian and Brent are cousins. Would you let your cousin sit in a jail cell if you could get him out?"

"All right." Kylie gave him that point. "But where did Ian get the money? Most law students don't have twenty-five hundred dollars in ready cash on hand. Unless, things have changed since I was in law school?"

"Guy, where did Ian get twenty-five hundred dollars to bail Brent out of jail?" Lauretta's voice trembled. She stared stonily at her husband, and Kylie was certain that this was the first time her aunt had heard the unwelcome news.

Their meals arrived at that moment, granting Guy a reprieve from having to answer. And while the plates were being set on the table, another guest was escorted into the dining room. The young blond hostess in her sprig muslin gown was flirting with him.

"Cade's here!" Guy gaped at him.

"You told him!" Artie accused, glaring at Kylie. "You promised not to, but you went ahead and did it anyway!"

But Kylie was as stunned as the others by Cade's arrival. She stared at him, watching him chat with the pretty hostess as they walked to a window table. She saw the moment he glanced over at their table for the first time, though Kylie was certain he'd known they were there all along. To Cade's credit, he didn't attempt to act surprised to see them.

Her hands in her lap, Kylie twisted her napkin into a tight coil as Cade ambled over to their table.

"Hello." He smiled laconically, his eyes locking with hers.

"What brings you all the way out here, Cade? The incomparable chicken and dumplings?" Axel Dodge asked caustically.

Cade shrugged. "I got tired of The Corner Grill's tuna on rye. Chicken and dumplings make a nice change."

Lauretta gave a nervous smile. "Won't you join us, Cade? If we push our chairs closer together, we can fit you in."

Kylie gave her aunt full marks for maintaining etiquette under pressure. Or was Lauretta motivated by fear? Until or unless he was dethroned at BrenCo, Cade Austin remained one of the most powerful men in Port McClain.

"Thanks, but I wouldn't dream of crashing your meeting." Cade's gaze remained fixed on Kylie.

"How considerate of you," Kylie said dryly. Even if he hadn't spoken a word to them, the meeting was effectively crashed. His arrival had the effect of a high-speed head-on collision.

She felt all eyes upon her and tried to tamp the surge of excitement that Cade's presence evoked within her. He was so clearly in the wrong, she reminded herself. He'd spied on her, and she did not care to encourage that sort of conduct.

"You followed me here," she said, her tone reproving.

"I didn't personally follow you, but I did arrange to have you followed," Cade admitted coolly, his hazel eyes glittering with challenge. "Pecoraro was off duty this morning and has been tailing you since you left The Corner Grill. He filled me in on your whereabouts."

"You got a cop to tail my niece?" Guy's lips tightened into a thin angry line. "I don't care who you are, Austin, you have no right to intimidate her!"

"Kylie isn't intimidated by me." Cade laughed off the notion. "And you'll have to agree that after last night, she needs protection from certain young goons who might decide that they haven't done enough to—"

"Cade, don't!" Kylie jumped to her feet. "Please," she added urgently.

She didn't want him to launch into a report of last night's misdeeds, she was positive her aunt knew nothing about any of it. Kylie wanted to spare her the knowledge, at least for now.

"What about last night?" Lauretta asked.

Guy, Artie and Axel Dodge remained silent, not even pretending to be curious, thus assuring Kylie that they knew all about last night's break-in. Whether they'd known before or after the fact was the next logical question to ascertain. Had they helped to plan it or been informed by the culprits later on?

"Conspiracy or cover-up?" Cade murmured softly, voicing Kylie's own thoughts aloud. Their mental attunement spooked her a little.

"We don't have to talk about it now," Kylie implored, glancing at her aunt's increasingly anxious face.

Cade followed her gaze and her train of thought. Again.

"No, not now," he agreed. He looked at the five plates of food sitting untouched on the table. "Eat your lunch before it gets cold." He made it sound like an executive order rather than a polite platitude.

After he'd left for his own table, an uncomfortable silence descended. Kylie stared down at the Peach Tree Inn's heralded chicken and dumplings, congealing under a pastelike gravy. She hadn't been very hungry to begin with, and the collective tension surrounding the table killed what little appetite she had. Listlessly, she stirred her fork around the plate.

"Guy, what aren't you telling me about Ian?" Lauretta's voice, shrill with anger and worry, filled the room.

Guy's unoriginal reply, "I don't know what you're talking about," only made his wife press harder.

Kylie knew a full-blown marital battle was brewing and wished for a return of the uncomfortable silence. Apparently Axel Dodge and Uncle Artie did, too.

"Perhaps you two ought to discuss this matter later?" Axel smarmily suggested a moment before Artie snarled, "Just shut up, willya?"

The silence was back.

Kylie made a pretense of eating. Cade caught her surreptitiously glancing at him and acknowledged her by lifting his eyebrows. She quickly looked away. When it happened a second time, then a third, her face flushed scarlet. She was so intensely aware of his presence she couldn't keep her eyes away from him. Worse, he knew it.

She felt restless and on edge. She wanted to march over to Cade's table and challenge him. How dare he have her followed? The more she mulled it over, the more irritated she became. She had been doing quite well at this meeting, holding her own without any trouble at all. Then *he* had arrived...

Kylie's gaze compulsively returned to him and this time when their eyes met, it occurred to her that Cade was experiencing a plight similar to her own. She'd caught *him* staring at *her* each time she'd looked his way. Cade was as aware of her as she was of him. He couldn't keep his eyes off her, and the realization exhilarated her.

While reminding herself that she was still vexed by his interference, another part of her—the romantic, dreamy side that had remained dormant until Cade had awakened those sweet emotions—admitted that she was glad he was here. She longed to bolt from this table and its four dour occupants and join Cade at his.

Her eyes lingered on his hand as she watched him lift his water glass. She studied his long graceful fingers, remembered their wickedly thrilling touch on her skin. Kylie quivered.

"I think Cade Austin's presence here defines the atmosphere you will be living under if you decide not to sell your shares of BrenCo." Axel Dodge's portentous tones finally broke the long silence. "The man is controlling, arrogant, and domineering. Freedom and independence will be nothing but lost concepts to you as long as you possess what Cade Austin wants, Kylie."

"Mr. Dodge, don't insult me with another fallacious argument." Kylie laid down her fork. "It's a waste of time."

"Heh, heh, we did mention that Kylie is an attorney," Uncle Guy gritted through his teeth.

Dodge looked annoyed. "Even if you hadn't, I'd've figured it out for myself by now."

Kylie knew she wasn't being complimented.

"Oh no, here he comes again," a morose Lauretta muttered under her breath. But when Cade reached their table, she flashed a megawatt smile. "I hope you enjoyed your lunch, Cade. Can we persuade you to join us for dessert?"

"Thanks, Lauretta, but I'll pass on dessert," Cade replied perfunctorily before turning his attention to Kylie. "I need a favor, Kylie."

"Anything we can do for you, Cade?" asked the ever-ingratiating Lauretta.

"Thanks, Lauretta, but I need this particular favor from Kylie."

Kylie tilted her head, waiting.

"I'd like a ride back to town, Kylie. Your cousin Bridget drove me out here," Cade paused, to let that register. "She dropped me off so I'm stuck without a car."

"*Bridget* dropped you off?" Artie muttered. He stirred uneasily in his chair and fiddled with his cutlery.

Kylie, an astute interpreter of body language, decided she'd never seen anyone look so guilty in her life. If she'd been defending Uncle Artie in court, she would already be mentally preparing for the appeal, positive that the jury was going to find him guilty on the highest count. Who wouldn't?

She stared at the faces around the table, her stomach churning as she thought of the despicable charges they were trying to talk Bridget into pressing against BrenCo. Her eyes flew to Cade's face. His expression was enigmatic, and she wondered how much he knew about the plot against him. He must know *something*. Mentioning Bridget seemed an obvious clue.

"So Bridget's receptionist duties now include chauffeuring you around?" Axel Dodge gave a tight, false laugh.

Cade made no reply. His face was an unreadable mask that any poker player would envy.

Artie and Guy looked stricken.

"I haven't seen Bridget lately," Lauretta remarked. "Is she growing her hair, I hope? The last time I saw her, it looked like it had been cut with a knife and fork."

Based on her own perception, Kylie again absolved her aunt of any knowledge of Brennan skulduggery. If Lauretta was feeling guilty, she would've been oozing with compliments about Bridget, not mocking her haircut.

"I'll ride back with you, Kylie?" Cade asked. It wasn't really a request, it was a statement of fact, and they all knew it.

"Okay." Kylie shrugged, trying for nonchalance. She wasn't sure if she'd pulled it off.

"Let's go." Cade held out his hand to her.

Kylie casually rose from her chair. Though she couldn't wait to escape, she didn't want to appear too eager. Jumping

at Cade's command would boost his male ego into the iono-
sphere, where *nobody's* ego belonged.

None of them tried to stop her from leaving. Cade's Bridget
salvo had served its purpose. The three men were exchanging
furtive uncertain glances.

Cade offered no further information. He came around the
table and took Kylie by the elbow, rushing her out of the
dining room, not bothering to play it cool.

"Did you have to make it so obvious that you were in a
hurry to leave?" she whispered as they headed toward the
door.

"I wanted to get you out of there before they stuck you
with the check," Cade said drolly.

"Oh!" Kylie stopped in her tracks. "I forgot all about the
check. I wonder if we were supposed to split it? Maybe I
should go back and—"

"Forget it." Cade moved closer to her, so close she could
feel his breath rustle her hair. So close she felt the heat radi-
ating from his big, strong frame. "After what they put you
through, the least they can do is to pick up the tab for your
lunch, which you hardly touched."

"They didn't put me through—"

"Save it, honey," Cade cut in again, pulling her along. "I
observed your group luncheon, remember? From where I sat,
a bad time was being had by all. And let's not forget last
night's water sports."

"Thank you for not telling Aunt Lauretta our suspicions
about last night," Kylie said quietly. "I don't know how Uncle Guy is going to explain Ian and the bail money to her, but
I'm glad I won't be around for it."

Cade pushed open the front door and wind whipped around
them. The sky was gray with the threat of more rain, but her
spirits lifted despite the gloomy weather. Cade had been right
on target about their *group luncheon*; the tension surrounding
their table had been as thick as the chicken gravy on their
plates. Being freed from it left her limp with sheer relief.

"I don't want to hurt Lauretta. Her son and her husband
are prepared to do that without any help from me." Cade put
his arm around Kylie's waist and walked her toward her car,

his body deflecting the force of the wind gusts. "I'm not trying
to hurt *anyone,* Kylie, but your uncles—"

She held up her hand. "Save the campaign speech. I wanted
to hear both sides and meet with all interested parties. Now I
have."

"And you've reached a verdict?"

She nodded. "Yes, but I want to talk things over with my
dad first. I'll call him tonight."

"Talk it over with me right now," Cade demanded.

"That's a conflict of interest. I want to—"

"This isn't a courtroom, Kylie, and you're not a judge who
must remain impartial to both sides." Cade's voice was hard.
"You've been playing that little game long enough and I'm
tired of indulging you. I know which side you're on, I know
you've decided not to sell your shares. I doubt if you ever
seriously considered it. Now stop trying to turn a business
decision into a melodrama by heightening the suspense. It's
very Brennan-like, of course, but most unbecoming."

"I am not one of your employees, and I do not take orders
from you!" The built-up tension and anger she'd managed to
suppress during today's series of family visits suddenly flared
to flashpoint. Kylie shrugged his hand from her waist and
moved purposefully away from him. "And stop the anti-
Brennan remarks. *I'm* a Brennan."

"Oh, don't I know it." Cade let her go but kept pace with
her.

In a more characteristic, contemplative mood, Kylie might
have viewed her burst of rage in a positive light. It meant she
felt comfortable expressing her anger with Cade, that she dealt
with him honestly, in a way she could not deal with her Brennan relatives.

But she was not feeling contemplative. More like combat-
ive. "I haven't been playing games and I don't need you to
indulge me in anything!" she added crossly.

That charge really smarted. Did it mean that everything between them so far had been calculated indulgence on his part,
a role he'd played for BrenCo's sake?

They came to a halt in front of her car. Cade leaned against
the hood, staring at her with a penetrating intensity.

"What are you going to tell your father, Kylie? That his

nephews tried to trash Gene's house? That his brothers are in cahoots with a scoundrel, that they're so unethical and corrupt they've asked Artie's own daughter to file false charges against Gene's company? That they've *all* tried to manipulate you and might've even put you at risk? How do you think your dad will react to that news?''

Kylie knew. "He'd go as ballistic as a missile on a nuclear submarine," she admitted reluctantly.

"Is that what you want, Kylie?"

"Of course not! I—I—" Her voice trailed to a whisper, and she stared bleakly at the thickening storm clouds in the sky.

Cade's point was a legitimate one. If she were to tell her father what was going on in Port McClain, he might well sever his ties with his extended family. And that would hurt her dad, badly. Though Wayne Brennan had little in common with Artie and Guy, she knew he loved his brothers. The Brennans were his family...and hers, too.

"I'm very familiar with the Brennan temper, and your father has a captain's share of it, even if he happens to be retired." Cade watched her intently. "It would be a kindness on your part not to tell him about the—unfortunate revelations of the past day.''

"You're right," she said softly. And then it struck her. "You *do* know about the false claims they want Bridget to make against BrenCo!" Just thinking about the treachery chilled her far more deeply than the sudden blast of cold air. "Did she tell you herself?"

Cade shook his head. "Noah did, this morning. Brenda told him about it last night. How did you find out?"

"From Aunt Bobbie. She is aghast. And scared."

And distrustful. *I see Noah using Brenda to get whatever information she hears about Artie and Guy's schemes and then passing it along to Cade.* Kylie recalled her aunt's suspicions and felt an anxious twinge. What if Bobbie was right?

Kylie pictured Brenda's face, aglow as she talked about her unorthodox date with Noah. "It would be terrible if Noah was simply using Brenda, pumping her for information to give to you. Cade, you—you didn't ask him to get close to her for BrenCo's sake, did you?"

Anxiety made her ask. Unfortunately, impatience and sarcasm fueled his reply.

"Yeah, sure I did. I set that plan in motion right after I ordered all the company water coolers to be laced with Agent Orange." Cade heaved an exasperated sigh. "Whose side are you on, Kylie? I thought that after last night, I wouldn't even have to ask."

"Is that why you made love to me?" she asked, the words sticking painfully in her throat. "To get me on your side? So I'll do whatever you want and you won't even have to ask?"

She was confused and vulnerable. Everything was happening so fast, the intimacy between her and Cade was all too new to her. Her feelings for him ran deep, but her confidence was unnervingly, uncharacteristically fragile. She thought she was in love with Cade but had no idea as to his true feelings for her. Sure, he desired her body. He also desired her BrenCo stock, and she didn't know which he wanted more.

She knew she probably sounded as panicky as Aunt Lauretta pressing for information about Ian, as suspicious as Aunt Bobbie speculating on everybody's secret agendas, as insecure as Brenda pondering Noah's desire for her.

She was pathetic! Kylie stared resentfully at Cade. He had reduced her to this!

"You've got things all figured out, don't you?" Instead of being reassuring, Cade was sardonic. "I find it interesting that you apply the innocent until proven guilty principle to everybody but me. You're willing to give your idiotic cousins and hysterical aunts and felonious uncles the benefit of every doubt, but you look for ways to incriminate me. I run a police state, I terrorize your family, I plot with Noah to break Brenda's heart, I trick you into bed for all the wrong reasons. And in addition to all that is your eco-terror that BrenCo is about as good for Port McClain as the oil spill is for wildlife, and you don't want any part of any of it."

"Well, *I* find it interesting that you proudly recite that list but feel no need to—"

"To what? Explain? Apologize? Deny?" He angled closer, his nostrils flared, his eyes sharp with anger. "No, I don't."

"Of course not. You're above all that. Because I'm a Brennan and you're Cade Austin, of a far superior caste," she taunted.

Impulsively, she darted to the driver's side of her car, key in hand, the way she'd been taught in her self-defense course back in Philadelphia. She'd aced her getting-swiftly-and-safely-to-her-car-in-a-dark-lonely-parking-area test.

The unexpectedness of her actions gave her a few crucial moments before Cade sprang to action. By the time his hand was on the door handle, Kylie had already locked herself inside the car.

She opened the window a sliver while the engine roared to life. "Being the human deity you are, I'm sure you'll have no trouble finding a way back to Port McClain," she called through the crack. "You can always command your lackeys at BrenCo to deliver your golden chariot."

"Kylie, stop the car right now," Cade commanded.

As if she were a lackey! Defiantly, Kylie hit the gas pedal instead. Cade wisely released his grip on the door handle before she pulled away.

Through the rearview mirror, she saw Axel Dodge emerging from the Peach Tree Inn with Uncle Artie at his side. Uncle Guy and Aunt Lauretta followed, and it was obvious that the couple were arguing.

"If the chariot doesn't work out, you can catch a ride back with one of them," she suggested and peeled out of the parking lot amidst an impressive squeal of tires.

Nine

An hour later, Kylie parked her car and walked through an icy drizzle to the Rock and Roll Hall of Fame in the heart of downtown Cleveland. The directional signs back at the entrance to the interstate highway had inspired her. She had a choice, to go east or west. To Port McClain or Cleveland?

A return to Port McClain meant waiting for her next run-in with Cade, which would inevitably end either in bed or in an argument. And if that wasn't daunting enough, Port McClain also offered the prospect of yet another encounter with yet another one of her relatives. Or maybe all of them.

An alternative destination did not seem like such a bad idea. Maybe she ought to take advantage of her proximity to Cleveland, where she hadn't been in years, and visit the music museum?

Her brother had driven down from Michigan the summer the Hall of Fame opened and sent her a postcard from there, recommending it. Sight-seeing was something of a family legacy. Wherever they'd lived, their parents had made it a point to take Devlin and Kylie to every local place of interest. Over the years she'd seen scads of arrowheads and suits of medieval armor and mummies. She'd seen battle sites, historic homes and graveyards, and art of every medium.

Kylie decided that now was the ideal time to take a tour of the history of rock. She desperately needed a breather, a diversion, a chance to regain her emotional balance—away from the powerful, provoking, tantalizing presence of Cade Austin. The absence of any Brennans in Cleveland only added appeal.

Approaching the impressive entrance plaza, Kylie entered the building, designed by renowned architect I. M. Pei. She recalled that Devlin claimed his primary site of interest was the Rhythm and Blues section. Being a blues aficionado would be right in keeping with Dev's ultracool image of himself, though Kylie couldn't remember him ever listening to a single blues song when he was not in the presence of his friends.

Lacking witnesses to impress with his hipness, when only his kid sister was around, Devlin Brennan turned on whatever radio station was playing the latest Top 40 hits or watched old sitcom reruns on TV. To Kylie, that was an indicator of his true tastes, which were decidedly mainstream and certainly not cutting-edge entertainment. She smiled with sisterly perception. Dev wouldn't ever want that information revealed!

Suave, detached Devlin. He was never without a girlfriend but none of his relationships became serious. Kylie wondered if he would ever drop his Mr.Cool façade long enough to allow anyone to get close to him. To get to know the real Dev within, the guy who knew all the words to all the verses of the theme songs from "The Facts of Life" and "Silver Spoons." Who mercilessly ribbed his younger sister, yet dropped his guard only with her.

"You'll probably be entranced by the One Hit Wonders, Kylie," Dev had kidded her over the phone shortly after his visit to the Hall of Fame. "Those are the groups who hit it big once and were never heard from again. Fits in with your penchant for society's forgotten."

Inside the main lobby Kylie glanced at the museum store, decided to visit it later, then took the escalator to the ground level and headed straight for the One Hit Wonders. She was pondering the fate of a group called Bob Kuban and the In-men whose one and only hit was a song called "The Cheater" when a voice sounded in her ear.

"I'm warning you in advance so you won't think you're being mugged, I'm right behind you. And I'm going to grab you so you can't run away again."

The advance warning did nothing to lessen her shock at the sound of Cade's voice and the feel of his hands on her shoulders. Kylie gasped and jerked, both audibly and visibly startled.

"Turn around," Cade directed and she did, slowly, gaping at him as if he were an apparition, her eyes round with amazement. He kept his hands on her shoulders anchoring her firmly in front of him.

For one of the few times in her life, Kylie was utterly speechless. Even a simple "hello" was beyond her.

"No opening statement, counselor?" Cade mocked her silence. "You're not going to ask me why I'm here? Or is that too much of a no-brainer?"

Kylie was still too befuddled by his appearance to reply.

"Are you wondering how I got here? Hey, maybe my golden chariot has wings." Those expressive, arched brows of his conveyed his disdain for that particular sally. "Or did I insist that Axel Dodge hand over his car keys to me back at the Peach Tree Inn?"

"You did?" She was awed by the sheer enormity of his colossal nerve. "And he did?"

"Obviously. He had no choice. I drove his car but I did let him ride with me."

"How magnanimous!" Her scattered wits were beginning to regroup. "You're all heart, Cade."

Cade did not disagree. "Dodge and I were both flummoxed when you headed toward Cleveland. He thought you were going to meet with a cabal of attorneys—shows how his mind works, hmm? I had no idea what you were up to. And then you came here."

His fingers dug into the delicate bones of her shoulders. "I still don't know why," he growled. "Are you going to tell me?"

"I didn't know you were following me." Kylie wriggled in

protest, but he didn't relax his grasp. "I never saw you, not once."

"That was intentional. You haven't answered my question. What in the hell are we doing here, Kylie?"

"If you'll loosen your grip, I'll tell you what *I'm* doing here."

"If I do, will you promise not to dash off? I'd hate to have to chase you through this place but I will if you make me. And I'll catch you, Kylie, have no doubts about that."

She had no doubts. His machismo was blazing, he was primed and ready to act. Kylie gulped. She really didn't want to race around the Rock and Roll Hall of Fame with Cade after her in full warrior mode.

"I'm not going to dash anywhere." She lifted her chin, hoping she looked proud and defiant. She was more than a little nervous, but was determined to hold her own. "I came to see everything, all the exhibits and artifacts and films and video clips, and I'm not leaving here until I have. So if you'll let me go, I'll get back to studying the One Hit Wonders."

Cade dropped his hands but stayed directly behind her, poised to capture her should she make a sudden move like the one she'd pulled in the parking lot of the Peach Tree Inn.

The clean fresh scent of her hair, mixed with the spicy allure of her perfume, wafted to his nostrils and his blood stirred in immediate response. As usual, her physical impact on him made him reel and while part of him resented her sensual power, that part kept growing smaller while a very crucial, very male part of him was growing considerably larger.

He glanced at the graceful curve of her neck, the soft, vulnerable nape. His lips had tasted the sweet silky skin there, last night and this morning. He remembered how she had shivered with pleasure and cuddled closer, encouraging him, subtly asking for more. He wanted to do it again, right here, right now.

Cade drew a sharp breath. If he clamped his hands on her shoulders and pulled her back against him, he could kiss her neck and her nape, then turn her in his arms and take her mouth the way he'd been wanting to, from the moment they had left Gene's house this morning.

Instead, the intervening hours had been filled with fury and frustration as he had coped with the latest, most dangerous aggravation that the Brennans had thrown at him. Working separately or jointly, they seemed to have an unlimited arsenal but Kylie Brennan was the most powerful of all...the only one he couldn't control, the only one he couldn't bully, threaten or cajole because she recognized exactly what he was doing and gave it right back in full measure.

And because bullying, threatening and cajoling were not what he wanted to do to her. He and Kylie had their own far more effective, far more satisfying methods of communication. If only they were communicating right now!

Kylie moved along at a leisurely pace with Cade following her, though walking was something of a trial for him. In his current condition, he should be sitting down—preferably with her on his lap, naked. Or perhaps lying down. He closed his eyes to fully appreciate the sequence of erotic pictures that idea conjured up in his mind.

Meanwhile, she seemed fascinated by the display in front of her, totally unaware that he was *burning* for her. Cade clenched his fingers, suppressing the urge to fasten them around her—anywhere. He tried to feign an interest in what she was looking at. And couldn't.

"Who the hell is Joey Powers?" he demanded testily. "I've never heard of the guy."

"Of course you didn't. Neither have I. Because he was a One Hit Wonder from 1963," Kylie explained. "His record was 'Midnight Mary.'"

"Never heard of that, either. Where's Elvis? And the Boss?"

"Not among the One Hit Wonders," Kylie said succinctly.

"No kidding." Cade scowled. "As long as we're stuck in this place, can't we find them? Or at least find someone that anybody's heard of?"

"I take it this is your first visit to the Hall of Fame?" Kylie eyed him knowingly. "Even though you're just an hour away and it opened back in 1995?"

"Thanks to you, this is my first visit."

"Unbelievable." Kylie frowned her disapproval. "If you lived in the Philadelphia area, you're the type who would never bother to go see the Liberty Bell or Independence Hall."

"And I wouldn't feel like I'd missed a thing," Cade admitted, without a twinge of shame. "I bet you've made pilgrimages to both the Liberty Bell and Independence Hall, probably within a month of moving to the city."

"That's true. Oh, look!" She pointed at Good Vibrations: The Making of a Song, an adjacent exhibit examining the creative process of songwriting. "That should be interesting."

Cade rolled his eyes. "I'm already riveted."

Kylie, the inveterate sight-seer, spent the next few hours viewing the exhibits and artifacts and films and video clips in the museum. Cade, whose lifetime record of sight-seeing expeditions could be counted on one hand, grew increasingly restless and bleary-eyed, but he doggedly remained at her side. She didn't allow herself to wonder why.

Her visit here was supposed to be a respite from thinking about Cade, from questioning his motives and weaving fantasies starring the two of them, Kylie reminded herself throughout the afternoon. Even though he was right beside her, never letting her stray more than a few inches away from him—maybe *because* of that—she concentrated fully on the Hall of Fame's sights and sounds.

And she learned a lot about the history of rock and roll. She even stored a few obscure facts about the blues with which she hoped to stump Devlin, that self-proclaimed bogus "Blues Fanatic."

The sky was dark when Kylie and Cade finally emerged from the museum. Fat, wet snowflakes were beginning to fall, lightly coating the street. Cade took Kylie's gloveless hand and tucked it into the pocket of his coat.

"Are you keeping my hand warm or keeping me from taking off?" Kylie quizzed, trying to keep things light and easy.

With nothing around to serve as a buffer, she was faced with all the thoughts, questions and fantasies she'd successfully kept at bay all afternoon. They seemed to engulf her now, the intensity both scaring and exciting her.

"You aren't going anywhere without me." Cade glanced down at her. "We have a date for dinner, remember?"

"Oh! I offered to cook dinner for you tonight at Uncle Gene's!" Kylie exclaimed, remembering her nervous invitation to him earlier that day.

"I won't hold you to that." Cade glanced at his watch. "It's getting late and I'm hungry. By the time we drove back to Port McClain and went grocery shopping I wouldn't be able to wait till the food was cooked. I'd probably end up devouring the stuff raw."

"I'm hungry, too," Kylie admitted. "I didn't eat much lunch at the Peach Tree Inn."

"No wonder. The food was inedible and the company was abominable. And before you take offense, I was specifically referring to Axel Dodge and not any particular Brennan."

He started to walk along the sidewalk and since Kylie's hand was in his pocket, she trotted along with him. "Your drive to Cleveland with Mr. Dodge must have been interesting," she murmured.

"For me it was. For the Not-So-Artful Dodger, it was as hellacious as I could make it. I let him know that I was aware of his plot to use Bridget to file false claims against BrenCo, that she'd already assured me she wouldn't go through with it, and that I fully intend to go after him. It was gratifying to see the sleazy little worm squirm."

"Will you go after him?" She gazed up at him. "Can you?"

"Oh, yeah." His grin was almost feral.

Kylie decided that if Axel Dodge was a little worm metaphorically, then Cade Austin was Bigfoot who'd squashed him during a short stroll.

"I have lots of connections, Kylie. *Legal* ones," Cade added, quirking his brow.

"I wasn't going to accuse you of mobster ties," she mumbled, flushing a little. Considering some of the things she'd said, she understood why he felt the need to clarify. "I'm sure you have *legal* influential friends in high positions."

"Especially in Columbus and Cleveland," Cade confirmed, naming the capital and largest city in the state. "And they will not approve of Dodge's methods of mixing blackmail with business. Be assured we'll find *legal* ways to make his life sheer misery."

"The ultimate misery for him will be having to pay exorbitant defense attorneys' fees." Kylie smiled her approval. "Talk about the punishment fitting the crime!"

"Someone as money-crazed as Axel Dodge deserves nothing less."

"Cade, what about Bridget and my uncles?" she asked quietly.

"Bridget and I had a long talk. She didn't do anything wrong, and after I mentioned what Noah told me, she volunteered information to prevent any wrongdoing from taking place. Which was very unBrennan of her. Ouch!"

Kylie had reached over to smack him with her spare hand. Cade pretended that he'd actually felt the blow through his coat. "Bridget will be rewarded for her honesty. She can choose between a cash bonus or extra paid vacation days," he added.

"Aunt Bobbie will be so relieved." Kylie was glad for her.

"You've heard of the carrot-and-stick style of management, haven't you, Kylie?" A gusty breeze blew snow around them, and they paused to catch their breath. "Well, Bridget got the carrot. Artie and Guy and their sons can expect the stick. That's all I'm going to say about any of them tonight. I'm tired of talking about them, I'm tired of thinking about them."

Cade reached down to smooth her wind-tousled hair away from her face.

The unexpected tender gesture sent glowing frissons through her. When he cupped her cheek, she placed her hand over his. "I feel I ought to apologize for my uncles, being of Brennan blood and all. What they'd planned was unconscionable."

He smiled into her eyes. "Not even the defense lawyer for the truly downtrodden can mount a defense for them, huh?"

"Especially since they wanted to use Bridget to do their dirty work. And most especially since they were motivated by greed. They were willing to turn Bridget into a criminal, just for money!" She was truly appalled.

"*Just* for money isn't the way their petty little minds work, Kylie. Try *anything* for money."

They started walking again. A few minutes later, Cade steered her to the front entrance of a hotel. "Here we are," he announced.

Kylie glanced around. The warmth and light of the lobby beckoned invitingly. It would be wonderful to get out of the cold, away from the wind and the wet snow shower. Her stomach growled, protesting the too-long interval between meals.

"Is their restaurant any good?" she asked conversationally, not caring if it was or wasn't. She was so hungry she could probably polish off a generous serving of the Peach Tree Inn's dubious chicken and dumplings, complete with their version of homemade gravy.

Cade drew her inside, leading her toward the registration desk. "The food here isn't bad, but we're not eating in the restaurant. We'll use room service."

His words hit her like an erotic atomic bomb. Heat exploded in every cell of her body, and suddenly she felt weak. All those feelings and desires she'd managed to suppress all day radiated through her, too powerful and intense to withstand any longer. She stood beside him in a daze, only vaguely aware of the transaction between Cade and the desk clerk as he registered for a room.

The lobby suddenly seemed stifling hot. Her skin felt ultra-sensitive, her clothes intolerably irritating against every inch of her body. She took off her coat, seeking some minor relief. Cade automatically reached for it, carrying it for her. His solicitousness pleased her.

"Any luggage, sir?" A bellboy approached them and eyed Kylie speculatively when Cade said no.

Under normal circumstances, she would've been mortified but at this moment it didn't seem to matter that the bellboy thought they'd sneaked into town for a shady tryst. Nothing mattered except being alone with Cade.

They held hands during the ride on the crowded elevator and her heart was thundering in her ears as he led her along the corridor to their room.

"I've never done this before," she admitted as he shoved the electronic key into its slot. "Checked into a hotel without luggage to—spend a few hours in a room."

For a second or two, her confidence faltered and she worried he would think she was cheap and easy—the terms her mother used to describe a woman who would check into a hotel to spend a few hours in a room with a man. No doubt Aunts Bobbie and Lauretta would agree with the description, achieving a rare moment of Brennan harmony.

"We're spending the entire night here, honey," Cade amended. "I already ditched work for most of the day, I might as well take it to the limit and stay out of town tonight. I didn't even leave Donna a number where I can be reached."

His confession bolstered her. "And that's unusual behavior for you?" It was heartening to know that she wasn't the only one acting so out of character.

"Unprecedented." Cade opened the door and pulled her in after him. "Donna might end up filing a missing persons report if I don't check in with her later tonight."

Kylie glided closer to him. All of a sudden, her thighs felt rubbery and she swayed slightly. "I need to eat something. I—I feel a little light-headed."

She assured herself that this was not a modern day mating ritual, a bedroom version of the dainty dropped handkerchief.

But Cade took it that way. He dropped both their coats to the floor. "You need to lie down, sweetheart." His voice was a sexy growl as he swept her off her feet and carried her over to the bed. He laid her down on it then sat on the edge, gazing down at her.

His eyes moved over her face and lowered slowly to her breasts that were already taut and swollen beneath her sweater. Kylie drew shallow breaths through her moistly parted lips. He was only looking at her, but she could feel the effects of his burning gaze every place her eyes lingered.

His palms closed over her breasts and he massaged them, fitting their shape to his hands, playing with them, teasing with his fingers. Kylie moaned. It felt good but it wasn't enough. She wanted more, she needed the exquisitely sensual feel of skin against skin. She knew the thrill of his hands on her bare breasts, the arousing feel of them nestled against the wiry mat of hair on his chest.

Acting on a wild primal instinct, she abruptly pulled off her sweater.

Cade smiled his approval. "Oh, yes, baby." He deftly disposed of her bra and then gathered her to him.

Somehow his shirt had become unbuttoned. His arms were around her and she pressed closer, savoring the male texture of his chest, the hair-roughened skin and hard muscle. The rounded softness of her breasts provided an enticing feminine contrast.

Cade caressed each one, his clever fingers stroking her nipples until she whimpered with pleasure ragged with urgency. Stretching out alongside her, he lifted one rounded breast to his lips and drew the hot pink little bud into his mouth. She felt his tongue swirl around it, then he began to suck.

Desire built and surged through her with each tug of his lips. She felt wilder and even more out of control than she had last night. It was as if her body now demanded the intoxicating release it had only found with Cade, as if she'd been in a constant subconscious state of readiness for him and needed less time, less stimulation to burst into full arousal.

They kissed madly, hungrily, shrugging off garments, pulling off others, until finally both were totally, splendidly naked.

"I want you so much," Cade groaned as he slipped his hand between her legs.

He felt the rich creaminess there, evidence of her desire that was as unmistakable as his own virile arousal. He had the physical proof that she wanted him but he wanted to hear the words from her beautifully shaped mouth.

"Tell me you want me, baby," he rasped, probing her lovingly, intimately, touching her in ways that made her want to scream with sheer ecstasy.

Maybe she did. Kylie was lost in passion, wanting to please him, to give herself to him and take him deep inside her. She saw no reason to be coy, to withhold anything from him, especially not the words he wanted.

"I want you, Cade," she whispered.

Emotional tears filled her eyes. She longed to tell him she loved him, too, because she knew that she did. But she wasn't so far gone not to realize that he hadn't asked that of her, that he might not care to hear a declaration of love.

"I want you so much." She kissed his mouth, his neck, his navel centered deep in the whorl of dark hair. "So much." Her hands caressed him, knowing exactly what excited him most. "So much, Cade."

He rolled her onto her back, handling her as easily as he would a doll, lifting her legs and positioning her to receive him. His hands slid up to join with hers, lacing their fingers as he kissed her with a possessive passion that only she had ever inspired in him.

He'd been wary at first and passed through various stages ranging from alarm to resentment but now, lying here with her, Cade accepted the unfathomable. He'd actually found her. He hadn't thought it possible that there was a woman alive who could interest him, who could engage his attention, who could captivate him as much as his work.

But she existed. She was Kylie Brennan and she wanted him, needed him as much as he wanted and needed her. Which was overwhelmingly. He couldn't wait another second. His body took over, and his mind ceded without a modicum of struggle. It felt fabulous to give up control, to simply give in to the driving force of their passion.

Cade surged into her, felt her welcoming wet heat clasp him. Both moaned, surrendering to the sensations of indescribable, incomparable bliss. Effortlessly, they commenced a frenzied complementing rhythm that sent them spiraling higher, into the realms of rapture. There they soared until both were consumed by spasms of pleasure so fierce that they helplessly exploded into a mind-shattering mutual climax.

Afterward, they lay together, Cade sprawled on his back, his eyes closed, while Kylie curled up next to him, her head nestled in the curve of his shoulder. She felt limp and replete, devoid of tension and energy, unable to do anything but lay quiescently at his side. One of her arms was flung across his middle, the other was tucked beneath her, her legs were splayed over his. She idly caressed him, with her foot, with her fingers, with her lips. She loved touching him, she loved looking at him, she loved *him!*

Minutes might have passed—or maybe hours. Kylie couldn't summon the initiative to raise her wrist and look at her watch. Time seemed irrelevant, the rest of the world didn't exist. There were only she and Cade, together in this moment. She never wanted it to end.

Cade didn't, either. A marvelous sense of rightness filled him. The world was exactly as it should be. Everything had fallen into a kind of cosmic order. As an engineer his precise, meticulously exacting mind revered order.

"It's finally starting to make sense to me," he confided

drowsily, speaking his thoughts aloud. His defenses were down, all blocks and barriers eliminated. He wanted to share everything with her, every thought, every insight, merging his mind with hers, just as their bodies had become one.

"Mmm" was all Kylie was capable of replying.

That was enough encouragement for Cade. "All this time, Gene's will simply didn't compute. It didn't fit in with the man I knew so well. I puzzled over it, I raged over it. Nothing drives me crazier than an equation that won't balance and that one was totally out of whack. Until now."

Kylie felt the first ominous stirrings within her. She was lying naked in Cade's arms, dazed by the all-encompassing force of her love for him—and his thoughts were of Gene Brennan's will?

"Until now?" she prompted carefully. She shifted her legs, moving them from his.

"Gene planned for this to happen, Kylie." Suddenly infused with a radiant energy, Cade rolled onto his side, propping his head on his hand. His hazel eyes were bright with exhilaration, inspired by his sudden epiphany. "Gene left you those shares to bring us together. By leaving them to you, he accomplished two things, both vitally important to him. He kept BrenCo family-owned, which is what he'd always dreamed and he kept his promise to me, giving me full control of the company."

"I don't think I understand." Kylie tried to swallow around the thick lump that had lodged in her throat and was growing bigger.

Unfortunately, she was beginning to understand all too well. When she looked at Cade, she saw the man she'd fallen in love with. When he looked at her, he saw her shares of BrenCo stock—and the way to get them. He was all but admitting that to her now.

Her whole body flushed and she was suddenly horribly embarrassed to be lying here nude under his avaricious eyes. She reached for her clothes, her movements slow and subtle. Luckily, they were accessible, laying in a heap on the floor beside the bed.

"Maybe you should explain." She managed to keep her voice steady, which was something of a feat when she felt on the verge of bursting into tears. The optimistic, idealistic part of her urged her to keep an open mind. Maybe she'd absorbed too much of the Brennans collective dark cynicism and was misinterpreting, finding iniquity where there was none.

"Gene wanted me to have BrenCo, he always said so," Cade shared his newfound insight with his newly discovered sexual and emotional soul mate.

For the first time since that wretched will had been read, he felt close to his good friend Gene, connected to his mentor once again. The sense that he'd been betrayed, that Gene had turned out to be yet another lying, backstabbing Brennan had vanished and been replaced with the wonderful glow of understanding.

Cade heaved a contented sigh. "But instead of specifying that in his will, he left the controlling shares to you and now I know why. Gene was matchmaking, Kylie! Nobody knew his brothers better than Eugene Brennan. He'd have calculated they would try something rotten enough to ally you and me against them. And once we were thrown together—well, what Gene wanted to happen, what he knew would happen, actually did. Instant chemistry."

During his rapturous recitation, Kylie had been quietly getting dressed. Now she rose to stand beside the bed, slipping her feet into her loosely laced shoes. Every word seared her, burning her hope into the ashes of heartbreak. The Brennans' dark cynicism was a pale shade of beige in comparison to Cade Austin's own personal brand.

"Instant chemistry," she repeated. "Translation—hot sex. Your theory is that my uncle knew of your prowess with women and with me being one of his moronic nieces—we all know the high opinion Gene had of his brothers' offspring— I would simply fall into your arms. Into your bed. Which I did. Congratulations, Uncle Gene." She lifted her eyes to the ceiling as if in heavenly salute to her departed uncle. "Your scheme worked. I was gullible enough to be swept off my feet by your brilliant, sexually irresistible protégé."

The edge in her voice sliced through Cade's hazy euphoric cloud. He jackknifed to a sitting position, his eyes round and wide as he stared at her. She was fully dressed and standing at the foot of the bed. His breath caught in his chest. "Kylie? Baby, what's wrong?"

She'd meant to simply stalk out of the room—she already had her car keys safely in hand—but the sheer arrogance of his question rooted her to the spot. "You're actually asking me that? Do you really want an answer or just more time to gloat over your temporary triumph? And I do mean *temporary*."

"Kylie, you—I—"

"You just admitted you took me to bed so I'd sign over my BrenCo shares to you. And then you had the gall to insinuate that it's part of some otherworldly plan! To hear you tell it, Uncle Gene is applauding you from the Great Beyond."

Cade ran his hand through his hair. "Sweetie, you've misinterpreted what I—"

"No, you misinterpreted! Your timing was atrocious, Cade. You got careless. You were so full of yourself, so proud of your conquest that you couldn't wait to brag about it to someone—even if that someone was me!"

He felt a sheen of perspiration cover his skin as a sickly apprehension seeped into every pore. He'd been babbling like he had been shot full of truth serum, and thinking back on what he'd said... Cade closed his eyes. It was possible that what he'd said could be interpreted in a way other than he'd intended. Clearly, Kylie had taken his revelation all wrong. He swiftly sought to set the record straight.

"Kylie, I was trying to tell you that we're so right together, that we were made to be together. You affect me like no other woman ever has or ever will. Sweetheart, you make me feel passionate and possessive in a way that I never dreamed I could. It's—"

"Since I'm the only woman who's ever owned controlling interest in the company you want, I believe I do affect you differently," Kylie interjected acidly. "Of course, you want to possess me—along with my BrenCo shares!"

"I'm not talking about BrenCo!" Cade's temper flared. "Will you drop the lawyering and quit arguing with every statement I make? Listen to me, Kylie! When I said you affect me like no other woman, I meant that you—you take me out of myself. Tonight, I completely lost control, I couldn't think of anything but getting inside you. That's never happened to me before and I—'' He broke off in a startled gasp. ''Kylie, I didn't use anything. This is the first time in my life I didn't stop and remember to use protection.''

She couldn't breathe, she couldn't move. Being body-slammed by a professional hockey player wielding a stick must feel similar to this, Kylie thought, dazed. For one terrible second, she feared she might faint but the rallying power of fury revived her, sending a gush of adrenaline surging through her bloodstream.

''Aunt Bobbie was right!'' she breathed as her aunt's dire warning blasted through her head. The words resounded in every lobe of her brain. ''You plan to get me pregnant and make me marry you so you'll be in the—the catbird seat at BrenCo!''

Cade uttered an expletive that according to the Rock and Roll Hall of Fame was now commonly recorded, but could not be broadcast over the airwaves.

Kylie construed his frustration and anger as further proof of Aunt Bobbie's ghastly theory. She couldn't resist the chance to extol the failure of his loathsome plan.

''It isn't going to work, Cade. For one thing, you fired your ammo at the wrong time of the month and you're not going to get another chance when the target is ripe! You see, *I'm* not as stupid as Uncle Gene thought and *you're* not as smart as he thought. So I guess we can call it a draw and forget—''

''I'm not going to forget anything and neither are you and we both know it,'' he interrupted tersely. ''Now come over here and let me—''

''Make a fool of me again? You really do think I'm an idiot.''

''I think you're upset,'' he tried to soothe her, but even he heard the bark of exasperation in his voice. ''You're confused and hurt and I'm sorry about that because the last thing I meant to do was to—''

''Clue me in,'' she finished for him. ''Yes, what a mistake! Sort of like Napoleon at Waterloo. Overconfidence got him, too. My grandmother, Mom's mom, the astrology buff, prob-ably said it best—'When the head swells, the brain stops work-ing.'''

Cade saw her inching toward the door. Now that he was aware of her propensity for speedy getaways, he could predict what she intended to do next. "Don't think of leaving this room, Kylie," he ordered, with far more authority than the situation warranted. She was fully dressed and upright, nearer to the door than he was. He had the added disadvantage of being naked and sitting in bed.

"Don't think your efforts have all been in vain, though." She met his eyes and for a moment the pain was so great, she wanted to crumple to the floor, sobbing. But she didn't. She'd had enough of being weak and foolish.

Holding his eyes, she casually scooped his trousers off the floor. She knew he hadn't seen her action, he was too concerned with maintaining eye contact. "I'm going to sell my BrenCo shares to you, as soon as possible. I want you to have them at the fair market price. That will be best for everybody, the Brennans and Port McClain. And—and me. Our attorneys can work out the terms of sale, although I don't think it'll be difficult."

She didn't stick around to see the smile of ecstasy, which would undoubtedly wreath his face, she didn't wait to hear him thank her profusely and perhaps offer a sporting "No harm done."

Clutching her coat and purse and his pants, she bolted from the hotel room, faster than she'd ever moved before. She heard him roar her name but knew he didn't stand a chance of catching her. After all, he was nude and by the time he managed to pull on the minimum of clothing, she would be in the lobby.

Where she left his pants. Kylie tossed them at the desk as she fled the building, figuring Cade would locate them eventually. Stranding him in Cleveland wasn't completely monstrous. He had his wallet; he could rent a car and drive back to Port McClain.

She had a bit of luck in the capricious weather. The snow had turned back into rain and the wind lessened to little more than a light breeze. Driving would not be a problem tonight. Kylie ran the whole way to her car; she didn't intend to waste a single moment of her head start.

She didn't know what she would do if Cade caught up with

her. Would he try to talk his way back into her heart, to charm the panties off her again? Literally!

Or maybe she was flattering herself. Suppose her statement of intent to sell her shares to him precluded any need to rush at all? Maybe Cade was so happy about the turn of events—not only was he getting her BrenCo shares, but he wouldn't be stuck with a Brennan mate in order to have them!—he'd ordered a hearty meal from room service and was breaking into a bottle of champagne right now, celebrating his victory.

Kylie felt tears stain her face and turned the heater on full blast as she rounded the bend to the highway ramp leading out of downtown Cleveland. Once again, the interstate directional signs forced her to make a choice.

Kylie made one.

Ten

A few hours later, she was knocking at the door of her brother's apartment in Ann Arbor, Michigan. She hoped Devlin was home although if he wasn't, she had the option of numerous motels where she could spend the night. But Kylie hadn't come to her big brother for lodging, she'd come for something else, something she'd never sought from him before.

She wasn't exactly sure what it was, but confusion and need and a long shared history with Devlin had caused her to choose the highway sign with arrows pointing to Michigan.

Kylie knocked again and pressed her ear against the door, to hear if there were any sounds of life within. The smoky sounds of a blues singer was vaguely audible. She caught her lower lip between her teeth. Uh-oh.

Moments later, the door opened and Devlin slouched against the door frame wearing only a pair of blue surgical scrub pants, the drawstring loosely tied. He was unshaven, his hair was tousled and his lips were swollen. Sensually swollen. The way lips looked after a marathon kissing session. Kylie remembered how enticing, how sexy Cade's looked when...

"Oh God, I shouldn't have come here!" she blurted out. "My timing is—"

"Incredibly bad, but that's nothing new." Devlin shrugged. It took a great deal to phase him. Obviously, the sight of his younger sister at his door close to midnight wasn't enough. "Come on in," he invited, stepping aside to admit her.

"Dev, who is—oh!" The tanned pretty blonde with enormous breasts and long, long legs sounded petulant. She was nude except for the teensy towel she held in front of her and when she spied Kylie, her eyes narrowed and her mouth thinned into a tight line. "Who are you?" she demanded in something close to a screech.

She sounded like a shrew and she didn't look quite so attractive anymore, Kylie noted, darting a quick glance at her brother.

"Help, she's morphed into a troll before our very eyes," Devlin murmured under his breath. "Looks like you arrived right in the nick of time to save me, Ky." He turned to the blonde. "Shanna, this is my sister, Kylie."

His ironic pronunciation of the word "sister" coupled with his daring bad-boy smile made it inevitable that Shanna would jump to the wrong conclusion. Kylie knew Devlin was counting on it; her brother had already lost interest in his towel-clad companion.

Shanna performed, as if on cue. "You're lying!" she accused in a shriek. "She's your sister like I'm your sister!"

Kylie groaned. Her acquaintance with Shanna had been less than sixty seconds, but that was long enough to know she was yet another one of Devlin's babes-of-the-moment. A Devlin Brennan babe-of-the-moment inevitably had an eye-popping body, which she was happy to show off and share, while her personality skills tended to be nonexistent or limited to histrionics.

Kylie caught herself in the middle of her rote characterization. She sounded disturbingly similar to Cade generalizing about the Brennans!

"I really am his sister." As penance, Kylie made a half-hearted attempt to reassure Shanna. Perhaps if she offered to show her photo driver's license as ID?

She didn't get the chance to suggest it.

"How dumb do you think I am?" Shanna demanded.

Kylie and Devlin exchanged glances. "What a lead-in!" Dev smiled lazily at his sister. "Can I answer it?"

"No," Kylie said severely. She walked toward his tiny kitchen, which also served as a passage between the wide living/dining area and the bedroom/bathroom suite. "I'm going to boil some water for tea. You have tea bags, I hope?"

"I always keep a box on hand, especially for you," Devlin said. "Not that you come to visit much. And while we're on the subject, what brings you here tonight?"

"You're going to let her stay?" Shanna howled while Kylie filled a battered teakettle she'd unearthed from a lower cabinet.

"What kind of a guy would I be if I threw my baby sister out in the street at this time of night?" Devlin asked.

The words were right, but his tone was all wrong. Dev had a gift for subtext; he would say one thing but his voice and his expression conveyed something else entirely.

"I know she's not your sister!" Shanna screamed, deciphering his deliberately false message. Just as Devlin had intended her to do, of course. His babes-of-the-moment were nothing if not predictable. "If you think I'll stay and watch you screw around with another woman, you're—you're—"

"Crazy?" Dev supplied helpfully. "Sick? Yeah, you could be right."

A few minutes later, an outraged Shanna was gone from the apartment, cursing and pulling on a minuscule cotton shirt, miniskirt and heels as she went.

"Whatever." Shrugging, Devlin closed the door behind her.

"You know, Dev, there really are women out there with common sense and brains, who aren't so easily manipulated. Who would actually say something normal like, 'You're Devlin's sister? Nice to meet you,'" Kylie pointed out dryly. "Ever consider dating one of them?"

"Nope. I keep those types as friends. In any other role, they want more than I have to give." He frowned wryly. "Okay, I'll be honest with you. They demand more than I feel like giving. I guess by your earnest, heartfelt standards that makes me shallow, huh?"

"You're not shallow, you just keep yourself so hidden I wonder if anyone will know to look for more." Kylie shook her head. "Meanwhile, you stick to your 'Baywatch' wanna-be types with their flair for bad drama."

"Yeah!" Devlin laughed.

"How did Shanna get so tan in Michigan in the middle of March, anyway? Does she live in a tanning booth? And she must have a few pounds of silicone in those—"

"Don't hold back, Kylie. Let's hear how you really feel about Shanna."

Chuckling, Devlin turned off the blues and switched on his TV set. An ancient episode of "Bewitched" was on and he flopped down in his big, wide BarcaLounger and stared at the screen.

Kylie joined him a few minutes later, setting a cup of tea in front of him. She'd bypassed his trendy assortment of hip, flavored coffees because she knew he liked tea with a teaspoon of sugar and splash of milk, just the way their mom had always fixed it for them.

"Do you still like Original Darren better than Replacement Darren?" Devlin asked, perplexed, his eyes glued to the actors on the screen. "I can't figure out why. To me, the two are interchangeable."

"Just like your girlfriends are interchangeable to you. I see a definite psychological link there." Kylie sipped her tea and settled back against the sofa cushions. "I've been in Port McClain," she murmured, staring sightlessly ahead.

"Ah, the Best Little Toxic Waste Dump Site in Ohio. Uh, sorry, sis. I know you're the current reigning queen of it all, thanks to Uncle Gene's will."

"I've kind of gotten to know the other Brennans better," she said tentatively.

"Is that good or bad? Say, did you ever find out who McClain is? Dad said he didn't exist but where did they come up with the name? There's McClain this and McClain that and there never was a McClain? What, did they just pick some random name out of a hat or something? I don't get it. And why call it *Port* McClain when it's not a port at all. Who ever heard of a port on a creek? That is one wigged-out place, Ky."

"I—I'm going to sell the BrenCo shares Uncle Gene left me," Kylie tried again. "To Cade Austin."

"Oh, yeah, the company prez. The beloved son Uncle Gene never had. Dad seems to like him okay, though."

"What did Daddy say about Cade, Dev?" Kylie poised on the edge of the sofa, watchful and alert. "Tell me everything."

Devlin waited until a commercial break to reply. "I don't remember Dad saying anything crucial about him. Why? Are you investigating the guy before you sell him those shares? Why not contact the EPA? Maybe they have a Most Wanted List, you know, like the FBI." He guffawed, enjoying his own joke.

Kylie sighed. Her brother had never been emotionally intuitive and he was running true to form tonight. He'd missed every subtle hint she had tried to give him.

"I went to the Rock and Roll Hall of Fame today," she said, giving up her attempts to confide in him. She and Dev were probably never meant to be confidants, anyway.

He was immediately interested and actually looked away from the TV while they discussed the various exhibits and their impressions of them. Kylie wasn't aware of how many times she mentioned Cade's name. He'd been with her at the museum and it was natural for her to quote him, to add his opinions and comments along with her own, especially since she'd found many too funny not to share.

Devlin was not so perceptively challenged that he didn't pick up on those frequent, affectionate references of hers. "Y'know, if I were supposed to guess—out of all the people in Port McClain—who would go with you to the Hall of Fame, Cade Austin is the last person I would've picked. It's easier to imagine Uncle Artie playing hooky from his turnpike toll-booth collector's job to stare at Buddy Holly's high school diploma than to picture Cade Austin paying homage to rock's roots. I thought the guy's interests ran strictly to incinerators and air pollution control."

That was all the encouragement Kylie needed to launch into the full story of her fateful visit to Port McClain—and her dizzying involvement with Cade Austin. She left nothing out, and Devlin listened attentively. He even switched the television set off, an almost unheard of occurrence as he deemed "background noise" enhanced his concentration.

But he seemed to have no trouble concentrating on his sister's revelations. He rarely interrupted her, letting her talk on and on, until she finally ended her story. Kylie slumped against the cushions, drained of energy and emotion, her blue eyes misty with tears.

"What do you think, Dev?" she asked, her voice quavering. "Doesn't it seem indisputable that Aunt Bobbie was right, after all?"

"Kylie, I don't know Aunt Bobbie all that well but my impression of her is—well, not only does she have both oars out of the water but a lot of time she's missing the rowboat, too. Get what I'm saying?"

Kylie felt a revitalizing flash of temper. She wasn't in the mood for Devlin's glib analogies. "But I told you what Cade did, Dev. And Aunt Bobbie warned me, she predicted it!"

"You couldn't have taken her seriously, Kylie, or you wouldn't have gone to that hotel room with him," Dev countered. "Come on, you admitted he didn't force you, you wanted to go with him."

She blushed, suddenly regretting what she'd confided. She'd said way too much, she decided, her discomfit rapidly increasing. "Never mind, I shouldn't expect you to understand."

Kylie grabbed the remote control and turned on the TV in an attempt to divert him. A rerun of "Charles in Charge" was on. That should do it.

To her surprise, Devlin didn't even glance at the screen.

"I understand pretty much, Kylie. You accused Cade Austin of plotting to knock you up when neither of you were thinking of anything beyond hitting the sheets. You said you were as hot for him as he was for you, so if you honestly forgot about snapping on the latex, the smart money says he forgot all about it, too."

"So you—you think I was wrong?" Kylie swallowed hard.

"Kylie, you left the guy stranded in a hotel room in Cleveland without his pants! Does that strike you as even remotely fair?" Dev gave his head an incredulous shake. "When it comes to a flair for bad drama, you give my 'Baywatch' wanna-be types some real competition."

Kylie covered her face with her hands. "It seemed like the right thing to do at the time," she murmured glumly. "It seemed like the only thing to do. I—I guess maybe I wasn't thinking very clearly?"

"I guess not," agreed Devlin bluntly. "Kylie, there's just one question I have to ask."

Kylie shivered, dreading it.

"What if you are pregnant? Any chance of that?"

"Well, there's always a chance, but I've always been regular, and it's definitely the wrong time of the month for me to get pregnant."

"Good." Devlin breathed a heartfelt sigh of relief. "Look, if I were you, when you know for sure, I'd let Austin in on the good news. Just drop him a postcard with a couple words to let him know. He must be sweating blood right now. I know I would be."

"You don't think that I—I should attempt to contact him otherwise?" Kylie asked wistfully.

"Definitely not!" Dev was emphatic. "Kylie, you would be setting yourself up for the worst humiliation of your life! I know how I'd feel if a woman did to me what you did to Cade Austin. I'd *never* want to see her again. I'd think she was a raving psycho, and I'd be down on my knees thanking God that I found out the truth about her."

Kylie winced.

"No, do not try to contact the man, little sis," Devlin ranted on. "Take it from me, he'll never forgive you."

"Because you would never forgive a woman who did something like that to you?" she asked dispiritedly.

"Never. A man can forgive certain women some things, like he'll forgive his mother and his sisters and maybe even his grandmother, just about anything. But when it comes to sex—forget about forgiveness. Why bother? There are always other women to treat you right, so why waste time with one who doesn't?"

Kylie stared dully at the TV screen. She felt queasy—the greasy cheeseburger and fries she'd downed during her drive seemed to have taken permanent residence in her stomach. The tea, now lukewarm, made her feel worse.

"Do you mind if I sack out on your couch tonight, Dev? I'll drive back to Philadelphia in the morning. I have friends there I can stay with while I figure out what to do next."

"Sounds like a plan to me. Although you know you're welcome to stay here for as long as you want."

"Thanks, but this place is too small for both of us. I'd cramp your style."

"So what?" Dev smiled. "I told you a guy can forgive his sister just about anything, even cramping his style."

But Kylie had already moved on in her mind. "I'll call Brenda and ask her to get my things from Uncle Gene's house and mail them to me. And I won't have any contact with Cade," she promised. "Our lawyers will handle the sale."

"Smart girl." Dev patted her shoulder.

Kylie planned to get up the next morning when Devlin did, for an early start on the long drive ahead. But though she awakened as her brother tromped through the apartment getting ready to leave for his shift at the hospital, she was too tired to move from the couch. She decided to rest a little while longer, only a few more minutes, then she would get up and be on her way. She wouldn't have to bother getting dressed because she'd slept in her clothes, a timesaver right there.

Pulling Dev's spare blankets more closely around her, Kylie closed her eyes for just a few more minutes of rest.

Sun was streaming into the apartment through the half-opened blinds the next time she awakened. Kylie sat up at once. She sensed it was late morning, even before a quick glance at her watch confirmed it.

Ten-thirty! So much for her early start to Philadelphia.

Then the pounding on the door started. At first Kylie ignored it, but when the bell began to ring insistently as well, she faced the inevitable. Whoever was at the door had no intention of leaving. Since mail and parcel delivery personnel did not carry on this way, Kylie resigned herself to the probability that the visitor must be Shanna or one of her fellow thwarted clones.

She walked slowly toward the door and attempted to smooth her sleep-mussed hair into some sort of order, using her hand as a makeshift brush. Kylie tried to brace herself for the encounter, fully expecting the door-pounding bell-ringer to accuse her of being a romantic rival for Devlin's attention. She held no hope that the babe would consider listening to reason. Dev didn't go for those types.

Without bothering to glance through the peephole, she pulled open the door while uttering a preemptive, "I'm Dev's sister, visiting from Philadelphia."

"I'm Cade Austin, and I'm going to wring your neck." Cade barged inside.

Kylie gaped at him. He seemed to have a talent for rendering her speechless.

He closed the door and folded his arms in front of his chest. "Well?" he demanded.

Her eyes hungrily drank in the sight of him. He was wearing a blue chambray shirt and jeans, and the vibrant virility of his presence struck her like a physical blow.

"You—you made it out of the hotel," she uttered inanely. Her mind was being bombarded with so many thoughts and feelings she could hardly process them, let alone coherently converse.

"No thanks to you," he said sternly. "You're damn lucky I've had time to cool down because if I'd've caught up with you last night, well, I don't know what I'd've done!"

Kylie rallied. "You come storming in here, threatening me, and you claim you've *cooled down?* As compared to what, an—an incinerator?"

"I'm not threatening you, and you know that, too." Cade fastened his hands around her waist and jerked her toward him. "Or at least you *ought* to know it. I'd better make sure before you go zooming off to God-knows-where because you've assumed I'm going to come after you with a baseball bat. Do you know I'll never hurt you, Kylie?" His voice softened a little, and his fiery hazel eyes met hers. "Do you know that?"

She felt her bones begin to melt, as his fingers began to knead the slender hollow of her waist. Her heart stopped aching and started to jump with mingled excitement and hope. According to her brother's logic, Cade shouldn't even be here. But he was, holding her, looking at her in a way that heated her blood and brightened her lowly spirits.

"Do you honestly believe that I tried to make you pregnant in a premeditated stock grab ploy, Kylie? That I would use you that way?"

"No," she whispered, her voice slightly raw. She'd cried last night as she lay alone on the couch and her throat was still a little sore from the strain. "I—I know that neither of us were thinking of anything beyond hitting the sheets. We both forgot about snapping on the latex."

Devlin's words came out of her mouth because she was too rattled to rephrase.

Cade's lips twitched. "I hadn't quite thought of it in those terms, but you're absolutely right."

"How did you know I was here?" she asked softly. She dared to lay her hands against his chest, her fear of rejection still inhibiting her. Devlin had been so sure that Cade would never want to see her again. It was hard to totally discount that, yet all her feminine instincts were telling her Cade would never not want to see her.

"I called your parents in Florida last night," Cade explained. "I—wondered if you would be heading there. I hoped you might've called them to let them know where you were."

"But I didn't." Kylie was puzzled. "The last time I talked to Mom and Dad was the night I arrived in Port McClain."

"So your mother said. I told her it was imperative that I get in touch with you—I didn't explain why. She suggested you might've gone to see your brother and gave me his address."

"And you made the trip to Ann Arbor, not even knowing if I was here?" Kylie gazed up at him, her blue eyes shining. "Why, Cade?"

"Why do you think, Kylie?"

She tried to move away, but he put his hands over hers and drew her arms around his neck. "Does this help you to come up with the answer?" he asked huskily, bending his head to kiss her neck.

Kylie clung to him, suddenly weak. She leaned her forehead against his chest to hide the sudden swell of tears in her eyes. "Dev said you'd never want to see me again, he said you would never forgive me for what I said and for leaving you at the hotel like that."

"Well, I wasn't happy about it," Cade drawled. "But not once did I consider never seeing you again. All I could think of was when I'd see you next. Kylie, I know this is too soon

for you and you'll probably try to talk me out of it, but—''
He paused and drew a deep breath. "I love you, Kylie. And
BrenCo has nothing to do with how I feel. Give me a chance
to prove it to you, sweetheart.''

She jerked her head upward and stared at him with wide,
startled eyes. "Why would I want to talk you out of it, Cade?
I love you so much, I—I—'' She felt tears streaming down
her cheeks. "Oh, Cade, it's not too soon. I feel as if we've
transcended ordinary time and…''

She stared at the ground, her face flushing. "That sounds
so banal, doesn't it? If Dev heard it, he'd roll on the floor
laughing. Or maybe throw up.''

"Well, I'm not laughing or throwing up.'' Cade lifted her
chin, raising her head to meet his eyes. "Will you come back
to Port McClain with me, Kylie? We'll take as long as you
need to be sure of us, but I'll be upfront and tell you right
now that my goal is to marry you. *Not* for your BrenCo shares,
let's settle that point, once and for all. Can you believe me,
sweetheart? Can we put the suspicions and misinterpretations
to rest for good?''

Kylie gazed at him and saw the man she loved, an honest,
honorable man who loved her. "I believe you, Cade,'' she
said softly. "I believe *in* you.''

He smiled a smile that made her heart sing. "And?'' he
prompted.

"And I would love to come back to Port McClain with you
and marry you as soon as we can plan a real wedding. I'm
already sure of us.'' Kylie snuggled closer to Cade, savoring
the warmth and reassurance of his masculine strength. "Do
you think I should have Brenda and Bridget as bridesmaids?
Polly, too. To try to achieve some family unity instead of
rivalry, for a change.'' She glanced up to gauge his reaction
to that.

He took it well. "If you want, honey. Maybe dealing with
the Brennans will be less maddening as a joint endeavor. In
some ways, you're already better at it than I am,'' he acknowledged.

"With certain exceptions. I'll leave the male Brennans to
you, to handle as you see fit. And I won't interfere.''

"Not much!'' Laughing, he lifted her off her feet and swung

her around, finally giving in to the relief and joy that seemed
to suffuse the very air they breathed.

"I love you, Cade."

"I love you, Kylie." He carried her to the sofa and sat down
with her on his lap.

"I think you were right about Uncle Gene and the will,
Cade." She searched his face with loving eyes. "He wanted
us to get together. If he hadn't died, he would've had to come
up with a plan other than the will, of course. Maybe he
would've tried to recruit me to work for BrenCo's legal department?"

"Never in a million years." Cade laughed against her lips.
She silenced him with a long and passionate kiss.

When Devlin returned later that day after a long shift at the
hospital, he appeared stunned to find the couple sitting at his
kitchen table, eating takeout from a nearby Chinese restaurant.

Kylie filled him in on the latest developments.

"You're going to marry her?" Dev gasped, staring at Cade
as if he'd just announced he had booked passage on a trip to
Mars. "After what she said, after what she did? Hey, I know
she's my little sister and I'd forgive her anything, but for *you*
to do it... Man, are you insane?"

"No, I'm in love," Cade amended, smiling at Kylie.
"You'll find out what it's like yourself someday, Dev."

"Not me!" Devlin proclaimed and turned on his TV set.
He lost himself in a rerun episode of "Full House" while
Cade and Kylie lost themselves in each other.

*   *   *   *   *

IN CELEBRATION OF MOTHER'S DAY, JOIN
SILHOUETTE THIS MAY AS WE BRING YOU

a funny thing
HAPPENED ON THE WAY TO THE
Delivery Room

THESE THREE STORIES, CELEBRATING THE
LIGHTER SIDE OF MOTHERHOOD, ARE
WRITTEN BY YOUR FAVORITE AUTHORS:

KASEY MICHAELS
KATHLEEN EAGLE
EMILIE RICHARDS

When three couples make the trip to the delivery room, they get more than their own bundles of joy…they get the promise of love!

Available this May,
wherever Silhouette books are sold.

Silhouette®
TM

Take 4 bestselling love stories FREE

Plus get a FREE surprise gift!

Special Limited-time Offer

Mail to Sihouette Reader Service™

P.O. Box 609
Fort Erie, Ontario
L2A 5X3

YES! Please send me 4 free Silhouette Desire® novels and my free surprise gift. Then send me 6 brand-new novels every month, which I will receive months before they appear in bookstores. Bill me at the low price of $3.24 each plus 25¢ delivery and GST*. That's the complete price and a savings of over 10% off the cover prices—quite a bargain! I understand that accepting the books and gift places me under no obligation ever to buy any books. I can always return a shipment and cancel at any time. Even if I never buy another book from Silhouette, the 4 free books and the surprise gift are mine to keep forever.

326 BPA A3UY

Name	(PLEASE PRINT)
Address	Apt. No.
City	Province	Postal Code

This offer is limited to one order per household and not valid to present Silhouette Desire® subscribers. *Terms and prices are subject to change without notice. Canadian residents will be charged applicable provincial taxes and GST.

CDES-696 ©1990 Harlequin Enterprises Limited

As seen on TV!
Free Gift Offer

With a Free Gift proof-of-purchase from any Silhouette® book,
you can receive a beautiful cubic zirconia pendant.

This gorgeous marquise-shaped stone is a genuine cubic
zirconia—accented by an 18" gold tone necklace.

(Approximate retail value $19.95)

Send for yours today...
compliments of  *Silhouette*®

To receive your free gift, a cubic zirconia pendant, send us one original proof-of-
purchase, photocopies not accepted, from the back of any Silhouette Romance™,
Silhouette Desire®, Silhouette Special Edition®, Silhouette Intimate Moments®
or Silhouette Yours Truly™ title available in February, March and April at your favorite
retail outlet, together with the Free Gift Certificate, plus a check or money order for
$1.65 U.S./$2.15 CAN. (do not send cash) to cover postage and handling, payable
to Silhouette Free Gift Offer. We will send you the specified gift. Allow 6 to 8 weeks for
delivery. Offer good until April 30, 1997 or while quantities last. Offer valid in the
U.S. and Canada only.

Free Gift Certificate

Name: _____

Address: _____

City: _____ State/Province: _____ Zip/Postal Code: _____

Mail this certificate, one proof-of-purchase and a check or money order for postage
and handling to: SILHOUETTE FREE GIFT OFFER 1997. In the U.S.: 3010 Walden
Avenue, P.O. Box 9077, Buffalo NY 14269-9077. In Canada: P.O. Box 613, Fort Erie,
Ontario L2Z 5X3.

FREE GIFT OFFER   084-KFD
ONE PROOF-OF-PURCHASE
To collect your fabulous FREE GIFT, a cubic zirconia pendant, you must include this
original proof-of-purchase for each gift with the properly completed Free Gift Certificate.

084-KFD

Silhouette Desire is proud to present an exciting new miniseries about the passions that rule a Montana ranching family, by bestselling author Anne Eames

A MARRIAGE MADE IN JOEVILLE
(6/97 SD#1078)

Word around Joeville, Montana, was that sexy loner Ryder Malone was suddenly planning to marry a very *unsuitable* woman with a fatherless little boy! All Savannah Smith knew was that this rugged cowboy had been the husband of her dreams since high school and considering that he'd introduced *her* to the wonders of passion mere nights before his shocking announcement, the only woman Ryder Malone was walking down that aisle with was Savannah!

Montana Malones—Three brothers whose lips are sealed with their secrets—till passion pries 'em loose. Don't miss **A MARRIAGE MADE IN JOEVILLE** by Anne Eames in June, and look for book two in December.

Look us up on-line at: http://www.romance.net

This summer, the legend
continues in Jacobsville

Diana Palmer

A LONG, TALL
TEXAN SUMMER

Three BRAND-NEW short stories

This summer, Silhouette brings readers a special
collection for Diana Palmer's LONG, TALL TEXANS
fans. Diana has rounded up three **BRAND-NEW**
stories of love Texas-style, all set in Jacobsville,
Texas. Featuring the men you've grown to love from
this wonderful town, this collection is a must-have
for all fans!

*They grow 'em tall in the saddle in Texas—and
they've got love and marriage on their minds!*

Don't miss this collection of original Long, Tall Texans
stories...available in June at your favorite retail outlet.

Silhouette®

LTTST

And the Winner Is...
You!

...when you pick up these great titles
from our new promotion at your
favorite retail outlet this June!

Diana Palmer
The Case of the Mesmerizing Boss

Betty Neels
The Convenient Wife

Annette Broadrick
Irresistible

Emma Darcy
A Wedding to Remember

Rachel Lee
Lost Warriors

Marie Ferrarella
Father Goose

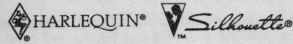